DISTORTED
Devotion

DEVOTION SERIES - BOOK ONE

PERSEPHONE AUTUMN

BETWEEN WORDS PUBLISHING LLC

Distorted Devotion

Copyright © 2019 by Persephone Autumn

www.persephoneautumn.com

ISBN: 978-1-951477-02-8 (Ebook)

ISBN: 978-1-951477-03-5 (Paperback)

Editor: Ellie McLove | My Brother's Editor

Proofreader: Rosa Sharon | My Brother's Editor

Cover Design: Persephone Autumn | Between Words Publishing LLC

BOOKS BY PERSEPHONE AUTUMN

Standalone Romance Novels

Depths Awakened

Sweet Tooth

Transcendental

Devotion Series

Distorted Devotion

Undying Devotion

Beloved Devotion

Darkest Devotion

Bay Area Duet Series

Click Duet

Through the Lens

Time Exposure

Inked Duet

Fine Line

Love Buzz

Insomniac Duet

Restless Night

A Love So Bright

<u>Artist Duet</u>

Blank Canvas

Abstract Passion

<u>Poetry Collections</u>

Ink Veins

Broken Metronome

Slipping From Existence

<u>Standalone Horror Novels</u>

By Dawn (published under P. Autumn)

For every woman who looks over her shoulder.
Who has had that gut feeling someone is watching her.
Following her.
You are not alone.

ONE

"THANK YOU FOR YOUR TIME, Ms. Jacobson. If you'll bear with me a few more minutes, I need to get a few more pieces of information from you."

My fingertips typed like a madwoman on my keyboard. On a roll, I gathered information from my tenth sale this month. Out of nowhere, a pen crashed into my desk, hurtled from outside my seven-by-seven cubicle.

Continuing my task, I ignored the projectile for the time being. "All right, Ms. Jacobson. I have all the information I need from you today. In the next week, you'll be receiving a packet of paperwork with further details in the mail. It will contain instructions on what you need to do to finish the process. Do you have any more questions for me today?"

She stammered as uncertainty rang in her answer.

"If you think of anything else, please don't hesitate to

call back and ask for Sarah Bradley. I'm happy to answer any questions that may arise."

Ms. Jacobson thanked me, her tone more chipper.

"It's been my pleasure, Ms. Jacobson. If there's nothing else I can assist you with today, I will let you enjoy the rest of this beautiful day. Thank you for choosing Hammond Life Insurance to protect your future, have a wonderful day."

Pressing the button on my earpiece, I disconnected the call. I finished typing a few last things before saving the new client profile. A rush soared beneath my ribcage as pride infiltrated in my veins. Two weeks into the quarter and I was on fire. This was cause for celebration.

I searched for the projectile pen which fell to the floor and rolled under my desk. A small slip of paper was taped to the barrel. As I peeled the tiny note from the pen missile, I saw a familiar scribble.

Lucky bitch! You're buying drinks tonight.

I scribbled back my response, more than happy to pay for a round or two of drinks tonight. Securing the note back onto the pen, I rose from my chair—my eyes peeking over the partition walls around me—and launched it back to the desk it originated from.

"Ow! At least I didn't hit you."

I stepped out from the confines of my second home.

Not as if I lived at work, but I put in my fair share of time. Like so many others, I embellished the semi-fabric cubicle walls with décor. Various pieces of bohemian art made the space more pleasant to stare at five days a week.

I eased through the sea of cubicles. In a handful of strides, I reached the plot of desk space given to one of my favorite people—Christy. Her workspace resembled the teeny-bopper magazines from our younger years—the walls splattered with vivid colors and celebrities she crushed on.

Her back to me when I rounded the corner, I stood quietly as her fingers typed with vigor. Lost in a trance with whatever task she had been assigned, Christy was clueless that I lingered just inches from her. I reached out and touched her shoulder. Her body jumped at the contact as a soft squeal erupted from her throat.

"Sorry, sorry, sorry. I didn't mean to scare you, chicky." I resisted laughing for... three, two, one.

Face shrouded in faux disbelief, Christy spun around with her fists on her hips. "And I'm supposed to take your word on that? Right after you hurled a pen at my head."

"If my memory serves correct, you fired the first shot. So..."

"True. But I didn't hit you. I only wanted it to land on your desk," Christy muttered.

"Sorry, I didn't mean for it to hit you. I took no aim. Forgive me?" My most pathetic puppy dog eyes and pouty lips groveled for forgiveness.

She turned back to her monitor and tapped the keys. "I forgive you."

The good friend I am, I allowed her a moment to finish whatever I disrupted. While she typed, I checked my watch. The digital face lit and displayed twelve-eleven.

"Hey, you want to grab lunch when you wrap up?" I asked.

Her fingers paused a split-second. "Yeah. Give me five minutes. I'll come get you when I'm done."

"Cool. See you in a few."

Falling in line with the masses, we stood at the deli counter and waited to order lunch. Carol's Deli took up half of the first floor and was always crowded.

"Number sixty-seven!" a petite woman hollered over the crowd, her eyes scanning the sea of faces. Her dark locks in a messy bun and masked by a cotton net.

"That's me!" I wiggled between a few people and stepped up to the counter.

"What can I get for ya, doll?" She poised her pen on the green order pad and smiled. I rattled off mine and Christy's orders. Tossing my call number into a wicker basket, I waited as she finished scribbling our order down. She tore the slip from the stack and read the order back to me. "Anything else for ya, hun?"

"Nope, that's it."

She reached under the counter and grabbed a numbered, plastic tent. As she jotted the number on the order slip, she handed me the table tent. "Have a seat, darlin'. Someone will bring your food out soon."

"Thanks."

Sifting my way through the throng of people, I stepped out of the hovering lunch crowd and found Christy. She snagged us a table by the windows—best table in the place.

"Food's ordered. Shouldn't be too long," I said as I slid into the chair across from Christy.

"Cool, thanks."

"So, I read your little note. Since I got another sale today, you think I should buy drinks tonight, huh?"

"Um, yeah. You're knocking it out of the park up there, chica. I bet you already exceeded your quota for the month. What was today? Eight or nine?"

My cheeks heat under her estimation. "Ten," I muttered.

"*Seriously?* How the hell do you find these people? Compared to you, I'm a slacker. I have four sales. Four. Soon, you'll set the bar and I'll be left in the wastelands." Her smirk a mix of jealousy and sarcasm.

"Shut your mouth. You're talking nonsense. My last three sales have all been referrals from other clients. Just doing things like usual." Christy loved harassing me, just for the hell of it.

I sat nowhere near the top of the sales list. That throne belonged to Agnes. Agnes started here before electricity was invented. Okay, slight exaggeration. In actuality, she started working for Hammond Life two years before I was born. Her twenty-eight-year tenure provided her top seniority amongst the worker bees.

If Christy thought highly of my ten sales, she would flip out when she learned Agnes's numbers. Last I heard, Agnes had already sealed the deal on twenty-two new clients. My shorter tenure with Hammond of two-and-half years was laughable — not even a tenth of Agnes' time — but I had a tiny following. Agnes had a binder full of contacts. I had four sheets.

She was an absolute legend among us.

"Well, everyone loves you. They're flocking to you in herds," Christy stated.

"Herds? That's extreme. It takes over ten to make a herd. Right?" This whole conversation is laughable. There were better things to talk about off the clock. This was our time, and I was done with the shop talk. "Enough about work and numbers. What d'ya want to do tonight? Drinks, dinner, a movie? Your call. I'll buy, seeing as I'm some master sales guru now."

"Not sure. I talked with Rick last night. He's headed out with the guys tonight, so I'm open. Maybe hang at my place? Have you talked to Liz today?"

Liz wasn't just our bestie, she also worked at

Hammond. We'd all started at different times, but fell into friendship easily. Funny enough, no one ever pegged us as friends—a free-spirited hippie child, an over bubbly, never-shuts-the-hell-up girl, and a punk loving goth. But our friendship bonded us like sisters.

"Haven't seen her. She must be in her fortress, hunting for prey."

We all made cracks about cubicle life. Jokes made work more tolerable. As did decorating. No two cubicles were the same. On any given day, you'd walk past Star Wars, Star Trek (and whatever you do, don't confuse the two or you'll never hear the end of it), Harry Potter, comic book paraphernalia, holiday decor, and family photos.

Christy giggled and heads turned. Her laugh a sweet, whimsical sound. "When we're done, let's stop by her desk."

"Sounds good. I vote we stay in. We can hang at your place. Watch a movie, eat takeout, drink a little. Whatcha think?"

"Perfect. I'm sure Liz will join. Want me to grab the provisions?" Christy tucked an escaped russet curl behind her ear under her thick, black-framed glasses.

"I'll grab food. You guys figure out drinks. We can sort it out with her."

A moment later, our lunch was delivered, and all conversation went out the window. My stomach grumbled loud enough for the next table to hear. As soon as the plate hit the table, I shoved a forkful in my mouth.

"Is there anything else I can get you ladies?" I shook my head, spewing a muffled *no thanks*.

He chuckled. "Let us know if you need anything else." As fast as he appeared, he vanished.

"You're a nut! Like a damn two-year-old, talking with your mouth full." Christy's musical giggle disrupted the chitchat near us.

"You know you love me. Just shut up and eat your sandwich."

I stepped inside Christy's apartment and my two favorite people greeted me.

Christy, in all her boisterous glory, bounded toward me. "Hey, bitch!" Wrapping her arms around me, she squeezed me tight like a stress ball. Then let go and disappeared around the corner. "You bring the food?" she hollered.

I trailed behind her as she walked to the kitchen. Christy and Rick's apartment was one of a few things I envied. They lucked out and got it for a steal. It had been remodeled and had the modern appeal everyone sought out. But her kitchen… it made me want to learn how to bake. Complete apartment jealousy.

Two plastic bags dangled in my hands. The scent of onions and garlic and grease wafted in the air as I set the Chinese food on the kitchen island. "Veggie Lo Mein, tofu and string beans, Kung Pao chicken, shrimp egg foo young, veggie egg rolls, tons of rice, crunchy noodles, and fortune cookies."

"It's as if you know the way to my heart." Liz's raspy tone rang out as she walked in from the living room. Right hand over her heart, she faux-swooned.

"Hey girl! Glad you made it," I said. I hugged her tight as if we hadn't seen each other in years.

"Although my body disagrees, I can't wait to eat everything. Just have to add a few extra miles to my run tomorrow."

"Liz, no one will know you ate a crap ton of greasy, delicious, carb-loaded Chinese food. There's nothing to worry about." Drawing an X over my heart, I continued. "Your secret's safe with me."

Her hazels narrowed and her slender lips scrunched. "I'm not journaling what I eat. Just don't eat much heavy stuff anymore. My body will punish me tomorrow, but it's totally worth it."

"Awesome. Christy, what are we watching?" She messed with the remote while I grabbed plates and utensils.

"I'll find it in a minute. Some new comedy on Netflix I added to the playlist. Got it… *When We First Met.*"

She dropped the remote on the table and came back to the kitchen, grabbing a plate and piling it high. A minute later, we headed out to the living room and sat sukh asana on cushy pillows around the table on the floor.

Christy brought a few beers to the table. I raised my bottle in the air and they mimicked. "Congrats for gaining ten new clients this month. And to us, reason unnecessary."

Our bottles clinked and we took a long pull from the brown bottlenecks. I didn't need a reason to hang out with Liz and Christy. Us spending time together was the same as breathing—both were essential. Whether it be Friday or Monday, anytime with Liz and Christy was perfect. Which reminds me of Monday...

"This just crossed my mind... you guys ready for the meeting on Monday?"

"Nope. We're not doing that now." Christy barked at me like a mother hen. Her eyes narrowed as she pointed a manicured finger at me.

"What?"

"Talking about work. The only exception was bringing up your sales. But it ends there."

"Yes, Mom." I stuck out my tongue, cocked a brow, and crossed my eyes.

My reward... A pillow to the face.

TWO

AS WITH EVERY other weekend in the history of mankind, this one ended too soon.

My alarm screamed an incessant buzz-wail combo and startled me from a deep sleep. What I wouldn't give for a little more sleep. But, like a good girl, I smacked the button and rolled out of bed. Sleeping another hour would have been easy, but a little voice whispered in my ear and reminded me to get off my ass and go to the gym.

Slower than typical, I slipped on my workout gear in the dark. I grabbed my gym bag after securing my hair, foregoing any extensive grooming until after. As I walked out of my apartment, I dropped my keys in my bag and walked to the gym in the middle of my gated apartment complex.

I loved having an all-inclusive gym—one of several reasons I lived here. The rent was reasonable considering the complex sat on the outskirts of Savannah. The gym—

loaded with more equipment than I would ever use—three pools, and several other great amenities sold me. The gated community the best perk. Safety was immeasurable, and I never had a worry here.

The gym's bright lights glowed in the morning darkness. It'd be another hour until the sun rose. Waking this early was worth it to miss everyone else in the complex. A shiver rippled through me as I tugged the metal door handle to the gym. A rush of warm air enveloped me and defrosted some of the early morning January air.

Moving past several muscle building contraptions, I headed for the row of treadmills, ellipticals, stationary bikes, and rowing machines. They formed a line, a break between them when it changed from one type to the next. A row of benches lined up a few feet behind them, butting against half-walled/half-windowed rooms. The rooms for yoga, Pilates, or other non-equipment classes.

After I set my bag on the bench behind the treadmill, I grabbed my towel, phone, and earbuds. My bag only held a few things—a change of clothes, water, keys, and an additional towel. Since I brought nothing I deemed important, I didn't worry about leaving it unattended. Plus, early hours in the gym equaled fewer bodies.

I stepped up and straddled the treadmill belt. After I pressed a few buttons, I started my warmup. Soon it would progress into a twenty-five-minute run. Running races for medals wasn't my thing, I only want to stay healthy.

Popping my earbuds in place, I scanned my music and

hit play. I picked an upbeat playlist since I needed to wake up and motivate. Today would be busy. Besides the normal hustle and bustle, we had our quarterly staff meeting. Numbers and graphs and goals galore. If I didn't wake up now, I would fall asleep once the power point started.

"You ready?" Christy stood across from my desk, pen and paper in hand. She tapped the pen like an impatient child. Christy was always happy-go-lucky, except when it came to work and meetings. Work smudged out her light.

"We do this every quarter. Not like anything spectacular will happen." I rose from my chair and grabbed a pen and paper.

"The day we're not prepared, a huge change will be announced. Mark my words." She pointed her pen at me and puckered her lips, nodding like a lunatic. What she took seriously made me laugh.

As we walked down cubicle row, I worked to lighten her mood. At the office, Christy was more fidgety and circumspect. The second she saw the conference room, Christy sucked in a deep breath. Today's meeting was for all the associates on our floor—all twenty-seven of us—plus our supervisors. Every quarter we sat in the same room, around the same round wooden tables, and picked at the sugar-laden candy in the center. Every meeting also involved a group exercise.

Liz waved to us from the chairs she secured for us. Bob from human resources and my direct supervisor, Marco, stood at the head of the room. Smiling, I waved at them as we walked over to Liz.

"Thanks for snagging us the good seats," I said.

"Hey, if we have to sit here for the next three plus hours, I'd rather not crane my neck or spin around every time something happens."

"Right there with ya," Christy added.

Like synchronized swimmers, we rolled our chairs out and sat on the faux leather. We had another ten minutes before the meeting started, meaning most of the staff wouldn't show up for another nine.

Not like I am a poster child for proper work etiquette, but punctuality speaks volumes. Arriving early gave hope to the meeting ending sooner. But no one cared.

More people trickled in—Sandy, Roger, Betty, and a few others I hadn't met. Most of my coworkers friendly, I'd chatted them up a time or two. In meetings or downstairs in Carol's Deli. Mom taught me to be polite to new people and make them feel welcome. We all remembered what the first day of school was like... *Does my hair look okay? What about my clothes? Will people like me? Do I know anyone here?* Mom reminded me everyone thought the same things and to not let such things impede making new friends.

The conference room grew louder as more people filed in and sat down, sparking conversations. I distracted myself and doodled while Christy and Liz chatted about some new haircare product. Beauty products weren't my cup of tea.

The garden of flowers on the top blue line of my perforated notepad grew—daisies and roses amongst a bed of lush grass—when a voice interrupted my artwork.

"Good morning, Sarah."

I peeked up from my doodle to find one of my coworkers standing too close to me. The buttons on his pale, blue dress shirt ready to burst open at his belly. "Good morning, Alan. How are you?"

"I'm good, thanks. How are you? You look nice today."

I tilted my head down, glanced at my chest, and tugged on the cream-colored fabric of my crocheted, bohemian top. "Thank you."

"Are you ready for hours of sleep-inducing speech? I didn't get enough sleep last night, so thank goodness we have this meeting today." He meant it as a joke. I knew this only because of the harsh chuckle—similar to someone who'd smoked for fifty years—exiting his throat.

To make light of his humor, I said, "Meetings... they're a necessary evil."

His laughter rang louder with exaggerated excitement.

Everyone nearby noticed—a few brows furrowed. What I said wasn't laugh-worthy, but to each their own.

Something tapped my hand, and I twisted to face Liz, the end of her pen hovered over my hand. Before I asked what was up, she pointed to the front of the room. Bob ready to start the meeting.

The conference room door shut, the heads of the meeting poised and ready as everyone wrapped up their conversations. As the voices faded into silence, I swore I heard *always getting in the way* resound from the table to my right. The table where Alan sat.

"All right folks, quiet down. It's almost over and then you can head to lunch." The stir of restless voices quieted once more and allowed Marco to finish. "This year's shaping up well so far, and we're only two weeks in. For those of you who are on pace to meet your quarterly goals, I thank you. Keep up the good work."

A hand landed on my shoulder and patted, and I jumped. "Good job, Sarah," Alan whispered too close to my ear. An uncomfortable tremor rippled through my body and my shoulders shook. With every ounce of courtesy I could muster, I responded with a thumbs up and kept my face turned away from his.

Marco's voice boomed over the slight uptick in the chitchat. "Give me one more minute, people." The room quieted one last time, allowing Marco his closing statement. "Thank you. For those below par, I don't doubt you'll meet your goals. Reach out to your previous contacts and ask for referrals. Talk to friends, family, and neighbors. There's bound to be someone. Thank you for your time this morning. Don't forget our annual luncheon is next month. Bob will get more information to you soon. Keep up the great work and let's blow this quarter out of the water! Meeting adjourned."

Like the running of the bulls, everyone bolted from their chairs and corralled out the door, eager to leave the conference room. Christy, Liz, and I hung back and waited for everyone to leave.

I thought the room had emptied. The room quiet except for our chatting about where to grab lunch, I startled when a chair rolled behind me and bumped my chair. That same awkwardness from earlier rested in my belly.

"Where you ladies going to lunch? I can't decide myself." Alan's voice next to my ear.

Christy glimpsed my face—unease rose from the pit of my stomach and highlighted my features—and answered for all of us. "We haven't decided yet. Too many options nearby."

Words escaped me as I tried to translate my nervousness. It was peculiar. Alan sat at his table, alone, for the last five minutes. I'd talked with him several times since I worked for Hammond Life and never once did I get a weird vibe from him. Today, though... Today felt different. Intrusive.

Was he eavesdropping? Our chitchat lacked substance, but spying made my stomach churn. My ass was sore from sitting so long, but I was determined to stay seated. The padded chair creaked beneath me as I redistributed my weight and waited for Alan to leave. The energy in the room was stagnant and eerie.

When he rose to stand, his body invaded my personal space as his voice thundered above me. "Well, I'm headed down to the deli. Hope to see you there."

"Cool. Enjoy your lunch, Alan." Christy's sing-song voice dismissed him.

A clock on the wall ticked three deafening beats before he pivoted away and walked out the door. Outside the room, I watched as he eyed me between the blinds a moment. Three breaths later, he spun around and headed down the corridor. I peered at Christy and Liz, my unease fading to the background. The discomfort from a moment ago replaced with mass confusion.

"What the hell was that?" Liz asked.

"Wish I knew. The whole situation was awkward. And you know it takes a lot to get me frazzled." The last part beyond true. My open and easy-going demeanor difficult to dislodge. Many of my friendships were forged due to my loving nature.

"We damn sure *won't* be going to Carol's today," Christy said, adamant.

"I am one hundred percent okay with that." Their agreement flooded me with relief and washed away any residual unease. "That being said, where should we go?"

The lunch crowd at the old bank-turned-restaurant was a madhouse today. Meeting days allowed us to venture farther for lunch. Since we had to endure hours of monotony, the company allotted us an extended lunchtime.

The waitress walked away with our orders. Miles of sunshine illuminated our table from the wall of windows. For a restaurant, the place wasn't huge, but had great personality and awesome food.

"So, what's up with Alan today? Is it me? It all seemed a little weird," Christy stated.

"He was trying to spark conversation, I guess. Maybe he doesn't have friends in the office. Who knows," Liz said, shrugging.

"You're so nice, Liz. The whole thing was still weird. Did you guys see him touch my shoulder when Marco talked about people being on track?" I wasn't sure of their focus when the speech was delivered.

"*Um, no. Really?*" Christy asked. Aversion tugged her brow and scrunched her nose.

"Yep. Awkward moment number one. When he first walked in and talked to me, it wasn't strange. More like water cooler talk. I was just being polite. But after... he wouldn't leave." This discomfort was odd. My outgoing nature a part of me as much as my hair or eyes or limbs. My extroverted mother ingrained it in me since birth.

"I read it all over your face. That's why I played coy when he asked about lunch," Christy said.

"And for that, you're my hero." I raised my hands above my head and lowered them, bowing to her.

"Whoa, whoa, whoa. Let's not go giving Christy a big head now. Put that shit away." Liz's hands swatted mine and stopped my display of worship to our friend.

"Don't be jealous, bitch." Christy giggled. "I did us all a favor. If Sarah wants to worship me, we should allow her to do so." Her eyebrow cocked as she stuck her tongue out at Liz.

"Whatever. On to something more fun. Let's talk about my birthday party. It's a couple weeks out. Thoughts on who to invite?" Liz fidgeted like a kid high on sugar.

My circle of friends was small and I prayed Liz didn't ask me to invite people. "I'll help decide food and drinks. You guys handle the invite list."

"Sounds like a plan," Liz said, pleased one task was

divvied. She was giddy we were one step closer to her big day.

"I'll talk to some people and get more names added to the invite list. How many you thinking?" Christy grabbed her phone and typed on a blank note screen.

"Only twenty-five or thirty. I don't want to piss off the neighbors. Hey..." Liz pointed at Christy. "Invite a couple of my neighbors, too. That way we're not only being nice, but we're also letting them know I'm throwing a party."

"Good idea," Christy said, not stealing a moment to peek up from her phone.

Seconds later, our conversation ended when our server arrived with our food. We lined up our plates like a buffet. Chopsticks in hand, onlookers probably thought we were fighting to the death. But this was our normal, and I loved it. I loved how we could be ourselves around each other.

But little did I know, someone else sat nearby. Someone who would turn my world upside down.

THREE

THE REST of the work week flew by, nothing notable occurring. I got another sale under my belt, by chance, and listened to Christy's tirade of jealousy.

When we weren't selling, we had a mountain of other tasks. Email correspondence the most boring of them all. Most of them follow-ups —*thank you for choosing Hammond Life* or *I haven't heard from you in a while, how's your family doing?* or *I'm sorry for your loss*. The latter being the worst.

Reports always needed filling out. Spreadsheet after spreadsheet. Endless boxes of numbers — sales, sales, sales. How many emails have I sent? Any responses? What marketing had I done? Am I on target? Blah, blah, blah. Box after box. So many numbers they all blurred together. If I spent less time on reports, I'd have higher sales.

"Ugh," I groaned as one last page of reports popped up.

I loved marketing and connected with so many people since working here. My top priority was to not be "the salesgirl on the phone". One of my favorite parts of my job was the conversations and learning about my client's lives. What brought them happiness.

Meeting new people was my bread and butter. As a child, my mother would always tell me I was too curious for my own good—often talking to strangers and making friends. As with any personality trait, extroversion is both a positive and a negative. Positive because it is how I meet so many great people—Christy and Liz included. Negative because not everyone you meet has the best of intentions.

It had been years since I had sensed something *off* about someone. This week rekindled that unfamiliar discomfort. But I did everything in my power to cast it aside. Dwelling solved nothing.

One afternoon shortly after I started working at Hammond, I was in the break room, I sat and read during lunch when Alan walked in and sat across from me with his lunch. I continued reading my book, engrossed in the words on the pages in front of me.

"Hey," he'd said. "You're the new girl Sarah, right?"

Although I wanted to devour the words in my paperback, I didn't want to seem rude, being one of the new girls on the block. So, I'd put my book down and sparked a conversation with him.

He'd seemed peculiar but harmless during our talks, and had a sweet demeanor. So, when he talked with me before Monday's meeting, I thought nothing of it. It was the mumbling comment I'd heard, followed by the hand on my shoulder, and the inquisition about lunch after apparently eavesdropping that didn't sit well with me. Several small things tangled my perception and caused me to second guess everything. The whole situation was abnormal.

But I could leave it at work. Except for Christy and Liz—and a couple other coworkers—I was a master at separating my work life from my home life. And I was adamant about keeping it that way.

One of the best parts about the weekends was not hearing the annoying buzz of the alarm clock. I woke early, but not hearing that god-forsaken noise made the entire day better.

Dragging my hair through the last loop of my hair tie, I startled when a knock broke the silence. Both hands on my ponytail, I tugged outward and tightened the band close to my scalp. Swiveling side to side, I took one last look in the bathroom mirror and fixed the sleeve of my snug sports top.

Two sets of pearly-whites greeted me when I opened the door. Their smiles brighter than the blinding sun.

"Morning, bitch. Ready to sweat your ass off?" Sometimes I wondered if Christy's father was a trucker. Or perhaps a sailor. Bitch rolled off her tongue like melted butter, no one seeming to care.

"Hey, sunshine. I need to grab my bag and I'll be ready. Either of you need water?" I asked before grabbing my bag from the couch.

"No, thanks," Liz and Christy replied in unison, followed by a fit of giggles from Christy. I swear, that girl thought everything was hilarious. She'd laugh at the most mundane things. And she was the friend who shared an obscene number of memes on social media.

"You guys practice that on your way here?" I asked through my own bout of laughter.

"Nope, we had more important topics to discuss. My party being top priority." Liz, a little girl getting her first pet; a sparkle in her eye and the broadest smile across her face.

"Cool. Well, let's chat about it more once we're in the gym." Stuffing my water in the bag, I slung it over my shoulder and headed for the door. "If we use the machines for about thirty minutes, we can catch the yoga class and use it as our cool down."

"Good with me," Liz said as her stride kept us all on our toes.

"Me too. I've skipped the last two." Christy's cheeks reddened.

"Awesome. Let's get the ball rolling. Treadmill or bikes?" My voice muffled as I pulled on the door to the gym, the familiar rush of warm air blew over us.

"Bikes," they said in unison. Again.

"You guys are too much for me today. And unlucky me, the day's just begun."

"Okay everyone. Now let's finish out today's session in shavasana. Listen to the soft sounds of the music and transition to focus on only your breath. Close your eyes. Center yourself. Feel your prana all around you." The subtle sounds of birds chirping next to a waterfall played in the background as our yoga class ended. "Great job, everyone. Until next time" —the instructor bowed at the waist, her hands in prayer position— "Namaste and enjoy your weekend."

"Namaste," the entire class repeated.

We sat on our yoga mats facing each other and waited for the other people in the class to leave. Some people bolted upright as soon as yoga ended. We always stayed a few minutes and enjoyed the solemn, peaceful moment after.

"So, ladies, what is on the agenda today?" Christy asked.

Swallowing back a mouthful of water, I said, "Well, I'd say showers are a must. Then we should finalize Liz's party. I have a few errands, but we should grab what we can for the party today."

Liz nodded. "Let's head home and shower and meet up after. My place?"

"Good with me," I said, grabbing my bag as we headed for the door.

"Me too, bitch." How Christy always used her favorite word, as often as possible, cracked me up. If I was ever on a game show and quizzed on the word she used most, I would win.

Weaving through the weights area, we headed for the exit. I threw my hoodie on and braced for the chilly morning air. Winter in Georgia wasn't as bad as some northern states—mostly because we weren't far from the Atlantic—but it was too cold to walk the hundred yards to my apartment in just a sports bra and leggings.

As we reached the door, a man entering held it open for us. Pulling up the tail end of our small conga line, I peeked up to thank him. I opened my mouth to say the words—two simple words—but froze, speechless. He looked past me and into the gym—meeting a buddy, or girlfriend, I'm sure. No way in hell a guy that handsome was single. The black cotton fabric of his hood masked half his profile. A hint of tanned skin and short, black stubble accented his jawline.

Trying to collect myself and not appear an idiot, I remembered how to speak. "Thank you. For holding the door."

Deep blue eyes swallowed me whole. My heartbeat skyrocketed as my breath disappeared. "You're welcome."

Before I spoke another word, he turned and walked off. Inside the gym he headed toward the weights and to meet whoever. Obviously someone more important than me. I had a sudden urge to lift weights.

"Sarah!" Christy shouted, her abrupt volume made me spin and jog to where she and Liz waited some fifty feet away. "Who's the hottie?"

I shook my head out of its foggy state and mumbled, "Wish I knew..." I really wish I knew.

Liz, Christy, and I sat on fluffy pillows around Liz's coffee table. Music blared in the background, but not loud enough to drown out conversation. Papers littered the table between us with various notes scribbled on them.

"So, I was thinking maybe we do finger foods." My ideas for the party food were basic. Keep it easy. Plenty of variety. Everyone stays happy.

Besides, munchies wouldn't be the focus of the night.

"Perfect. Anything in particular?" Liz asked.

"Wings, veggie trays, small deli sandwiches, chips and dips, a small cake. Simplistic with no assembly required. I'll get the wings from Tatiana's Pub. We can keep everything in the kitchen and let people grab it when they want. Do we have a head count yet?" Liz and I glance at Christy.

Christy opened an app on her phone and scrolled a moment. "I've reached out to all the usual suspects. As of now, thirty-two. Not including us. There's still plenty to hear from."

Liz may have said only thirty people, but I could see forty plus showing up and her not caring. Her parties are all about fun. The more people, the better.

"Awesome. I'll order food based on that. I'd rather run out than have leftovers for the trash," I said.

Liz nodded, her mind somewhere else. "What about alcohol? Christy, you want to make a run with me? We can grab a handful of bottles, some beer, and mixers. Split the bill?"

"Sure thing. When d'you want to go?" Christy asked as she continued to scroll through her phone. No doubt she had a spreadsheet or party planning app.

"Tonight? This weekend is the perfect opportunity to get as much done as possible. I don't want us fumbling for shit at the last minute."

"Tonight works for me. Maybe you and I go to the liquor store while Sarah gets the food sorted out and then we chill after." Christy's statement hung like a question, but was more of a request.

Every killer party Liz had thrown came with a lot of legwork. It was a process. But worth every minute.

"I'm game. I'll place orders for the trays then grab stuff from the store. Let's meet back here, order takeout, and binge watch a TV series."

"Yes." Both of them replying in unison. Again. And that was all it took for the three of us to fall into a fit of laughter. Without a doubt, we were three peas in a pod.

The rest of my weekend passed by as it always did. Gym. Laundry. Grocery shopping. A little cleaning here and there. Chilling on my couch with my current paperback. Most of the time, I went with the flow. Some things planned. But most not.

Weeknights and weekends weren't always this laid back, but having time to myself was invaluable. Next weekend, we'd be swamped with the before, during, and after party. As amazing as it'd be, we'd be overwhelmed leading up to it. So downtime now was essential.

Most weekends, we went out to a bar or nightclub and

partied. It wasn't all booze and sex. Although there was plenty happening. But most of the time, it was just friends enjoying each other's company in the center of nightlife.

Rick, Christy's boyfriend of four years, was with us often. On occasion, he'd bring a couple of his buddies. There was never the sense of obligation to pair up, but we welcomed the protection against any unwanted attention.

Eric and John — Rick's friends — had drool-worthy bodies. Muscular frames, clean cut, enough charisma to keep you coming back for more. But they weren't *my* boyfriend material. After hanging out a few times, Eric asked me out and I declined. Guilt blanketed me for days, but honesty was more important. He was attractive and sweet and had a great personality. But he wasn't my type, and he'd become more of a brotherly figure rather than a love interest.

Weeks afterward, he shied away, unsure how to act near me. But things loosened up again. We'd chatted and hung out like siblings, and he'd protect me in an instant if someone bothered or pressured me. Eric was my big brother from another mother — and father — and our bond morphed into something I shared with no one else.

It had been a few weeks since we'd all hung out, but he'd be at Liz's party. He never missed her parties. Most people didn't. Anyone invited would be a fool to not show. When Liz threw a party, people talked about it for weeks after. Liz's parties morphed into a nightclub. Alcohol always flowed freely in plastic red cups. Every inch of the house would be packed. Sweaty bodies grinding against one another. Lips tasting while everyone got lost in the music. I loved every minute. Anyone who attended knew it would be a memorable night.

Grabbing my paperback, a glass of water, and my sunglasses, I stepped out onto my tiny back porch. Settling onto the plush chaise, I reached for the blanket at the foot. The temperature warmer than expected for early February, but I draped the thick throw over my legs and settled in for four or five chapters.

Absolute heaven. I lived minutes from the city, but couldn't hear it. Not even from the edge of my first-floor porch. I'd fallen asleep reading on this lounger several times. Everything about this place is perfect.

But perfection has its flaws. Even my homey slice of heaven.

FOUR

ALTHOUGH I HAD BEEN HERE hundreds of times, I was lost.

"Where's the collapsible table?" I hollered from the garage. Boxes of random stuff stacked in small mountains in every direction. Liz's garage is a live version of Tetris, the piece falling from the top, flipping around and fitting in the empty spaces.

"It's near the washing machine, behind the Christmas decorations. Do you see it?" Liz yelled back to me, her voice closer than expected, yet nowhere in sight.

I wiggled my body through the maze. The empty trail led to what was most important—the washer and dryer, water heater, electrical panel, and a few boxes she got into more often.

"I see it. But I have to move shit to get to it. You have way too much shit out here. Time for a hoarder intervention. If not a garage sale." What really had me curious was why Liz had so much boxed-up shit in the first place.

"Move whatever you need to. We'll discuss my over-abundance another day. Do you need help? Last time I wedged it in nice and tight."

"That's what she said," I belted out and Liz laughed.

I grabbed the edge of the table and jostled it side-to-side until I loosened it from its holding cell. A moment later, the table slid out of its prison. I lugged it through the maze and into the house.

"Table acquired." I drew out the words and exaggerated my breath. It may have been a joke, but anyone who stepped foot in the garage got a workout.

Liz smirked at me and slapped my arm. "It's about time. I thought maybe you died in there and I would have to call somebody." She stuck her tongue out at me and zeroed in on the tip of her nose.

"Shut up. Besides, you'd have to call a search party to find me in there." I cocked my head and smiled goofily at her. "Anything else you need before I pick up food?"

"Christy? We missing anything else? Sarah's leaving in a minute."

Christy had been so quiet for the last fifteen minutes, I'd almost forgotten she was here. "Not that I can think of." Engrossed in the living room furniture layout, Christy moved couches and chairs and tables all over the place, making more room for the future crowd.

Some of the smaller pieces would be stowed in a bedroom. The more space we had, the more bodies we'd have inside. On occasion, Liz's parties trickled outside when the crowd became too much. But we tried to control the noise and keep everyone inside.

"M'kay, I'll be back in thirty to forty-five. Message me if you think of anything," I said.

Christy shot me a thumbs up as I walked out the door.

Cars lined the street for blocks. Liz's front yard a makeshift parking lot. The thumping vibration bounced around you no matter where you stood in the house. Friends inched closer and talked over the music. Bodies gyrated in the center of the room and rubbed against one another. Red disposable cups of beer, wine, and mixed liquor littered every available surface.

Christy stood near the front door talking with a group of unfamiliar people, Rick's arm wrapped around her waist. Her head threw back in laughter at something a guy with short, blond hair said. Her boisterous nature detectable across the house.

I spotted Liz in the middle of the living room, sand-wiched between a man and woman, their bodies synchro-nized to the electronic rhythm booming off the walls. Liz wanted a relationship whenever she found the right person, but having fun was her current philosophy. She had patience and believed everything happened when it was meant to. And one day she'd find her mister or misses right. When she did, they would be the luckiest person alive.

I wandered from the open kitchen and headed to the makeshift bar. I tossed my beer bottle in the trash can and grabbed a cold beer from the cooler below. Something brushed against my back—a hand maybe—but when I turned around, no one was near me.

The front door opened and more bodies piled into the house, their faces hidden amongst the tall sea of people. Weaving through the foyer, I recognized Eric and smiled. His eyes lit up the second he saw me. He jutted his chin in my direction—his version of hello—and I returned his sentiment. I yelled over the crowd and music, but no way he heard me.

A glass shattered and stole my attention. I peered back to the kitchen, a group of women laughing at the mess. A guy nearby grabbed a paper plate and started picking up the shards. After I located the broom, I helped him clean up.

The beat of the current song faded just enough to transition into the next. Thumping bass kicked off the next song and the rhythm seeped into my bones. One of my favorite songs ripped from the speakers and I started dancing.

I wove between the throng of bodies and sidled up

beside Liz. A second later, Christy joined us. No matter where we were, when the three of us hit the dance floor, we were unstoppable. A ménage à trois of dancing—our hips locked together, hands groping each other, bodies moving in one fluid motion. We called ourselves close friends, but in actuality, we were the friendship version of soul mates.

"There's my ladies!" I shouted at their smiling faces.

The opinions of everyone watching never mattered. I closed my eyes—Christy at my back, Liz facing my front—as the song washed away the world around us. More times than not, we danced like this. It never bothered Rick. He owned Christy's heart, and she owned his. We were three friends who enjoyed life and music. Plain and simple.

The beat shifted and the bass vibrated the walls and deep inside my core. Instinct took over and I clutched Liz's hips, my legs grazing hers. I thrust into her as my body swayed side-to-side and my hips circled. Sweat pricked my brow and a flush spread from my neck to my navel. Liz and I had an intimacy unlike most friends.

Her hands traced down my arms and slid along the hemline of my shorts as her thumbs tucked into the waistband. A tingle spread across my exposed skin and I inched closer to her. Anyone with clear vision probably thought Liz and I were lovers or girlfriends or whatever. I gave no fucks what anyone thought.

Liz and I were best friends. She made me happy in my own skin. Was someone I confided in. There had been conversations between us at the start of our friendship, about dating. We never classified ourselves as girlfriends or being "together," but we enjoyed each other's company. And we had fun. If either of us was lonely—neither of us dated much—we hung out.

We enjoyed ourselves in other ways when it was just us. The first time we dined out then came back to my apartment to watch a movie. Turned out the movie had more sex scenes than not. One thing led to another, and we ended up naked on my couch, our mouths and hands all over each other.

From that moment forward, we weren't only best friends, we were the occasional fuck buddy. No strings. We never set any obligations because one of us might date. In some ways, we had a pact. While single, we were fair game.

So, when Liz's mouth landed on mine, my lips separated and invited her in without hesitation. The warmth of her lips and tongue mingled with mine and lit my body on fire. Christy walked in on us kissing once, so it never fazed her when it happened. And she never asked us if we were more than friends. She loved us, regardless.

"Mmm." Liz groaned as her tongue caressed mine. Whiskey and cola and sin danced over my taste buds. But I wanted to taste more of her.

The crowd hooted as wolf whistles reverberated throughout the room. Guys danced nearby and rooted for us. Weaving through the music, people expressed their opinions on our lip lock. *Damn that's hot* or *fuck me!* or, my all-time favorite, *got room for one more in there?*

No, we didn't. When Liz and I were together, it was only us. We may not be in a legit relationship, but we were monogamous.

The song slowed and transitioned to the next. Liz broke our kiss, and I opened my eyes. A thin sheen of moisture layered her almond skin. Her hazel eyes glowed, and a lustrous smile accentuated her features. I licked my lips, already missing the taste of her. So I leaned forward and gave her one last kiss.

"I need water." My throat scratchy.

She nodded and shouted over my shoulder to Christy, "Water!"

As quick as we appeared on the dance floor, we were off and headed to the kitchen. Half my water disappeared in a flash as my body screamed for relief.

"Hey, ladies! Not sure if I've ever been privy to what I witnessed out there, but that was pretty fucking hot." Eric's voice boomed and startled us.

"Of all the times we've been out, you've never seen us dance?" Liz cocked her head as a snide smile pushed up her cheeks.

"Sorry, Lizzy. I'd definitely remember you and Sarah making out."

My face heated. His words didn't embarrass me, but they put our arrangement in the spotlight. I shifted from foot to foot. Not that I cared what people thought. But I didn't want our display to be an open invitation for something else. I may be a free spirit, eyes-closed-while-I-dance-in-a-field kind of girl, but I'm not sleazy.

I zoned out while Eric and Liz talked. Their conversation trailed off as I chugged my water. A moment later, I was mesmerized by a pair of familiar blue eyes. The same dark blues I'd glimpsed at the gym last weekend. A set of blues I thought I wouldn't see again.

"Excuse me a minute." I dismissed myself from our little group and met the blue-eyed stranger halfway. His sapphires tugged at an invisible force inside me. A volcano erupted beneath my sternum. Who was this guy? Why did my pulse go from zero to a hundred at the sight of him?

"Hey, I'm Sarah. Don't think we've met." I extended my hand and hoped he'd take it.

"Jackson. Eric's friend." His palm blistering against mine. Small callouses toughened the skin at the base of his fingers. The blend of smooth and rough textures oddly arousing.

"Nice to meet you, Jackson. I might be losing my mind, but I swear I saw you last weekend."

His lips curve up a little, displaying a lopsided smile. "You did. At FitPlex. Thought I'd never see you again. Glad that didn't turn out to be true." If possible, his smile grew infinitely bigger.

"So it was you who held the door as my friends and I left."

Something stirred in his eyes as he kept them locked on mine. "My client lives in your complex, and I was meeting him."

"Client?" God, I was mesmerized by how he watched me. As if I would disappear if he looked away. But I didn't want to look away either.

"Personal trainer. I work at one gym, but travel for some clients. Depends on their schedule. What about you? What distracts you during the week?"

It's not lost on me he stepped an inch closer. "Life insurance sales and service. Not so glamourous, but it pays the bills."

His eyes scanned the room for a beat. "This party's kinda crazy, in a good way. How often does your girlfriend throw them?"

His question innocent. No added insinuation. No crude tone. Just a simple question. That he asked without prejudice made me like him more. "We're just friends. Best friends. Tonight's for her birthday, which is days away, but people are over every couple of months. Tonight's a little crazier than the norm."

"Sorry. I didn't mean to assume. I saw you on the dance floor with her. The kiss." I might be wrong—it's hard to see in the darkened room—but I think he's blushing. For a breath, he averted his gaze. For some reason, this plucked at my heartstrings.

"No worries. I'm sure you're not the only one with the idea floating through their head. It doesn't bother us. It's difficult to explain without a long story." He accepted this and the lines that highlighted his face a moment ago smoothed out. "What about the other guy? Is he your boyfriend?"

My eyes tightened and lips pursed. *What the hell was he talking about? What other guy?* "I'm not sure who you're referring to."

His eyebrows pinched together as he tilted his head. "There's a guy that's been your shadow since I've been here, until a few minutes ago. Older than you. Wears glasses. Couldn't see much else under his hoodie. He watched every move you made."

My stomach twisted. His description was so vague it could be anyone. But who the hell would be following me? Christy and Liz invited so many people. And I didn't know everyone on the list. More than likely, people brought other people not in our circle of friends. Tomorrow I'd ask Christy and Liz.

"Not sure who he was. Christy and Liz handled the invite list. Definitely not my boyfriend." I spewed word vomit all over him. Time to put the focus back on him. "What about you? Girlfriend?"

His cheeks plumped as the corners of his mouth perked up. The sexiest dimple popped on his right, while a dazzling flash of white lit up his face. His smile belonged in movies or advertisements. Between his set of sapphire eyes and his radiant smile, I melted into a puddle.

"No girlfriend. Can't seem to find the right girl."

How was that even possible? He was gorgeous. If gorgeous was a proper term for a sinfully delicious man. He wasn't one of those personal trainers who sat on the sidelines. His biceps Herculean—the muscles defined and straining under his black cotton t-shirt.

"Don't mind me while I stand here, baffled. How can you not have a girlfriend?"

If possible, his smile grew bigger. And I melted more. "I've seen my share of beauties, but I'm also a fan of intelligence. Any girl can make herself pretty. I like the women I can talk with and it not be all about them. They're more difficult to find than you'd think. Having a sense of humor helps, too."

"Man, you're asking a lot from us females." I held my poker face as long as possible and watched his expression morph into concern. Just when I thought he would cut ties and run, I burst out laughing. His face and shoulders sagged, relief clear in his posture.

"That wasn't funny. I just thought of a hundred awkward ways to break off our conversation." His frown vanished and his dimple reappeared. Sigh.

"I thought it was pretty damn funny." I laughed, and he shook his head.

"Ha-ha. So, Sarah, what do you like to do?"

Continual conversation. Body leaning forward. Smile on his lips for days. This guy was hitting on me. No doubt in my mind. That fact did crazy things to my insides. Flutters erupted in my belly. Perspiration covered me like a too hot blanket. And my eyes refused to leave his.

When I figured out how to speak again, my voice came out breathy. "You know, a little of this, a little of that."

"That tells me nothing," he chuckled.

"Maybe I want to be mysterious." My playful, flirty side popped up as I batted my lashes.

"Well, it's working. At least tell me something. Anything. Perhaps some of your favorites?"

"My favorites?"

"Yeah. Like movies or books, food or flowers. Anything."

It was cute how we barely knew each other, and he didn't hide his eagerness to learn more. We met ten minutes ago, but something inside me said we'd known each other a lifetime.

"Hm. Let me think a minute. It's not every day a girl gets put on the spot." I paused, pretended to wrack my brain, and dig deep for the answers. "Let's see... I love smutty, romance novels. A girl can never have too many sunflowers or daisies. I'm content getting lost in the woods. And my favorite color..." I stared into the depths of his exquisite gaze. "Without question, blue."

The music faded away and the room grew void of sound as our own little bubble sucked us in. His eyes locked onto mine. Subliminal questions floated in the air. Desire invaded the small gap living between us. I wanted to kiss him. Hard.

My gaze traveled to his throat and locked on his Adam's apple that bobbed as he swallowed back words left unsaid. He broke the silence between us after ten rapid beats of my heart.

"I'd like to get to know you better." He peeked down as he drew his phone from his pocket and unlocked it. "Can I get your number?"

Eyes glued to his brightened phone screen a moment,

he shifted and met my stare. A silent prayer etched on his irises. Begging me to take his phone and enter ten numbers under the contact.

My eyes dropped to the screen as I reached out and took the phone from him. I typed my name and added a sunflower emoji before entering my phone number. I didn't know Jackson, but he intrigued me. His sapphires the bait, and I was hooked.

I handed his phone back and peeked up to study his expression. His eyes glued to the screen, a smile from ear to ear, he tapped a couple of things before locking the screen and returning the phone to his pocket. My phone vibrated in my back pocket and I checked the notification. An incoming message read *Thank you. Jackson*.

Our little happy bubble burst a second later as Eric sidled up on my right. "Hey, I see you met Jackson." Eric's eyes darted from Jackson to me and back to Jackson. "You ready to go, bro? I have to help Pops out in the morning. I'll be useless if I don't get at least four hours of sleep."

"Sure, man. It was great meeting you, Sarah. Till next time." Jackson's addictive smile reappeared.

"You, too. Bye, Eric. See you soon," I said. Eric picked me up and squeezed me as if I was choking and needed the Heimlich maneuver. I smacked his shoulders. "Put me down, dumb ass!" We definitely bantered like siblings.

He set me back on my feet, leaned in and planted a kiss on my cheek. "You know you love me. Later."

Jackson walked behind Eric, looking over his

shoulder at me before he walked out the front door. His beautiful blues the last thing I saw. Again.

Is it possible to ignite into flames and melt into a puddle at the same time? Because that's exactly what my insides did.

FIVE

IT'S BEEN three uneventful days since Liz's party. Three drag-ass days since Jackson walked out of Liz's front door. Three quiet days since I gave him my number. And I haven't heard a word.

No text.

No call.

Complete radio silence.

For the umpteenth time, I unlocked my phone and stared at his text message. *Thank you. Jackson.* It's there. In its own little light gray bubble. Verification, once again, I didn't imagine the whole thing.

Why ask for my number if you don't plan to use it? Several times, I'd contemplated reaching out to him. Sparking conversation. My fingers hovered over the keyboard, eager to type something. Anything. But I stopped myself, every single time.

He asked for my number. So, he should make the first move.

That's it. Period.

"Hey, bitch. Holly told me to tell you there's a delivery for you at reception," Christy said. She walked back to her desk, but didn't sit.

"Delivery? From who?" I asked, a little too loud over the sea of cubicles.

"Don't know. I was headed back in and was told to tell you."

"Thanks, Christy."

As I walked to the elevator, I tried to recall any recent orders I placed and had shipped to work. Nothing.

A sharp ding signaled my arrival to the first floor and the elevator doors slid open. Two steps out, a turn to my right, and my feet halted in their tracks.

I hope those are not for me.

My feet ambled as I took more time than necessary to cross the reception area. With each step, I prayed I made a false assumption.

They're not for you. They're not for you.

I dropped my shoulders, inhaled deeply, and schooled my expression as I approached the counter.

"Hey, Holly. Christy told me I had a delivery."

"Hey, girl. Yep. You're looking at it." Her fingers pointed to the massive bouquet of sunflowers on the counter next to her. My stomach churned at the display. "They're beautiful. You're so lucky. Wish I had someone who sent me flowers."

"Me too," I mumbled.

Her brows pinched in concern. A second later, the concern vanished. "Maybe it's family or something. Or a secret admirer." She shrugged and glanced at the flowers with longing.

As I picked up the flowers, I inhaled their sweet fragrance. "Not sure. I'll keep ya posted."

"Talk to you later," she said as I headed toward the bank of elevators.

When was the last time I got flowers? Had I ever had flowers delivered? And who sent them? I had no clue.

Unless... No. It couldn't be. We met days ago. Knew nothing about each other. Although, he did ask about my favorite flower.

Maybe it was a test. Maybe he was just curious. Or... Would a guy who knew me for all of three minutes send me flowers? How? I never mentioned *where* I worked.

I didn't remember hearing the elevator chime, but the doors whisked open to the third floor. I clutched the flowers to my side as I beelined for my little cave.

Every set of eyes locked on me, watched me, as I walked past with a gargantuan arrangement of bold yellow flowers. Being discreet was impossible. The sunflowers gorgeous, but the attention undesirable. I didn't want an onslaught of inquiries, but knew someone was bound to ask who sent them.

Four partitions away, a scruff voice made the first comment. "Wow, Sarah! Those flowers are vibrant. What a lucky girl!"

Ugh.

Turning my head as I passed, my feet slowing a smidge. "Thanks, Stuart." That's all I said. Stuart stood and watched me. The way he stared sent a shiver down my spine and I increased my pace. Had Stuart always looked at me that way? Why did I get so many weird vibes recently? Was it me?

The flowers were beyond gorgeous, but the receipt of them strange. Awkward. And had me feeling a little unhinged.

Two more steps and I'd be in my work safe place. I set the mass of sunshine on my desk and startled at the sight of Christy and Liz.

"Holy shit, girl! Who are those from?" Christy's octave and volume loud enough for the entire third floor to hear.

"Oh, Jesus! You scared the shit out of me," I said as I clutched my chest.

"Sorry. Who sent the flowers?" Christy asked again.

"Not sure. Haven't looked at the card. Gimme a sec."

Pushing a few of the blooms aside, I retrieved a small envelope from the plastic prong. I slipped my finger beneath the flap, opened the envelope, and slid out the card tucked inside.

"Who are they from?" Liz and Christy did that whole talk in unison thing again.

My eyes scanned over the words on the card. "Uh... I'm not sure. There's no name. And the message is kinda... weird." That was putting it lightly. The message was creepy, if I was honest.

"What's it say?" Liz more inquisitive than Christy, for a change.

"It says, 'A beautiful girl deserves beautiful flowers. I love seeing your face glow like the sun, day in and day out.'"

"So... sounds like it's definitely not from the hottie you met at my party. Unless you've seen him since," Liz said.

"Nope. Been hoping he'd call or text. Haven't heard a word."

Always the optimist, Christy said, "At least you have pretty flowers to look at the rest of the week."

"I suppose."

I hated telling her I wanted them off my desk. That I was uncomfortable receiving flowers with creepy, unsigned messages. The flowers a constant reminder someone watched me. Daily. Bile rose in my throat.

We sat quiet a moment. Liz and Christy took the silence as a hint to go back to their desks. For once, I was more introspective.

Christy patted me softly on the shoulder, her eyes gentle as she got up and left. Liz hung back a moment and stared at me, intrigued.

"You sure you're okay? You look bothered."

I slumped in my chair. My thoughts scattered like glitter in the wind. Not that I didn't like the flowers. They were a burst of sunshine. The sentiment bothered me. No name or indication of where they came from bothered me. All of it just sat *wrong* with me.

The context put me on high alert. Whoever sent the

flowers saw me often, perhaps daily. Only two people saw me on a regular basis. One went back to her desk, the other sat across from me.

"I'm okay. I guess it's the last line that has me thrown. Like this person sees me every day. Other than you and Christy, I don't see anyone often." Christy and Liz weren't my only friends, just my favorite.

"I'm sure it's nothing. Maybe it means something else. To them, at least."

"I guess... It still feels weird."

"Want me to take them?" For the first time in fifteen minutes, I smiled. Liz offered to do this task and I immediately sagged in my seat. I loved my best friend.

"Please. What're you doing with them?"

Liz tapped a finger on her lips. "Hm. I'll set them in the break room with a sign. *Free flowers.* They'll be gone in no time."

In seconds, the nausea vanished. A veil of discomfort lifted. "That would be amazing. Thanks, Liz. You're more than the best."

She half-smiled and her plump bottom lip curved up. Liz peeked over my cubicle walls, scanned left and right, before snatching the tainted flowers and quickly kissing me. "Anything for you. Later."

Within a heartbeat, she left with the ominous flowers. It's crazy how the simplest thing soured my mood. Flowers should bring smiles. Today, they didn't. Instead, they left a gap. A void.

Curiosity clung like a shadow. I needed answers.

Somehow. Someway. Few people knew my preference in flowers. Mom. Dad. Maybe Christy and Liz. A few guys I'd dated, but months had passed, and I can't picture any of them sending me anything, let alone flowers.

And then there was Jackson.

Sliding open my desk drawer, I retrieved my phone. Jackson and I hadn't spoken since Saturday, but asking him seemed a logical place to start.

Opening my text history, I tapped on the message he'd sent me Saturday. *Thank you. Jackson.* I'd saved his number to my phone and hoped his name would've popped up before now. But it never did. How on earth was I supposed to ask him if he sent me flowers? What would I say? *Hey, did you send flowers to my job with a super creepy message?*

Ugh. This sucked.

My fingers hovered over the screen as my brain scrambled to type something not embarrassing. Think, think, think. My fingers tapped away and typed out a message. For a second, I lingered above the send arrow.

Sarah: Just wanted to say hi.

Corny. The lamest text message in existence. But I sent it. I dangled the bait and waited for him to bite.

I set my phone down and went back to what I was working on before the flower fiasco. A vase full of unpleasantries wouldn't disrupt my day. Not today.

Knee deep in my call list, I waded my way to the end

just as my phone vibrated and Jackson's name flashed on the screen.

Jackson: Hey. How are you?

Sarah: Doing good. Working like a fiend. How are you?

Jackson: Doing good. Just finished with a client. I'm bummed you messaged first. I was planning on reaching out to you tomorrow.

Tomorrow? If he'd sent the flowers, he would've messaged me today or tonight, to see if I'd gotten them. Right? So maybe they weren't from him. But I had to be certain and ask. Time to turn the awkwardness up to high.

Sarah: I have a strange question. Please don't freak out. By chance, did you send me flowers at work?

An eternity passed as I waited for his response. Did I scare him away? God, I hoped not. He was sexy and intriguing and mysterious. I wanted to see him again, but had to ask if he'd sent them. If he did, why the strange message? My phone buzzed.

Jackson: Sorry. Wasn't me. But now I have a competitor for your attention. I may need to up my game.

I read the text three times and smiled. Relief eased my

troublesome thoughts and resuscitated me. Thank god the note wasn't from him. The likelihood of things moving forward would've decreased exponentially.

But now a new concern followed me like a storm cloud. Who knew me well enough to send something so personal? The million dollar question.

Sarah: I'd like to see what's entailed in this competition. Sorry for the weird question. I got flowers with an odd message and no sender name.

Jackson: If I send you flowers, you'll know they're from me. I have another client in a couple minutes. Can we talk later?

Sarah: Definitely I'm off work at 5ish. Sweat a lot today 😓

Jackson: Maybe later…

Maybe later? Huh? Not sure what he meant, but my mind went straight to the gutter. For the rest of my day, I thought about Jackson, his deep blue eyes, and his mysterious body… hot and sweaty. A fantastic visual for the rest of my day. And my mood shifted in seconds.

Work breezed by with no further discussion regarding the flowers. Liz, Christy, and I had lunch downstairs. I shared the flirty banter I had with Jackson and let them over-analyze the texts.

Christy was head-over-heels about a new guy in my world. She rambled on and asked questions I couldn't answer. She rattled off fairy tale stories about how she saw my future. Tons of sex. Marriage. Babies. Her scenarios laughable.

Liz was excited for me, but seemed on edge. Almost as if disappointed. Or sad, perhaps. She and I would have a *date* night soon. Just the two of us. Where we would talk openly and get everything out.

Maybe I read her wrong. Maybe something else bothered her and it chose this moment to bleed out. Assumption was the enemy. So, I vowed to learn the truth.

I loved Liz. My best friend. More so than Christy. We'd shared fun and passionate times. But we talked about them. In full detail, no holds barred. Agreed they were only fun. Agreed to no strings. But maybe, when I wasn't paying attention, it evolved. I didn't want to hurt her. Ever. No matter what happened with either of us.

When Christy got up to use the restroom, I told Liz I wanted to hang out. So, before Christy returned to the table, we planned to meet at her house tomorrow night.

Simple enough... Dinner, conversation, and TV reruns. I just hoped everything went according to plan.

SIX

PEEKING through the frosted glass like a Peeping Tom, I spotted Liz inside. A shiver danced over my skin, the cool night air not the cause. For reasons unknown, I was frazzled. I had never been nervous around Liz. More the opposite. Liz grounded me. Kept me centered.

I hesitated a moment. I glanced down at my fumbling fingers, closed my eyes, and took a few cleansing breaths. Liz was my best friend. My nervousness was ridiculous. We'd done this hundreds of times—dinner alone, enjoying the other's company.

As I opened my eyes, I centered myself. This was Liz. Nothing had changed. We were still us. Comfortable in our own skin together. Watching her blurred silhouette another second, I rapped on the blue wooden door.

"Come in!"

I opened the door and stepped inside. Liz was a force of nature as she scurried around the kitchen and focused on cooking. A pot and pan sizzled on the burners. Wooden utensils off to the side for each dish. Steam wafted throughout the room and spread delicious aromas of garlic and herbs and something sweeter. When Liz took over the kitchen, everyone prepared to be wowed.

As I stepped farther inside, I set a bottle of wine on the kitchen counter. "Smells amazing in here. What's for dinner?"

She paused her feverish stirring to glance my way, a sultry smile lit her face. "Thanks. Grilled rosemary chicken, garlic pearled couscous, and roasted carrots."

More times than not, it baffled me why Liz worked for a life insurance company. Her skills in the kitchen blew my mind. She could take the simplest ingredients and turn them into a succulent work of art. No matter how many times I complimented her cooking and told her she should do more with it, she always told me it was something she enjoyed. And she didn't want to ruin that joy by doing it as a job.

"How much longer?"

"Maybe ten more minutes."

"Okay. I'll set the table. Want a glass of wine?" I waved the bottle in the air as if teasing a dog with a toy.

Her eyes beamed as much as her smile. "Wine would be great."

Liz and I danced around each other in synchronicity. She bounced between the sink and stove as I grabbed everything else we needed for dinner. The coffee table set, I tossed fluffy pillows on the floor. Back in the kitchen, I grabbed glasses, the wine, and Liz's snazzy wine opener. A pop echoed, and I set the wine on the counter to breathe.

"Anything I can help with?" I'd run out of tasks and saddled up beside her.

The aroma of herb roasted carrots drifted through the air. Liz gave the couscous one final stir and said, "Just grab plates. Everything's ready."

We portioned out dinner, then headed to the living room. Settling onto the pillows, Liz flipped on the television and picked a random series to binge on Netflix. I poured the pale hued wine into our glasses. An unfamiliar, awkward silence stretched between us. Did Liz feel as out of place as I did? We weren't usually like this, but things were on the verge of change. I didn't want our dynamic to change. Losing Liz wasn't an option.

Leaning over my plate, I closed my eyes and inhaled. My mouth watered instantly. Fork in hand, I was prepared to dive in, until I noticed Liz in my periphery. She nudged carrots around her plate like a toddler, trying to mask how much she hadn't eaten. Discussing the change between us was inevitable, but I never wanted us to become uncomfortable. Liz meant the world to me and I valued our friendship.

"You okay?" Two words—a simple question—slipped from my lips slow and soft.

"Yeah," she mumbled, her dinner still making circuits on her plate. "Guess I was more surprised than expected when you brought up talking with Jackson. Showing me the texts made it real. I'm not sure why this shocked me. Someone as amazing as you..."

She left her thought hanging wide open. I understood where her head was; mine was there too. "I get it. We have more than your average friendship. We don't just hang out and shoot the shit. And although we've talked about not getting too deep with things, we can't change reality. That we've been intimate."

We sat there, eyes locked and loaded with questions, and watched each other. No words exchanged. No movement. Silent and still. She searched my eyes, scanned their depths, and looked for answers neither of us had.

Her pinky brushed my hand and my pulse picked up. The soft touch thrummed in my veins. Liz's eyes said a thousand things, words we'd never spoken aloud. Her chin dropped, eyes locked on our near touch, her voice a hair above a whisper. "I can't lose you."

I pinched her chin between my thumb and forefinger and brought her line-of-sight to mine. Our lips a breath apart. "You'll never lose me. No matter what."

Her eyes glazed over from the threat of tears. "Promise?"

As my best friend—my person and someone I relied on—how could she think we'd be anything less? Even if our lives changed, she would always be a part of mine. "I promise."

She closed the gap between us. Her lips encompassed mine as her tongue swiped my lower lip. I opened up to her and she caressed and stroked her tongue against mine.

In this moment—lips joined, hands hugging curves—a mile long list of questions popped into my head and asked why.

Why hadn't we taken this to the next level? Why hadn't we tried to be more? Why did we hide our intimacy from everyone? People saw us kiss. At bars or clubs and the other night at her party. But that was the extent of our exposure. Behind closed doors, though, our level of intimacy was intense. An intensity we hid. We'd been friends two years before we evolved to where we are now. So, why?

Her hand slid under my shirt, fingertips traipsed up my abdomen and caressed my lace bra. With subtle tenderness, Liz fondled my nipples through the lace. I twisted and propped myself up on my knees and tugged my shirt over my head.

"Can't lose you," Liz mumbled when our lips reconnected.

Her hands slid down and trekked to my backside. On their ascent, Liz unfastened my bra. My arms dropped, and the lacy material fell between us, exposing my pebbled nipples.

My body burst into flames when Liz's lips abandoned mine and traveled down my neck, along my collarbone and over my breasts. Her mouth and fingers greedy as she sucked and squeezed. I was mad with hunger and yanked her cotton shirt off her body. The second her bare flesh was exposed, my desire grew tenfold. No obstructions. No extra steps. Nothing except skin and heat and passion.

When her mouth was back on mine, I sucked her lower lip. Ravenous, I licked and nipped my way across her creamy chocolate-colored flesh. Desire pooled between my thighs as my clit throbbed. My mouth traced the lines of her skin, landing on the firm peak of her breasts. I latched onto her nipple, sucking and scraping the flesh, salivating at the sweetness of her skin. A moan echoed from her chest and my core clenched.

"You won't lose me," I groaned. We might not have moments like this in the future, but only now mattered. Because right now, nothing had changed.

Liz's warm fingers ran from hip to hip and traced an invisible line along the linen fabric. A slight tug at my waist loosened the strands securing the material and Liz's fingers grazed over my lower abdominals.

My mouth explored her body and left no part untraveled. Liz's fingernails etched the sides of my spine, my back bowing and lungs gasping for breath. Lust and heat and yearning surged within me. I needed more of her. Now.

She drew my lips back to hers and devoured me as if starved her whole life. Her hand slid between my skin and the linen, and skimmed the small lace triangle, stopping when she discovered my damp folds. A low growl rumbled in her chest, the reverberation spiking the insatiable hunger in my core. Her fingers circled a slow tempo.

Breath hot on my neck, Liz panted harder with each loop. "Fuck! It drives me wild when you're wet like this."

Her teeth sunk into the plump flesh at my shoulder and I arched into her touch.

Liz's hand slid from my waistband, a small cry escaping my lips at the sudden loss. She stood and extended her hand. I took it as she stood me up and dropped to her knees, grasping my pants and yanking them down.

Starting at my ankles, her fingers traced invisible lines up the outside of my calves, over the contours of my thighs and hooked into the thin lace of my panties. Hungry eyes locked on mine as the lace fell to the floor.

Liz grasped my bare ass and squeezed with authority. Her mouth hovered inches from the groomed patch between my thighs. I panted when her breath coasted over my skin and teased my clit. My pulse pounded and my skin heated. I wanted her hot tongue to run the length of my slit. Wanted it to circle my most sensitive place. To lick and lavish my clit and folds. My core ablaze, I wanted her to forgo dinner and eat me.

She peered up, hazels hooded and ignited. I framed her face with my hands, the tips of my fingers clawing her siren red hair. Liz leaned forward, inhaled deep, and licked from the junction of my thighs up. My back bowed, and I thrust my pussy into her.

The room faded away as my body landed on the plush sofa cushions, the cool fabric prickled my skin. Liz forced my legs apart and rubbed along my thighs from knees to cleft as her mouth peppered kisses.

Lips kissed. Mouth sucked. Teeth bit. She consumed

every ounce of me, pausing at my core. As she hovered over the soft, pink flesh, her breath came in hot bursts and I trembled, unsure how long I could withstand her teasing.

My fingers combed through her hair as her hazels lifted and met my stare. Voice gravelly and foreign to my own ears, I said, "Fuck me. I need to feel you."

Frozen in place, she gaped as I placed my hand over hers and inched it toward the wetness between my legs. Liz forfeited control a moment and sat slack-jawed as I traced her fingers over my slit. After a few strokes, I shifted forward and thrust gently into her fingers, goading her to take over.

One more stroke and her fingers took control again. My hand shifted to her breast and fondled the plump flesh. As my body crept forward, her fingers tempted and teased my entrance, circling the bundle of nerves above.

She sat up on her knees and aligned herself better with my body, fingers stroking my folds over and over. On the next twirl of her fingers, I drove my hips forward and forced her fingers inside me.

"Yes…" The single word a litany on my lips. My breath faster, harsher.

Liz's mouth crashed down on mine as her tongue dove in and stroked vigorously. Her fingers pumped like pistons in and out of my greedy pussy. But I craved more. I picked up the rhythm and rammed harder as Liz kept pace. Hungry to plunge my fingers inside her, my hands skimmed down her torso and past the skimpy loose-fitting short shorts. Propping myself up, I slid my fingers beneath the inseam and growled when I grazed her hot, bare skin. Moisture coated my fingertips. A new desperation coursed through my veins and I buried my fingers inside her.

Our bodies gyrated to a ferocious beat. Hands and fingers frantic to touch. Orgasms rocketed as friction stroked like a wanton beast. When her orgasm clamped down on me, I no longer resisted my own.

My body ignited like a star being born. Heat incinerated the landscape of my skin, screams ripped from my lips and she swallowed them whole. Liz bit my shoulder and dug her nails into my sides. I loved how impassioned we were when we came undone together.

When she stopped shaking, Liz collapsed against my abdomen. We laid half on the couch, our limbs tangled and the room a haze of rapid breathing and undiluted sex. She scooted up and rested her forehead on my chest, jostling every few seconds to nestle the crook of my neck.

"So much for dinner, huh?" Liz said.

I burst out in laughter, my body shaking uncontrollably. A second later, she joined in. Arms squeezed tight, our bodies trembled in happiness. So much for talking about relationships and emotions. I guess we'd play it by ear and see how the future unfolded.

Bringing her closer to my chest, I added, "That's what they make microwaves for, right?"

SEVEN

DINNER WITH LIZ turned into sex with Liz. Dinner was eaten, but it wouldn't have mattered if it wasn't. After being up far too late, we skipped watching television and talked. We spewed everything we'd bottled up and discovered that we've had more than a simple best friend friendship for quite some time.

By the end of our chat, we decided to keep our previous 'agreement' in place. Both of us had immense feelings for each other, but didn't want a romantic relationship together. Hard to admit, we were both scared to break something perfect. Something completely us.

And though I cared deeply for Liz, I explained my desire to pursue things with Jackson, but needed her reassurance. Her happiness was my happiness. If things didn't pan out with Jackson, perhaps Liz and I would try for more—without ruining years of friendship. But I still had unease about altering the current Liz-Sarah dynamic.

After hours of chatter, the night transitioning into early morning, I decided to stay at Liz's place. In the morning, she'd let me borrow clothes for work. It wouldn't be the first time. After our intense conversation tonight, it didn't seem right to up and leave. Instead, I wanted the press of her warm body against mine, and to have her arms wrap around me and hold me while we slept.

As I stepped out of the ensuite bathroom, my heart raced.

The comforter laid askew on the floor. Liz's almond-hued, nude body sprawled across the bold, red sheets as her fingers rubbed between her thighs. Magnetized, I stared as her fingers circled the spot above her slit with vigor. Her folds glistened from the moisture.

"Oh, god," I moaned as I took in the sight of her.

An ache furled at the junction of my thighs. The intensity almost unbearable. Dampness seeped from my core and slid down my legs. *Fuck me.* Liz stirred things in my body incomparable to anyone prior. I'd been with men and women over the years. But being with a woman was unparalleled. A distinct hunger. One I hadn't known until Liz.

Tugging my shirt over my head and shoving my pants down my thighs, I bared my wanton flesh to her once more. There was no use in denying her, or myself. Although I was eager for what might happen with Jackson, we weren't anything more than two people agreeing to get together at this point. Until that changed, I would enjoy life.

Planting my feet near the edge of the bed, I gawked as her fingers circled her clit then slid between her folds. The ache between my legs morphed into a powerful beast. It clawed and growled and begged me to not hold back.

I slid a hand down my stomach, through the trimmed patch of curls, and ran them along my slick skin. My eyes darted between Liz's lust-spelled gaze and her greedy fingers. Arousal coated my fingers as I propped one leg along the edge of the bed and played with my clit. With each stroke, my fingers disappeared between my folds.

Liz's back arched off the mattress, her fingers moved faster, pumping in and out of her pussy with an insatiable hunger. Her moans louder with each stroke, edging my orgasm further. Our eyes locked, neither of us able to look elsewhere. Both of us chased our orgasms. I pinched a nipple with my free hand, tugging the firm nub and twisting while I drove into my pussy harder.

My eyes scanned Liz's body as she inched into a more upright position. My eyes glued to hers, her fingers worked her clit harshly in my periphery.

"I'm so close," Liz said, her eyes glassy as her face and chest bloomed scarlet. Her legs trembled, a sign she was about to come. An undeniable visual. One I wanted to participate in.

Her jaw fell slack, eyes hooded and focused between my legs. My clit slick as I swiped rapid circles. I moaned, the reverberation raspy in my throat. A second later, Liz whimpered. Our cries of pleasure in sync.

And then she screamed in pleasure—a familiar and alluring cry. The guttural howl sent me over the edge and I rode the high with her.

The air a mixture of her breath and mine, our lungs burning for oxygen. Liz dropped onto the mattress, her legs sprawled with her arms at her sides. Her chest rose and fell in rapid succession.

I want to make her come again.

I planted one knee on the bed, then the other, and crawled up to hover over her. My lips inches from hers as I gasped. "Need to taste you."

She nodded. "Yes."

I kissed her with intimate tenderness, climbed off her body, inverted my position, and mounted her face. Lips to folds. We consumed each other into the early hours of the morning, nowhere near satiating our desires. And without a care in the world.

The hours at work trickled by. Phones at a lull. Reports up-to-date. And my inbox had no new messages.

The company frowned upon cell phone usage in the office, unless work related, but I was beyond bored and had another hour before the day ended.

Checking no one managerial hovered nearby, I deduced it safe to sneak a little phone time in without a slap on the wrist. I opened my desk drawer and snagged my cell. After unlocking it, I checked social media and cleared out a handful of notifications. I played my turn on a round of Words with Friends. Then started perusing my surplus of personal emails.

Once bored with my phone, I peeked up at the clock and noticed only ten minutes had passed. This sucked. The monotony endless. Bored out of my skull and tired as hell, I just wanted to go home, slip on some comfy PJs, and crash in my bed. My fluffy pillows and cozy comforter were in for a major cuddle session soon.

A buzz jolted me from the daydream. I glanced down at my phone and saw a text notification. After unlocking my phone, I tapped the notification.

Jackson: Hey, how are you? Ever find out who sent the flowers?

Jackson. Part of me jumped up and down like a four-teen-year-old girl because the boy she liked called her. But another part of me lingered in a strange funk as Liz popped into my thoughts. A twinge of guilt churned in my core at my excitement, especially after what happened between us last night. I didn't want to betray my friend and her feelings, but reminded myself we talked about me wanting to date Jackson. Liz would always be there for me, regardless. It would be idiotic to deny this connection with Jackson.

Sarah: Nope. Probably some lunatic. Who knows? I gave them away. Didn't want to keep them.

Jackson: Didn't think you'd answer right away. Thought you'd be at work.

Sarah: Still at work. Being rebellious. Bored out of my mind. Was messing with my phone when you messaged.

Jackson: Gotcha. Anything new?

Sarah: Same old, same old. How'd your sweat session go?

Jackson: Just another day doing what I do. Sorry I didn't reach out last night. Crashed early. I was beat.

Sarah: No worries. I hung out with Liz last night. Crashed at her place. Stayed up way too late.

After I hit send, I smacked myself in the face. Literally. Did I just tell him I slept at my friend's house? The same friend he saw me making out with. That we were up too late. I closed my eyes, squeezing them tight while I mentally beat myself up. Did I kill my chance before I got one?

Jackson: You two hang out often?

Sarah: Yeah. Best friends and whatnot. We're pretty tight.

Jackson: That's cool. How would I fit into that equation?

I was unsure how he meant the question. Was he asking to be a part of what we had? Or, was he asking what would happen between me and Liz if something happened with him and me? Time to tread lightly.

Sarah: I'm reading that question more than one way. Can you be a little more specific? Sorry.

Jackson: If I asked you out on a date, how does that work? Would you be dating both of us?

Sarah: I told you, we're friends… with a few extra benefits. We have an agreement. Easier to explain in person.

Jackson: Maybe we can grab dinner one night soon and you can explain it to me.

And there it was, right smack in front of my face. The question I'd been eager to hear, or in this case see. And yet the question had my stomach twisted up like a pretzel.

Although Liz and I talked last night, I had to share what just happened. That Jackson made his move. The chess pieces in motion. And I planned to accept his invitation.

Sarah: I'd really like that. Between now and this weekend probably isn't the best idea. V day and all.

Jackson: Valentine's Day doesn't scare me. But you're probably right. Every place will be packed. What about next week, Tuesday?

Sarah: Tuesday sounds great. When? Where? Details.

Jackson: All in good time. I'll let you get back to being a rebel. Okay if we talk later?

Sarah: Definitely

Jackson: Cool. Till then…

My cheeks burned as a megawatt smile stretched across my face. If I was ten years younger, I'd be a hormonal lunatic—screaming with my girlfriends, resembling the nerdy girl who got asked out by the quarterback. I wanted to share my excitement with Christy and Liz. Wanted my thrill to be theirs too.

I popped my head up, scanned the sea of cubicles, and spotted no one walking within proximity. Plopping back into my seat, I opened the group chat between me,

Christy, and Liz, my fingers jittery as I typed. Christy would be excited, no doubt about it. I only hoped Liz would be, too.

Sarah: Guess who scored a date next week?

Christy: No fucking way, bitch!!! I will need more details.

Liz: That's awesome. The three of us should get together before then and coach you 😊

Sarah: As if I've never dated before 😶 V day dinner this weekend? Is Rick taking you out C?

Christy: We're going out the day after. Too many people out that day. I'll ask him if it's cool that we hang on V day.

Sarah: Awesome. Keep us posted.

Christy: 👍

The next two days at work snailed along. Liz, Christy, and I had lunch both days, the two of them giving me their best advice on my upcoming date. They behaved as if I'd never gone out with anyone. Ever. It was sad and laughable.

"Give me something to work with here," Christy said over lunch today. She wanted to know all the ins and outs of where Jackson was taking me, hoping she'd be able to rifle through my closet and pick out my attire for my date.

"If I had details to share, you'd be the first to know."

Jackson had yet to disclose where he was taking me. Our texts during the week had been brief. But the second I mentioned we'd been texting back and forth, Christy stuck out her hand and begged for my phone. She was eager to read what our hungry little fingers had typed, word for word, and not my interpretation. As much as I loved Christy, I denied her. If I let anyone read them, besides me, it would be Liz.

I trusted Christy with my life, but her outlook on things was overzealous, and I wasn't mentally prepared for that experience. With things slowly evolving between me and Jackson, I wanted to share things in fractions, not wholes. If she read our text history, I would never hear the end of her over-analyzation. And the last thing I wanted was for things to be picked apart.

The end of the week passed, and the three of us agreed to hang out at Christy's place on Valentine's Day. It was a two-fer. We got to hang out, chat girl stuff, and they could infiltrate me with whatever dating advice they deemed necessary. And Christy would still be home with Rick, in case he wanted more time with her on the cards and flowers holiday.

The whole evening was packed with laughter, good food, and great company. Liz and I sat on the couch, while Christy sat on the floor facing us. Rick joined us shortly after we started eating, cozying up to Christy. They were so damn adorable.

As the conversation flowed, Rick threw out dating tidbits the three of us would never think about. He pitched his version of what would make a great first date from the male perspective. Sex was the one thing I waited to hear but didn't. He told me every first date he'd ever been on, he was super nervous. He worried about every little detail and sex was the last thing on his mind. Call me fascinated.

Sometimes, as women, we forget men are human, too. Behind the bravado and physique, they can be on edge like us, their emotions scattered. A constant wonder if they've said the wrong thing. Uncertain if they should kiss a woman on the first date. It's a challenge to remember we're all capable of the same things in that first moment... Love and fear.

Four-thirty-three. "Could this day be any slower?" I mumbled at my computer. The clock ticked by at a snail's pace as the workday wrapped up. Not checking the time every other minute proved difficult. In less than two hours, Jackson would pick me up from my apartment and whisk me off to a nice restaurant somewhere in the city. Tonight's date had me antsy and over-the-moon. Something about the way Jackson looked at me made my body sing.

We'd messaged back and forth over the last week, talking about dinner and solidifying our plans. There had been light flirting, the occasional innuendo, and consistent interaction. I tried to get a better read on him through his texts, but he didn't give much away. But I was eager for more before he knocked at my door. And he kept me hooked, teasing me with bait on occasion.

Somehow, I made it home in record time, and had more than an hour to look presentable for our date. I reached into the shower, cranked the lever to the far left, and let the water heat. I peeled off my standard Hammond Life polo and khakis before I stepped under the hot stream. Snagging the hair tie I kept in the shower, I secured my hair in a messy top bun.

The water pinked my skin as my muscles loosened and relaxed. I stood there a moment, mind blank, while my body let go of the day's tension. Normally, I wasn't so tightly wound. Was I really that nervous about our date tonight? Maybe. My stomach had been in knots since I woke up.

My last official date/relationship was months ago. And over the last several months, single life had been fabulous. Unlimited time hanging out with friends. Christy and Liz packed my life and heart with happiness, and I wanted for nothing. Dating Jackson wouldn't occupy a vacancy that had magically appeared. More like he was a new branch on our little family tree. At least a small part of me hoped as much.

When I'd told Christy and Liz that Jackson planned to take me to an eclectic bistro, Christy insisted on choosing my attire. As if I were incapable of fulfilling such a task. "I can dress myself," I'd said to them both. Christy rolled her eyes. Liz smiled.

On a wooden hanger, a soft, cream-colored linen dress hung on the back of my door. Thin straps held the halter in place, tied around my neck and exposed most of my bare back. The billowy material skirted over the floor, my khaki flats peeking out as I walked. Sifting through my jewelry, I located the perfect piece to add a little flare and offset the light color.

I slipped the necklace over my head, lifted my hair over the cord, and allowed the chunky, raw lapis lazuli to rest on my sternum. Whenever I wore my lapis, I always felt more connected and energized. I hoped I wouldn't need the extra boost tonight, but a lady could never be too prepared. From the short time we'd seen each other in person, plus the easy flow of conversation through our text messages, a mysterious chemistry ebbed between us. A magnetic aura brought us together and opened our eyes to new possibilities.

For tonight's date, I left my honey blonde locks loose. The strands tickled the skin below my mid-back. As I stared at my reflection in the bathroom vanity, my heart galloped like a pack of wild animals beneath my ribs.

Why was I so nervous?

My ring finger ran across my lower lip as I spread my glossy balm. A buzz from the intercom startled me, and I sprinted for the door. Pressing the answer button on the speaker, Jackson's voice broke the silence in my apartment. "Hey, I'm at the gate."

"Give me a sec." I pressed the button to open the gate, a beep blared from the box. "I'm in the building just before the curve, bottom floor."

"See you in a few." The breeze muffled his voice.

I ran back to my bedroom, going to the full-length mirror beside the bathroom door, my hands brushing down my sides. Twisting left then right, I inspected my appearance from head to toe, and tucked a few strands of hair behind my ears before setting them free again. Before I left the room, I snagged my purse, a loose-fit knitted sweater, and my phone. I plopped down on the couch, my right knee bouncing as I waited for my date to knock at the door.

From the moment we entered the restaurant, I was convinced I'd worn the wrong attire. Saying it aloud would only state the obvious. This place edged closer to fine dining than artsy bistro. I needed more material over my skin. Perhaps something more formal in appearance. Something to cover the mass of bare flesh displayed on my back. Compared to everyone in the room, I was naked. Even if I put on the more-than-comfortable knitted cover-up—which hung limp over my arm—I'd be inadequate. Lacking the coverage I suddenly craved, I wrapped my arms around my center and hugged myself tight. For an outgoing woman, I shied up in an instant.

"You okay?" Jackson's warm fingertips skirted the exposed dip along my spine.

"Uh... I think I'm a bit underdressed," I said and glanced at him. Clad in denim and a dark turquoise button-up, his sleeves were rolled up and hugging the distal end of his biceps. My mouth watered at the observation. The pop of blue accentuated his sparkling eyes as they stared into my soul, my heart ballooning in my chest. I inhaled deep and relief flooded me as I snapped out of my fantasy and realized our ensembles were on equal ground.

"You're not. This place appears more extravagant than it is. One of the reasons I like it." Jackson's fingertips traced up and down my lower back, the soft, subtle motion comforting me. The corners of his mouth curved up, and his smile sparked an unfamiliar heat in my body. A spark which slowly ignited a forest fire.

My arms relaxed as my hands loosened their grip above my elbows. As I scanned the other patrons nearby, I breathed easier and relaxed my shoulders a bit. "Thank you."

"For what?"

"For calming my nerves. And helping me see I blend in. I'm usually not this nervous."

"Sarah, you could never blend in... You're a sunflower in a field of daisies. You light up the room." Heat blossomed on my cheeks. His reference to my favorite flowers, and using them to explain how he sees me, left me speechless. I opened my mouth, wanting to say something other than thank you, but snapped it shut. No perfect words. No witty comeback. My mind frozen. Vocal cords out of service.

The hostess guided us to our table. Various pieces of art adorned the white walls along our path. Paintings, sculptures, drawings. Red curtains connected along parts of the ceiling and created a look like theater curtains. Each wall space had its own art theme—animals, landscapes, fruits, vegetables, wines, abstract, and so on.

If someone explained the interior of this restaurant to me, I would call it gaudy. But it was quite the opposite. Everything on display tasteful. In here, it was all about placement. They used strategy to place each piece. A form of Feng Shui. Once you stepped back, it was easier to see.

Jackson pulled out my chair, his fingertips grazing along my shoulder and down my arm a few inches after I sat. When his touch vanished, my body pled for more.

Crisp, white linen blanketed our table. A large, rectangular candle rested in the center, the wooden wick crackling under the flame. A small vase sat off to one side —dozens of daisies, tall sprigs of rosemary, and stems of a fine leafed fern nestled in the glass.

I scanned the other tables nearby, each of them lit with similar candles but absent of flowers. It'd be silly of me to assume he bought them or had them delivered, but no other tables had flowers. The arrangement was perfect and beautiful, and I itched to lean forward and smell them.

"Did you have the flowers delivered?" I asked, curious.

"Kind of. When I called to reserve a table, I asked if it was possible to add daisies to the table."

Again, for the second time tonight, I had no words. For a woman who spoke openly, it was odd to have nothing to say. Jackson pulled out all the stops and dazzled me. I wasn't a difficult person to impress since I enjoyed the simplest things. But his tactics definitely weighed in his favor.

"They're beautiful. Thank you." My cheeks tightened from my unstoppable smile. Heat bloomed across my face as my eyes diverted down to my menu. What was it about Jackson that brought out this new shyness?

"You're most welcome." The dimple on his right cheek appeared when I peeked up at him.

A server had come and gone, our food and drink orders placed. Under normal circumstances, I wouldn't drink on a first date—wanting to keep my wits about me—but tonight felt anything but normal. I ordered a glass of wine, hoping the burgundy liquid would settle my nerves and fill me with my normal courage. I wasn't a quiet person under normal circumstances, but with this man... everything was different. I was different. In a good way.

Jackson sat across from me, hands steepled at his mouth, elbows on the table, inquisitive eyes boring into mine. His hands lowered from his lips, lips I had trouble looking away from. His tongue peeked out, the tip running over the center of his lower lip, tugging it in and trapping it under his teeth a moment.

As if someone caught me peeping in a window, I gazed anywhere but at his mouth. My line of sight shifted up to his sapphires, their hue brightened by with amusement.

"See something you like?" Jackson asked.

He had no idea. "Mmm..." It was the only response I

mustered, reaching for my wine to give my mouth a distraction.

"Perhaps we should distract ourselves with conversation," he teased and poked fun at my lust driven observation. It wasn't my fault he was beautiful, in the most masculine ways. Could any woman *not* stare at him?

An idea hit me. Hopefully it would be enough to distract my wandering eyes. "Perhaps. Seeing as you already know a few of my favorite things, I think it's only fair I'm given the same."

"Fair enough. Ask away." His invitation sat open as he leaned forward and gave me opportunity to ask anything.

"Let's start off with the basics... Favorite color, book, flower, place. The good stuff." I plastered on my best corny smile, knowing he would meet my probing inquisition with humor. I wasn't wrong.

A throaty, deep chuckle bounced in the space between us as his smile crinkled the corners of his eyes. "The good stuff. Let's see. If I had to choose a color, I'd have to say green, like an evergreen or an emerald." He paused for a sliver of time, enthralled, and stared straight into my soul. When his voice reappeared, it seemed as if I'd awoken from hypnosis. "I don't really have a favorite book, but I read mysteries when I pick one up. Flowers... it's really hard for a guy to choose." His index finger tapped his lips as if he were in deep thought. "Purple calla lilies. My mom loved calla lilies, more so of the white variety. They were in the house often when I grew up. I don't really have one specific place I call my favorite, but I love hiking in the mountains. Something about being away from everyone and everything is invigorating."

"I'll make note later. Good to know a man who isn't afraid of owning his love for flowers." The words rolled off my tongue like a whimsical tune as I winked at him.

"A real man isn't afraid to own who he is or what he likes." My joking extinguished by his semi-serious tone. "Why be someone I'm not. My turn?"

Interesting. As each layer of Jackson is peeled away, I became more intrigued. "Ask away," I say, repeating his earlier words.

"If you could eat anything, contents aside, what would it be?"

"Italian food. Pastas, breads, all of it. I haven't met an Italian dish I didn't like. What about you?"

"Without a doubt, good old-fashioned American home-style cooking. My mom used to make the best shepherd's pie. She also made a mean biscuits and gravy."

I loved how he loved his mother. Nowadays, people got caught up figuring out who they were, often separating themselves from their history. In good times or bad, our history made us who we were today. He'd referenced his love for her twice in the last few minutes and that warmed my heart.

"She sounds like an amazing woman."

"She was. I've met no one else like her," he murmured, something in Jackson's tone akin to heartache.

"Was?" I hoped I wasn't rehashing something painful, or yet something better left buried. We were just getting to know one another, and I didn't want to stir the kettle of old emotions.

"She passed away a few years ago. She was outside, working in her garden, and had a heart attack. My dad didn't realize what had happened for a short time. By the time she made it to the hospital... it wasn't good."

I picked up on his desire to stop talking about her. With each word he spoke, the light in his eyes faded a fraction. "I'm sorry to hear that happened to her. No doubt she's still nearby, watching over you."

He watched me as we sat in silence a couple minutes. The way he studied me was calculated, his eyes working to read my unspoken thoughts. As with most people, he didn't want pity. And I had no intention of giving him any.

"Thank you. She would've liked you. Before she passed, she told me she wanted me to find a pretty girl. Someone not scared to be herself, no matter who was around."

The sentiment enveloped me in a veil of emotions. Three times. No words. Would anything about him not surprise me? Was there an undesirable bone in his body? I doubted it. Jackson wasn't just a pretty face. His soul seeped out, grabbed hold of mine, and reached parts I didn't know existed.

In an attempt to shift us back to lighter topics, he continued our game of twenty questions. "Favorite type of music?"

"That's an easy one. I love all music. I listen to rock or

electronic the most, but I think all music has its place. You?"

"Rock in all forms. Depends on what I'm doing, or my mood. I'll listen to almost anything, though, as long as it doesn't sound like crap."

"I'll agree to that."

It was peculiar. Even though we knew nothing about each other, as I listened to Jackson speak and tell me details about his life, it seemed as if I'd known him years. We were strangers, yet a part of me felt more connected to him than anyone else. It baffled and intrigued me.

Lost in my own headspace, I hadn't realized the server arrived with our dinner until it was placed in front of me. The savory aromas distracted me enough to halt any further questions. For now. I still had so many questions to ask him, but they could wait. Plus, he wasn't going anywhere soon. Not if I had a say in the matter.

Jackson parked his Jeep a few spaces from my front door. He cut the engine and let the darkness encapsulate us. If I considered myself out of place or uncomfortable earlier tonight, I was mistaken. A low hum coursed throughout my body. My thoughts ran a marathon alongside my heart.

I fiddled with my fingers, not sure where to put my hands. Silence stretched the space between us, neither of us sure what to say next. First dates were always tricky. Do you kiss your date? Do you not? There was a mysterious, invisible list of first date dos and don'ts in the world. Depending on whom you asked, different rules would be applied.

Right now... I had zero clue how the evening would end.

I liked Jackson. A lot. He had a great personality. He was charming, funny, down to earth, outgoing, and very nice on the eyes. Just because I thought those things about him didn't mean he reciprocated. I'd have to test the waters, get my feet a little wet, and see where it led us.

"Thank you for a wonderful evening. I had a great time." My voice blended in with the chirping cicadas outside.

He opened his door, exited the Jeep and walked around to my door, opening the door for me. "It was my pleasure. I had a really nice time, too."

Our footsteps clapped against the pavement as we walked to my front door. The pace of our stride nowhere as fast or loud as the beat of my pulse beneath my ears. His fingertips toyed with my bare back, the small strokes flamed the spark in my veins. When we reached the door, I fished through my purse for my keys, then unlocked the bolt before turning back to face him.

Under the soft glow of the porch light, part of his face masked in shadows, the sapphire of his blues burned radiant. My eyes shifted away from his, dropping down and locking on his mouth, watching his lips as he watched me.

His calloused fingers traced my spine, gliding up and stopping when he reached the length of my hair. He flattened his palm against my skin and my body jolted to life. Barely a breath passed between us before he seized my chin with two fingers and lifted my lips to his.

Warmth radiated from every inch of him and poured into me.

His lips on mine was all-consuming. My front porch disappeared. The singing cicadas gone. All traces of the outside world vanished. No sights. No sounds. Just a hint of his scent—a heady blend of spice and fresh cotton.

It was him and me. Kissing as if we were the last two people in existence.

I reached behind me and turned the knob. I backed us into the confines of my apartment and kicked the door shut. Our lips locked, my hands traced the line of muscles along his biceps as I walked backward and he followed. A moment later, the backs of my knees bumped the couch.

Reality struck Jackson a second later, and he broke our kiss, framing my face in his palms. "You have no idea how bad I want this." His breath heavy on my mouth.

"I'm not stopping you." Truth be told, I may have wanted him more than he wanted me.

"It's not my style to go to bed with a girl on a first date. Or even a second date. But with you... It seems like I've known you my whole life." His words lured me in further, and my desire for him grew tenfold. That he felt the same attraction and familiarity added fuel to the flame.

"I want you. Now." My desperation for his touch spilled out before I stopped myself.

Our eyes locked, the question of what would happen next weighed heavy in the air. I ached for him in a way I'd never ached for anyone else. We barely knew each other, but Jackson filled a void inside me and made it whole. A void I never knew existed. The desire for his connection was powerful and heady.

"I know you do. But not tonight. Not on our first date. I want you to be sure and I want it to be unlike anything you've ever experienced." A smirk lit up his face, then turned serious in an instant. A hint of significance at what was happening between us.

His lips brushed over mine one last time, then he inched back and pivoted to leave. When he reached the door, my words ran after him. "When will I see you again?"

He turned his head, just as he swung the door open. "Soon. I promise. Sweet dreams, my Sarah." And then he walked out the door.

EIGHT

THE MEMORY of my date with Jackson cycled on repeat in my head for days.

I reached up and pressed my fingers to my lips, recalling the heat and intensity of his mouth on mine. He had been such a gentleman the entire evening. As much as I wanted to take our date to the next level, he declined my advances. He wanted to take things farther—desire clear in the way his lips devoured mine—but he needed us to start slow. Get to know one another.

Men like Jackson… they were one in a million. A rare gem. Does this make me lucky? While my head said yes, my body screamed no.

As frustrating as stopping had been, I was thankful for his desire to wait. Instant gratification wasn't all it was cracked up to be. Anticipation… now that made life much more enticing.

Every night this week, I'd gone to bed imagining his

lips on my skin. I recalled the way his tongue tangoed with mine. The way his mouth worshiped mine, as if I was his dying breath. If his lips had me that worked up, God only knows how I'd react when his hands caressed my skin and I stripped him bare for the first time. Hell, I couldn't stop daydreaming of what his broad shoulders and strong core looked like under the snug fabric of his shirt. Not to mention the way his jeans hugged his hips and legs, highlighting all the best parts.

"Hey, bitch. We carpooling to the luncheon?" Christy's bubbly voice popped up, and I jumped in my seat, snapping out of my daydream.

"Yeah. Let me grab my purse." My hands fumbled to open the desk drawer while my mind shifted gears back to the present.

"You seem flustered. Everything okay?" Christy asked.

I worked to mask the rising heat in my cheeks and nodded. If I spoke right now, my voice would crack and Christy's questioning would commence.

The annual company luncheon was something they required us to attend, but no one enjoyed. Hours of speeches and slideshow presentations, accompanied by buffet food and boredom. At least it was a change of scenery and I wouldn't be answering any more calls or emails today.

I loved my job, and I performed well. But sitting in a room with close to two hundred people, hearing last year's sales numbers and this year's company goals, was sleep worthy. The only thing we hoped for was a decent selection of food.

I hooked arms with Christy and we all but skipped down the path through cubicle central and headed for the elevator. "Is Liz riding with us?"

"Of course she is. Bitch, you think I'd forget about her?"

Christy and her incessant need to use the word bitch. No matter what kind of day I had, this woman always made me laugh, just like now. "I don't think you could forget about anyone. That's why I love you so much."

Someone's elbow jabbed into my back, a heavy, unwelcome breath heated my neck. The doors to the convention room remained locked for a few more minutes. The mass of Hammond Life employees grouped together like a concert mosh pit, ready to shove when the time presented itself. A gentle weight skimmed the loose locks of hair on my back, followed by a light tug on the strands. As I turned to see who was standing behind me, the large wooden doors opened and everyone propelled forward, eager to breathe cooler air.

"Jesus. You'd think this was a rat race or the running of the bulls," I said to Liz and Christy, who had been driven into my right side.

When we were ten feet into the room, the crowd dispersed and we all breathed a little easier. Everyone split off into four lines. The banquet hall was a spacious room with large, cloth-covered tables and metal-framed, padded chairs. Our names displayed on tent cards in front of each place setting. At the center of the table sat a small bouquet of greenery and simple wildflowers. Banquet employees stood at the head of the four lines, asking our names and directing us to the table number assigned to us.

Christy, Liz, and I were seated at the same table. We appreciated whoever was responsible for the seating arrangement. No doubt I would enjoy the company of anyone at the table, but it was always nice to sit with your favorite people. We had only seen each other a couple times since my date with Jackson, and I missed time with my best friends.

We arrived at table eighteen, our tent cards displayed but not side by side. After moving a couple people around, we ensured we sat next to each other. Taking our seats, we waited while the line diminished. As soon as everyone located their seats, the meeting would begin. The quicker this party started, the quicker the day would end.

"So, I feel like we haven't talked in a lifetime." Christy rolled her eyes, her face highlighted in faux exaggeration. "I neeeeed to know more about your date with the hottie. Details, please." She leaned toward me, her elbows on the table and fingers steepled in front of her mouth. She bounced in her chair—literally. Excitement oozed from her pores.

"There's really not much to tell." My face heated as my legs clenched. Right now, I was thankful the tablecloth hid my lap. "We had dinner. We kissed. He did the gentlemanly thing and went home. The end."

Talking about my date with Jackson made me want to crawl into a hole and hide, which was foreign to me. I was unsure if it was the date's simplicity. Or because I liked him a lot. Maybe I didn't want to prattle off details with Liz by my side. Perhaps it was all three blended together. The urge to share bubbled in my bloodstream, but I didn't want to rub it in Liz's face. Just now, the thought of Jackson's supple lips pressed against mine, my core temperature rose a few degrees. Nowhere in proximity and Jackson affected me.

What exactly does that mean?

"I'm sure there was more to it than that. Why're you being so prudish?" Christy's inquisitive mind was bound to drive me insane. I loved Christy's nature, but couldn't handle the probing right now. Not with Liz here.

"Seriously, there's not much to tell." *Please leave it alone.*

This time, Liz chimed in. "Sarah, are we not best friends? Don't we share everything? Tit for tat. It's an equal exchange. For all of us."

Was Liz sending me a hidden message? Letting me know I could express my feelings for Jackson without hurting her? Our eyes locked as I gauged her mood and the definition behind her words. When she registered my silent pondering, she winked one of her dazzling hazels.

I hadn't realized, until now, how important it was for Liz to accept my potential relationship with Jackson. That she would be okay with hearing me talk about someone else. It was one thing to discuss the possibility of me dating Jackson, but it morphed into something different when I actually went on a date. Knowing she would still be the same Liz either way... it meant the world to me.

I gazed at the white plate in front of me, a cloth napkin folded into a bird rested in the center. My mind drifted, wondering what poor soul had to fold hundreds of napkins a day as their job. Sucking in a deep breath, I spilled the sorted details of my date, my voice growing louder the more I shared.

I told them about dinner. My nervousness when I felt underdressed. How his hands occasionally touched me and it set me ablaze. How much he loved his mother. Our quiet ride back to my apartment. And the kiss. The kiss that had me wanting him like he was my last meal. Part of me thought I had him on the cusp of agreeing to take it farther, but he had been a gentleman. His desire to wait, the most delicious form of torture I experienced. I loved it and hated it.

"For the last week, I've been losing my mind. I've been deprived. We've been talking every night, but his schedule is packed. I hope we can see each other between now and the weekend."

Feedback screeched throughout the room, everyone

covering their ears and halting conversation. "Sorry, everyone. Thank you, all, for joining us today to celebrate Hammond Life. In a moment, we'll let you all grab your lunch. Please hang tight while the concierge walks around and signals for your table to go to the buffet. After everyone has gotten their food, we'll begin the conference. Thank you."

We returned to our conversation. They sent tables to the buffet in numeric order, a few minutes elapsing between each. Minutes into our more detailed conversation about my date, a hand tapped my shoulder. Startled, I spun in my chair and spotted Kyle—a middle-aged man whose cubicle butted against the back of mine —behind me.

"Hey, Sarah, how are you? Haven't talked to you in a while."

"I'm good, Kyle, thanks. Been a little busy, but otherwise good."

"Glad to hear it. I saw those flowers you got the other week. They were super pretty. A gift from your boyfriend?" His face shifted for a second. If I hadn't been looking him in the eye, I would not have caught it.

My poker face slid into place. I was somewhat protective about what I shared with my coworkers. An old habit I started years ago. And with the recent delivery, my defensive side appeared more frequently. Staying generic with my response, I said, "They were pretty. But not sure who they came from. Wasn't my boyfriend. So, I ended up giving them away."

I swore, for a fraction of a millisecond, anger glinted on his face. But it vanished before I registered its validity. So, I played it off as my imagination. Maybe all the paranoia about who sent them got to me.

"Such a shame to give away such beautiful flowers," he muttered and turned back to his table as if someone garnered his attention.

My gaze reverted back to Liz and Christy, their eyes glued on me, mouthing *weird*. A slight chill made me shiver from head to toe. Kyle was one of the sweetest guys in the office. He had a handsome face, brown hair, and a full beard. What he didn't have in physical features, he made up for with his kind nature. Sure he was different, but weren't we all? But something about his tone and body language a minute ago didn't sit right with me.

I took out my phone, texting Christy and Liz in our group chat.

Sarah: Not saying anything else. Later, when it's just us.

They both checked their phones and nodded. A man wearing a white dress shirt, black vest and black pants stepped up to our table. "When you're ready, you may proceed to the buffet." I couldn't get up fast enough.

Sarah: How's your day been?

Jackson: Lots of sweat and tears. No tears from me though. First client was having a rough day.

Sarah: Pain is beauty. JK. I hope they're okay.

Jackson: Me too. Life stuff that they're trying to not worry about. How was your day?

Jackson and I had these chats daily now. Although we'd only been on one date, we conversed on a regular basis. Some conversations just idle chitchat. Others more in depth. But with each exchange, my eagerness to see Jackson grew.

Sarah: Boooorrrring. Annual company luncheon. Crap food, long winded speeches.

Jackson: I suppose we must have dinner again. Have some better food to balance it out.

Yes! Now we were getting somewhere.

Sarah: Sounds like a great plan to me. Name the time and the place.

Jackson: You available tomorrow?

Is that even a question? I don't want to come off as desperate, so I paused a moment before responding.

Sarah: Calendar says I am 😊

Jackson: Let me figure out the details. I'll message you in the morning.

Sarah: I'll be patiently waiting.

Jackson: Good night, Daisy.

Sarah: Good night xo

Why did I love it when he called me Daisy?

I stabbed at my salad, spearing the veggies with unnecessary vigor before shoving them into my mouth. My teeth gnashed loudly as I answered Christy's latest inquiry. "I don't know where we're going yet. He asked if I was available tonight and said he'd message me this morning. No other details yet."

"I'm sure it means nothing." Her words tried to soothe me. "Maybe he's just been super busy with work this morning and hasn't had a minute to pick up his phone."

"Christy's probably right. Anyone who ignored my girl would be an idiot." Liz draped her arm over my shoulder and squeezed.

Using my fork to push the remaining contents of my salad around the bowl, I bobbed my head. Their words soaked into my consciousness. "You're both probably right. I've never been this worried about a date before. I feel ridiculous." My juvenile behavior laughable.

"You feel that way because you like him. Just keep sending out the positive vibes and let everything happen how it's meant to." I glanced over at Liz, her words softened my heart more for her. She really was an awesome friend and wanted nothing except the best for me.

We finished the rest of our lunchtime talking about Christy and Rick and how things were in their world. Rick was her happily ever after. Doing small gestures to let Christy know how much he loved her. For their post Valentine's Day date, he arranged an elegant dinner in the park. Heater lamps kept them warm in the chilled air.

Followed by a horse-drawn carriage ride. Christy still swooned over the whole evening.

Stepping out of the elevator on our floor, the three of us split up and headed for our designated workspace. After we parted ways, I heard my phone chime in my purse. I snagged it, switched the phone to silent and discovered the long-awaited message from Jackson.

Jackson: You okay with dinner at my place?

Sarah: I'm good with that. Just let me know when and where.

Jackson: Anything you can't or don't eat?

Sarah: Nothing too heavy. Trying to maintain my girlish figure. Not a big red meat eater.

Jackson: Cool. I can work with that.

His address populated the next bubble on the screen, followed by a request for my presence at six thirty. A bevy of doves took flight in my chest as excitement for our date had me a little light-headed. As I reached my desk, I sat down and inhaled a few deep breaths.

I wasn't sure what had me more excited. A second date with Jackson. Or that our second date would be at his place. I pressed my fingers to my lips to hide my exuberant smile from no one. My mind ran laps around the possibilities of the evening ahead. And with each lap, my heart raced a little faster.

I stood outside Jackson's door for at least five minutes. Arriving much earlier than expected, I stared at the grain lines of the large oak door. In a moment of realization, I prayed he wasn't on the other side of the door, watching me through the peephole. Because I surely appeared a fool.

My fingers wrapped around the cool metal door knocker, tapping it a few times and crossing my fingers he didn't open the door too fast. I ran my hands over my hair and smoothed any out of place locks. By the amount of time it took Jackson to open the door, I determined there was no way he'd witnessed my loitering.

"Hey. Come in, come in." He reached for my hand, enveloping it in his before he pressed a tender kiss on my lips. "Food's almost ready. I'll give you the tour in a sec, just need to watch the stove another minute. Don't want to burn anything." Letting go of my hand, he jogged toward what I assumed to be the kitchen.

I followed behind him, walking through his living

room and past a wall opposite the front door, into a spacious kitchen. The walls, cabinets, and floors a mix of black, white, and marble. It was modern and masculine. Beyond the kitchen, a pair of glass doors were open. A screen door kept pests out but allowed the cool evening air to break the heat of the kitchen.

"From what I've seen, you have a really nice place," I said as I leaned against a counter and watched him move around the kitchen. Jackson focused on a task was a delectable visual.

"Thanks. I can only take credit for the decor though. I rent the place. Haven't found quite the right place to purchase yet. I figure something that permanent, I should be ready to stay in one place for years. Know what I mean?"

"Yeah. I love Savannah, but I'm not sure if it's where I want to live for the rest of my life. Who knows? Maybe something will jump out at me one day and I'll know where I'm meant to be."

His eyes studied my face a moment as he assessed my words and held back some of his own. Did I say something off-putting? Did I insinuate? I really hope I didn't just stick my foot in my mouth. How could I break up the awkward silence closing in around me? Around us?

"Is there anything I can help with?"

A dazzling smile highlighted his square jaw, my body temperature rose from the single expression. "The food will be done in a sec. Why don't you go out onto the patio while I plate everything. Pour yourself some wine. I'll be there in a minute."

"Okay."

Sliding the screen door open, I stepped out onto the patio that stretched along the entire back of the house. Off the kitchen, a wooden, planked table had several votive candles illuminating the place settings and an arrangement in the center. Jackson had woven two sunflowers between the candles, along with several daisies scattered around their stems.

At one end of the six-person table, I noticed a metal pail with a bottle of wine nestled in ice. I retrieved the wine from the chilled bucket, liquid courage necessary sooner than expected. Pouring Chardonnay in the glasses on the table, I shot back half the contents of mine before topping it off.

I sat back in the handcrafted, Adirondack-style wooden chair, the grain matching the table, and ran my hands along the lacquered surface on the armrests. The air still crisp as winter lingered, I wrapped myself in the blanket Jackson must've placed in the chair.

I closed my eyes and took a moment to absorb the atmosphere. The mixed scents of Jackson's cooking, his masculine smell on the plaid cotton, and the oak trees beyond the screened porch filled my nose. Miscellaneous forest insects sang to each other as the sun set. My stomach flipped like a hammock as I waited for Jackson to join me.

Tonight was my second date with Jackson and an overwhelming burst of elation soared in my chest.

We'd talked on and off over the last week. Some small talk, work stuff, and a little flirting. From what I could tell so far, Jackson was a pretty laid-back guy. He was also ambitious and gorgeous as sin. I hadn't pegged him as a romantic. Sitting at this table, the glow of the candlelight flickering in my periphery, the decadent smell of our dinner... my heart swelled as butterflies started a hurricane beneath my diaphragm.

The screen door slid open and Jackson stepped out with two plates in his hands. The aroma and artfully displayed food had me licking my lips and my mouth watering instantly. As he set his plate down, he shared tonight's menu. "Shrimp scampi with spinach pasta, maple roasted rainbow carrots, and a small balsamic dressed salad."

I leaned forward, inhaling deeply as the aromas wafted from my plate. "Everything looks and smells amazing. Did your mom teach you to cook?"

His eyes softened at the mention of his mom, his lips curving up into a gentle smile. She must've been an incredible woman to live within him so deep. "She taught me some basic stuff, but mostly she taught me how to cook family recipes. Biscuits, roasts, her version of southern delicacies. I have several recipes. I might have to break them out again sometime." He spoke about her with such reverence. There's no way I could fathom his loss and the pain of missing her.

"I think I would've loved that kind of stuff when I was a kid; making things in the kitchen with my family. My parents lived the hippie life for a while—simplistic. I wouldn't change anything about my childhood, but it would have been fun to do some of those things, too."

The candles flickered with the occasional breeze. Our food disappeared from our plates. The time followed right beside it as we talked more about our lives. Conversation with Jackson was as effortless as breathing. He was open and spoke his mind, emotions included. He seemed passionate about everything in his life. Nothing entered his life without giving him purpose. That concept had me itching to ask him how I gave him purpose.

Why hold back? Curiosity weighed my thoughts as I hesitantly asked, "So, you say that you don't do anything that doesn't give you purpose or have meaning." I sucked in a breath, holding it for five heartbeats before releasing it. "How do I fit into that equation?"

He studied my face, pondered over the words I left unsaid. "When I saw you at the party two weeks ago, you lit up the room. Like a spotlight pointed you out to me."

"Are you sure it wasn't my body rubbing up against two other women that lured you in?" I laughed, the sound bouncing around us.

"Well, I can't discount that. That was hot." A million-dollar smile flashed across his face. "But that wasn't the sole reason. Before you danced with your friends, I saw you. You were wandering around, keeping tabs on every-thing and everyone. I caught your profile, your smile hiding a bit behind your hair. I wanted to walk up to you, but I didn't. The guy I mentioned that night, he'd been near you for a while. And, although he didn't look like he was your type, I stayed back. It wasn't until I didn't see him anymore that I realized he must not have been with you."

Like was not a potent enough word to describe how Jackson saw me. The way he described that night, he looked at me in an incomprehensible way. He had seen me. Wanted to talk to me. But kept his distance because he thought someone had claimed my heart. *Seriously*, how did I get this lucky?

Date number two. Speechless. Once again.

The rough scrape of his chair legs grated over the concrete floor as he stood. He grabbed his plate and mine. "I'll be back in a second. Grabbing dessert." He pressed his lips to the top of my head and then disappeared into the kitchen, leaving me to swim in the sea of emotions he stirred inside me.

His words from after our first date came to the front of my mind. Ever the gentleman, he didn't want to taint our first date with sex. He wanted to drag out the anticipation, to be sure it was something we both wanted. That it wouldn't hinder us from our future. I peeked over my shoulder and watched him move around the kitchen.

This man was doing everything and anything to impress me. And I fell for every single maneuver. I rose from my chair, the blanket falling behind me as my feet ambled forward, with a single destination in mind. Sliding the screen door open, I stepped into the kitchen, walked up to his back and traced my fingers along his triceps.

He stopped assembling our dessert and his breath hitched. My hands coasted up and down the lines of his muscular arms. Twisting to peer over his shoulder, I glimpsed his profile. Jaw slackened and sapphires sparkling with hunger. He set down our dessert and spun his body to face me. His hands glided up the sides of my face, the gentle touch strong as I leaned into it.

"You are going to make me break my own rules," he stated in a deep, raspy tone. Jackson's eyes smoldered with unspoken desire.

"I want you to break them," I begged as I stood on my toes and pressed my lips to his. A beat later, his lips parted and his tongue mingled with mine.

His hands danced down my neck and traced my collarbones before gliding down my arms to my waist. He deepened the kiss with a throaty hum as his tongue devoured me. A new synergy formed between us and a fire burned hot in my core. A moment later, Jackson hoisted me up in his arms — my feet dangling a beat before I locked them around his hips — and we were moving.

Our mouths continued to dance in synchronicity as he held me close. His feet padded against the hardwood floor, turning past corners before he stopped. A soft yarn rug warmed my soles when I set my feet down and his hands framed my face as our kiss intensified.

My fingers skirted the firm lines of his back, dipping and tracing before my palms flattened to discover the sculpted tone of his muscles. I fondled my way down his back and hooked onto the loops along his waistline. Slipping my hands under his shirt hem, I hummed my appreciation against his lips. His heated skin seared me like wildfire as I shoved his shirt over his head.

Nothing but our labored breaths floated in the air. With my palms splayed on his bare chest, I leaned forward and kissed the skin below his clavicle. He hissed under my touch, his chest rising and falling faster. Skimming my palms over the pronounced ridges of his abdominals, my tongue peeked out. I licked and sucked over his pec before landing on the taut peak of his nipple. I captured the bud between my teeth and tugged.

His sharp intake broke the silence before his hands gripped my arms and drew me back. A second later, I flew through the air as he launched me onto the bed. Adrenaline pumped through my veins and made me rabid, my fingers eager to remove the clothes shielding the rest of him from me. He opened the bedside table drawer, grabbed a condom and tossed it on the bedding before resuming his position.

His hands glided up the length of my legs, slipping under the loose cotton of my skirt. He hooked his fingers into the tight band of my panties as his remaining digits grabbed hold of my skirt. Quicker than I could say *yes*, he yanked hard and exposed my wanton flesh.

His breath hovered over the apex of my thighs. The rapid exhalation of air from his lungs coated my skin in goose-flesh, driving my appetite to insatiable levels. Jackson's hooded eyes locked on mine, the intensity of the moment causing his sapphires to resemble an onyx.

"Please," I whisper-begged.

The pads of his fingers grazed down the sides of my torso—a trail of sparks in its wake—as he shed the rest of my clothes. His mouth worshipped my flesh, nipping and sucking. My back bowed off the mattress, craving more with each stroke, lick, and fondle.

Fumbling to remove the final barrier between us, I unbuttoned his shorts—my hands and feet working together to push them to the floor. A tidal wave of heat spiked in me when I learned Jackson was naked. *Did he always go commando? Or did he plan for things to progress between us tonight?* Either way, it didn't matter. I wanted him more than anything in this moment and nothing hindered me from having him.

When he pressed his steely erection against my abdomen, a new fever dampened my skin. I reached down and wrapped my hand around his length, watching as he bit back a moan. The action caused him to jut farther into my grip, his length grinding over the tight bundle of nerves between my legs.

"Oh, god," I mumbled as my back bowed and my breasts crushed against his chest.

His mouth smashed mine, tongue thrusting inside; greedy and ready to consume every ounce of me. Jackson's hand slid between us. His fingertips circled my pulsing clit, a slow, lazy rhythm before adding more pressure. Low in my belly, my orgasm grew hungrier with each swipe. Just as I hit my climax, he shifted his fingers and dipped them between my folds, coating them with my arousal before repeating the process.

"Fuck, that's good," I groaned, breathy and loud before I sunk my teeth into the crook of his neck.

"Not yet..." His fingers stopped. Jackson kissed his way down my body, his tongue leaving a trail from sternum to apex.

I propped myself up on my elbows, my breath shallow bursts, my core begging for release. Jackson's lust-hazed eyes stared back at me, drunk at the sight of me. A second later, his tongue lavished me, flicking the tight bud at my core. His fingers clamped onto my nipples and rolled back and forth, the harsh pinch had me crying out and driving myself more into his eager mouth.

Jackson had a magical tongue. And the way he used it was a superpower. I had no clue what he was doing, how he maneuvered between my thighs, nor did I care. The only thing I cared about was him worshipping my body.

"Holy shit. Don't. Fucking. Stop. Oh. My..." I closed my eyes tightly as I cried out into the darkness.

My core temp was thermal—a volcano ready to erupt. The skill of his magical tongue had me on the brink. When my orgasm hit, it was a sonic boom. Intensity rippled in waves from my convulsing body. The faint tearing of the condom wrapper was barely discernible with my pulse racing in my ears.

A second later, Jackson inched up my body and hovered above me, his eyes locked on mine. After a ragged breath, he dipped down and devoured me. The taste of my orgasm salty and intoxicating as our tongues swirled together in a rhythmic dance. A groan vibrated in his chest and he drove his hips forward, adding the perfect amount of friction between his cock and my clit. My desire to have him inside me escalated by the nanosecond. As if my thoughts displayed on a marquee, he shifted down then thrust inside me. My head tipped back and my torso arched up as I learned what Jackson's strength and prowess entailed.

Our bodies froze—his length fully inside me—as he waited for my eyes to open. He leaned down, his breath hot on my ear. "Being inside you is incredible. Perfect," he said. My groan in response was very unladylike and animalistic.

He reared his hips back slowly, stopping before the tip slid out, and then thrust forward again. Both of us gasped as we took in the moment. My eyes rolled back, and I savored every sensation as Jackson filled me completely.

It had been months since I had been with a man, and my body stretched to accommodate him. Not that any man before Jackson even compared. His magnitude filled me in the most delicious of ways. Each stroke lit me up like the Fourth of July. When he slid out, I dug my nails into his broad shoulders and anchored him to me.

Something shifted between us. His ravenous expression stared down my body before he leaned into the crook of my neck and clamped down, sucking at the tender skin. Hard. One hand, then the other, slipped beneath my butt and squeezed. Tingling started at the ends of my limbs, flowing inward until it converged into a bonfire at my epicenter. My nipples pert. My core ached at the loss of him. Desire ambushed my mind. Delirium on the verge of taking hold.

Before I even said a word, he rammed back into me. Hard. The intensity is incomparable.

My nails dragged down the rippled sinew of his back. With my lungs crying for air he buries his length to the hilt inside me. He reared back—faster this time—and slammed back into my pussy. Slam after slam, he set a fevered tempo that had us both clawing at one another.

His breath hot on my ear, labored and heady. "You... are so... fucking... exquisite." He sucked my earlobe before clamping down and tugging it with his teeth.

Short, high-pitched cries reverberated from my throat and echoed in the room. I clasped Jackson's glutes and relished each of his thrusts. A deep-rooted fire ignited, burning hot and intense, ready to incinerate. It inundated every molecule. My skin pinked and dampened in the darkness. My limbs trembled at the ferocity. And my mouth watered, begging to taste Jackson on my tongue. Every fiber inside me screamed for more.

"Harder. Fuck me harder," I said, my voice indiscernible. My hoarse cries filled the air as I wrapped my legs around his waist and locked my ankles together.

His tempo increased and an electric charge filled the room. One hand encased the back of my neck and locked me in place while he pounded into me viciously. My screams surrounded us, multiplied with each drive forward, and Jackson's growl turned feral.

Pressure and pain and pleasure gnawed my shoulder as Jackson's teeth broke my skin. It was the last straw as I detonated into oblivion. My walls clenched and milked Jackson's cock.

"Holy fuck," he said, breath ragged. A second later, his moan pierced the air as he came inside me.

Holy fuck was right.

NINE

THE BUDDING relationship between Jackson and I had been nothing short of freaking awesome.

To say otherwise would understate the obvious—a once in a lifetime guy. Jackson was more than a pretty face plastered on a magnificent body. So much more. Yes, women got lost for days looking at him, but he had the kindest heart. The way he put others first incomprehensible. Not to mention, his smile warmed my skin and melted my panties.

A few weeks passed since our first date, not a dull moment in our foreseeable future. Jackson mastered the art of wooing. I imagined his mom was the culprit behind how he treated and respected women. He loved her in a way so different from how I loved my parents. My mom and dad loved me to the ends of the earth—and vice versa —but were content being on their own, even in my younger years. The chivalry Jackson displayed was completely natural. A part of him. And everything he did had my heart swooning and my core dampening.

It wasn't just the sex, either. Although, sex with Jackson was a euphoric experience. A high never rejected. Jackson was the whole package. Kind. Gentle. He treated me like a lady in public and a freak in the bedroom. That, all by itself, was a tremendous turn on and made my thighs tremble. I loved how our lives slowly merged. Selfless in nature, Jackson always thought of us as a whole. Every trait he exhibited made him downright tantalizing.

Since the night we sealed our souls, we went on a few more dates. One at a bar-and-grill during karaoke night. We both learned neither of us could sing worth a damn. Another in the park—our picnic turned into something children's eyes shouldn't be privy to. Needless to say, our picnic ended quick. And, three nights ago, we shared a date night with friends. Me, Jackson, Christy, Rick, Liz, Eric, and Jackson's friend Rob, a personal trainer. All of us had a night full of laughs, beers, and bowling.

Never in my lifetime did I think I'd be so lucky as to find someone like Jackson. My perfect match. You hear stories of your friends, acquaintances or colleagues finding that one person. The one they can't stand to be away from. Someone they call, text, or FaceTime whenever they have a free minute. The one person who is in every molecule they breathe, every beat of their heart, every sensation throughout their body. Someone they can't live without. A person who makes them a better version of themselves.

Our relationship new, our beginning still happening, but I couldn't imagine my world without Jackson. Far too soon for the infamous *l* word, but I was very much *in like* with him. And he was very much *in like* with me. When together... the air in the room pulsated with energy. Raw and passionate and potent.

Hopping out of my Beetle, I walked to the mailboxes for my building and waved at a neighbor. Her chihuahua yipped at me and she scolded him. "Stop barking at the nice lady, Stanley." A second later, she apologized and walked off. Why were the small dogs always the noisy ones?

"Whatever," I said to my mailbox. I popped my key into the aluminum door and discovered a pile of unwanted advertisements along with some envelopes sandwiched in the crease.

As I walked back to my apartment, I flipped through the envelopes.

Crap.

Crap.

Bill.

Crap.

Something. Although, not sure what.

A plain, white envelope sat in the stack, my first name typed in the center. Not typed on a computer and printed from an inkjet. No. Someone typed this on a typewriter, the paper behind the font embossed with faint ink. *Who even owns a typewriter anymore? And how was this in my mail-box?* There was no indication someone mailed it—no return address, no mailing address, no stamp. Only my first name.

My stomach churned at the sight of my name pressed into the paper. Something didn't sit right as I held it in my hands.

I stared at the ominous rectangle as I walked to my apartment. It singed my hands and piqued my curiosity with each step forward. After stepping inside my apartment, I set my keys and purse on the entryway table then opened the envelope, wary to discover what lay inside. A folded piece of paper sat nestled inside the flap. After a moment's hesitation, I retrieved the thin sheet and unfolded it, an entire page also typed on a typewriter.

My beautiful Sarah,

Oh, how I dream about your beauty. The way the sunlight accentuates the golden glow in your hair. How your laughter lights up a room. The way you love others without effort. You are beautiful in every sense of the word. Every time I look at you, you take my breath away. Every time I smell you, you intoxicate me. Every time I hear your voice, I tune out every other sound. You make the world a better place. You make my world worth living in. One day, you will see. One day, you will be mine.

XO my beautiful XO

I dropped the envelope and letter, kicking them away when they landed on my feet, the words blistering my skin. I pressed a hand hard against my sternum as I gasped for breath. A newfound pain seared my lungs and stabbed my heart.

What the hell was this? Better yet, who the hell sent it?

Newsflash... it wasn't mailed. Somehow, some way, a random person placed this envelope in my mailbox. A locked mailbox. And whoever they were... they knew precisely where I lived. My hands trembled at my sides as a chill prickled my skin, spreading throughout my body. Whoever this phantom was, they made me feel a pervading sense of menace that swallowed me whole.

My life had been invaded, and I shuddered at the idea of someone watching me. I rushed to the door and locked the bolt before sliding the chain in place. Next, I dashed to the four windows in my small apartment, checked the locks, and cranked the handle tight on the blinds. Within seconds, darkness engulfed me. Double checking that the lock on the patio door was secure, I yanked the loose string and jumped as the blinds crashed down.

At a loss, I collapsed to the floor and cried into my palms. *What should I do?*

I should tell somebody. Someone whose cognitive skills function right now. Because mine vanished the moment I read the letter. Someone to give me advice on how I'm supposed to handle a situation of this magnitude. It's not every day you have to deal with someone sending you flowers or creepy notes and letters.

I glanced down at my trembling hands, the tremors strengthened with each passing minute. I stood, wiped the tears away, and inhaled deeply. Step by step, I trudged back to the foyer. When I reached the menacing note, I stopped and stared a moment. *It will be okay.*

Bending down, I picked up the letter and envelope between my thumb and forefinger and held them at arm's length. I walked over to my desk and dropped them, then slowly backed away. Heading back to the entryway, I snatched my purse from the table and riffled through it for my phone. After unlocking it, I opened my contacts and froze.

Who do I call? Jackson? Liz? Christy?

I eliminated Christy first. She would be equally lost. As I squeezed my eyes shut, I imagined her tugging her hair, freaking out, and screaming in my ear. After thirty minutes of screams, she'd tell me to call someone else. Plus, she and Rick were together, and I didn't want to disturb them.

I contemplated calling either Jackson or Liz for a solid five minutes while my eyes seared a hole in the threatening paper on my desk. Liz knew me better than anyone and would rescue me in a heartbeat. But I hesitated over calling her first. Our relationship didn't warrant me going to her when I needed rescuing. We were friends. Best friends. But still friends. We opted to not go down the strings-attached-relationship avenue. And I needed to keep things between us clear. For her and me.

I scrolled to Jackson's name, pressed the phone icon and listened to the slow, torturous ringing. After the third ring, which felt like the twentieth, Jackson answered.

"Hey, babe. What's going on?" His voice sweet and charismatic on the other end. I'm happy that I called him.

I remained tight-lipped. What should I tell him? *Hey, I got some creepy letter in my mailbox today. Can you help me figure out how it got there?* I ran through countless stupid lines. Tried to decipher how to speak my unspoken words. But my brain was mush and incapable of decision making.

"Sarah? Are you there? Can you hear me?"

"Hey, sorry. Yeah, I spaced out for a second." My tongue fumbled over my words.

"You okay? You don't sound like yourself," he said as worry etched his tone and concern rang evident.

"Um... I got something strange in my mailbox today. Can you come by? I'm not sure what to do." Normal enough, *right*? A legitimate statement and question. Plain. Simple.

"What kind of strange thing? I'm just finishing up. I can be there in thirty minutes."

"It's easier to show you. You'll understand when you get here." I bit on one of my fingernails, a habit I always found disgusting but I did it without realizing I was doing it.

"Okay. I'll be there soon."

"Thanks."

I checked the clock. Jackson said thirty minutes. Thirty minutes wasn't so long, was it? As I scanned the windows in the living room, I exhaled into the darkness. *I'll be safe until he arrives. He'll be here soon.*

Twenty-three minutes later, a knock at my door startled me. Creeping to the door, I pushed up on my toes and checked the peephole. Jackson. *Thank god.* I unlatched the chain, twisted the deadbolt and turned the knob. As he stepped past me, I scanned the mini front yard and parking lot in front of the building. From what I could tell, no one lingered behind the bushes or stared at my door. In fact, no one was anywhere. Odd? Or was my paranoia hiking up a notch?

"Why is it so dark in here?" Jackson asked as I shut the door. The moment he turned and his eyes met mine, his hands framed my cheeks. He studied my face, seeking answers for my red-rimmed eyes and blotchy skin. "What's wrong? What strange thing was in your mailbox?"

"It's on the desk," I muttered. My eyes shifted to the side as I gestured behind him.

He pivoted and stared at the letter a moment. Two of the folds stood up straight. The envelope beneath. Jackson placed a gentle kiss on my lips then walked over to the piece of paper that shook me to my core.

I bit my nails as his eyes scanned the typewritten lines.

His face redder with each word read. By the end, he picked up the envelope and turned it over in his hands. Jackson stared at it and noticed that only my name pressed into the surface with ink. As if I missed something, he lifted the envelope flap and peered inside to look for some missing piece. Another page. Some scrap of evidence I missed, perhaps.

"We need to call the police. Maybe this is the person who sent the flowers." Coming back to me, he cocooned me in warmth. His protective embrace comforted me. And I felt some other nameless, powerful emotion as well.

"I'm afraid," I whispered into his chest. Words I never thought I would say. "What are the cops going to do? File a report? Will a report *catch* whoever this is?" I had no idea. And even fewer answers. Zero. Zilch. Nada. No expertise in this area.

"I have no idea how this whole thing works either, babe." Goosebumps prickled my flesh as he took a step back and held my cheeks in his palms. "But we can't do nothing. We have to try." He leaned back in and placed a sweet, brief kiss on my forehead.

I stared past Jackson to my tattered oak desk, my eyes watering as the disturbing words jumped off the letter and threatened me. My pulse skyrocketed and my limbs shook as panic seeped into my veins. As frightened as I was, Jackson had the right idea. "Okay." I gazed back at him and nodded. "Let's go to the police. But will you drive? Don't think I can."

Jackson's strong arms hauled me forward and pressed

me into his chest. His heat encased me like a fleece blanket on a cold evening and slowly eased my fear. "Of course. I'll do anything for you."

We walked out of the police station with a detailed report in hand. Thankful Jackson had his arm around my waist, my body needed his guidance while my brain registered this was actually happening. That this whole situation was real. That I had a... *stalker*. Just thinking the word made me nauseous.

A female officer asked me endless questions, many I fumbled to answer.

"Do you have any former partners where the relationship ended bad?" Not that I can think of.

"Do you know anyone who would want to cause you harm?" No, I was always nice to everyone.

"Have you had any recent arguments or debates with acquaintances, friends or family?" No, like I said, I'm nice to everyone.

The questions went on for two hours. They asked to keep the letter and envelope in the hopes of getting prints other than mine and Jackson's. I happily handed it over to them and told them I had no desire to see it again.

The officer also suggested I behave as if I never received the letter, more so when outside the privacy of my home. She had two theories. The first theory—the letter came from someone with a crush. Perhaps the person wasn't certain how to come forward and speak with me directly. The second theory was more disturbing and had me wanting to lock myself away and throw out the key.

The second theory—this person knew me. Someone in my present or from my past. And this person didn't have a crush, but a deep-rooted infatuation. Disillusioned to the extent they believed I was their girlfriend or lover. Extensive enough that they would do anything within their means to bring us together. Even if that involved hurting someone—including me. With Jackson being a new love interest in my life, it most likely provoked whoever and kick started their initiative.

Neither theory desirable, but I crossed my fingers and sent a silent prayer to whichever deity listened. If I could choose one of the two, I'd pick the first. *Please don't let it be the last.*

The couch cushion dipped next to me as Jackson set a buffet of Chinese takeout boxes in front of us. He grabbed a couple forks and plates from the kitchen, set them on the coffee table, and unfolded all the containers. My stomach groaned and begged me to grab a fork and dive in. My brain, on the other hand, had a million mile per hour marathon on what I should be doing. Eating didn't seem like a priority. Eating was the last thing my body wanted, but I opted to ignore it.

Jackson laid a hand on my knee, his thumb strumming back and forth lazily. As minor as the motion was, the gesture soothed me. "I know you probably don't feel like it right now, but you really should eat something. Your head is probably drowning in thoughts. For a bit, try to resurface."

He was right. As easy as it was to dwell, I had to be strong. This would pass, I just needed patience. I nodded, my eyes glued to the white and red cartons. "I'll try. Nothing too heavy though."

His fingers gave my knee a quick squeeze before they released me to grab a plate. "How about steamed vegetables and a little rice?"

"Yeah. That sounds okay," I mumbled, donning a half smile.

He scooped a spoonful of rice on the plate and added some veggies on the side before handing it to me. "Let's start with that."

Jackson picked up his plate and shoveled food from each box. He covered his dish with more than three times what I had. When he finished building the small mountain, he sat back and scooted as close to me as possible.

Once situated, he grabbed the remote and brought up the guide on the television. After scrolling a minute, he selected a show for us to watch. Jackson chose something that, I'm sure he hoped, would lighten my mood. Tension blanketed the air like a humid summer day. And the television served as background noise while I nudged broccoli and carrots with my fork, the tines occasionally scraping like nails on a chalkboard.

Jackson finished dinner first. I forced myself to eat bite after bite. We curled up on the couch afterward and watched hours of rerun episodes of *Friends*. His face lit up the couple times I laughed. Every once in a while, his strong arms squeezed me tight. After everything that happened today, all I craved was to not worry. Jackson did everything in his power to make this a reality. Mission accomplished.

As my eyes grew heavy, Jackson's weight shifted beside me. Next thing I knew, his arms were scooping me up and I was being carried into the bedroom. Cradled tight against his body, I inhaled his fresh and spicy scent and relaxed.

Our relationship still so new, but he was nothing short of sweet and caring. Jackson helped me undress, then tucked me in under the comforter. He stepped back and toward the door. *Was he leaving?* I didn't want him to go. I didn't want to be alone in the confines of my apartment. Not when someone outside these walls, who had an unhealthy obsession with me, might come after me at any time. Instead, I wanted him to slip under the bedding and lay down beside me. Bundle me up in his protective arms and hold me throughout the night.

I reached out and clutched his hand. I whisper-begged, "Please. Stay with me?"

His gentle eyes studied me, a small pinch glinted the edges. I squeezed his hand tighter as he struggled with staying or leaving. He sighed while bringing his free hand to stroke my cheek. "You have no idea how much I want to stay. I need to know you're safe. But I don't want to take advantage of the situation."

Sincerity laced each word he spoke as his watery eyes stared down at me. Jackson's tender nature astounded me. I had heard stories of women being taken advantage of in times of vulnerability. Far too many. But Jackson wasn't one of those types of guys.

I gripped his hand tighter and pleaded with him. "Please. Just lay with me. Hold me. I just need you next to me." No doubt my gravelly voice screamed desperation, but I no longer cared.

He removed his hand from mine, stepped back and dragged his shirt over his head. A second later, his shorts fell to the floor beside his shirt. I peeled back the comforter and made room for him. The mattress sloped, and I rolled closer to him as he encased me in warmth. I sighed and relaxed into him.

In this micro-blip of time, a stampede of emotions warmed my heart.

I was safe. Someone cared for me. And he would protect me.

"Thank you," I whispered as my eyes grew heavy.

Jackson pressed a kiss to the crown of my head. "Anything for you," he spoke softly against my hair. "Anything."

TEN

DAYS PASSED, nothing new came to light. No unannounced gifts. No notes or letters. No updates from the police. It's almost as if nothing had happened.

Aside from work, Jackson and I spent every waking — and sleeping — moment together. For the first time in my life, I craved someone at my side. Hungered for strength and courage from another. And Jackson stood eager to be at the front of the line. Ready to shield me from pain and lift my spirit. To give me the sense of security I so desperately yearned for.

We took the officer's advice and used the weekend as an opportunity to distract ourselves. When it was just the two of us, we were in heaven. But we also didn't want to become one of those couples who shut everyone out. Hanging with friends our livelihood, one of many things we shared in common, and one characteristic neither of us planned to change.

At lunch yesterday, I told Christy and Liz about my and Jackson's plan—a friend's night out. I invited Christy, Rick—if he was free—and Liz. Jackson asked Eric and Rob. Our plan—hit a couple bars or clubs around Bay Street.

Without question, Jackson and I agreed to not mention the letter I received to our friends. The less who knew, the better. We didn't need multiple sets of eyes and ears prying through my life. Plus, if it was someone close to us—which the officer suggested as a possibility—it was better to act as if I never received the letter. Maybe it would lure the culprit out into the open.

"Hell yeah, I'm in, bitch. I'll check with Rick and get back to you." Christy's exuberance lifted my spirits and made my cheeks burn. Too many days had passed since I'd smiled. Days since something other than dread flooded my veins. Christy's energy was the exact medicine I needed filtering through me. If anyone was capable of relieving the stress weighing down my heart, and dulling the craziness in my head, Christy won every time. Never a dark cloud in her blue sky. She always stumbled upon the silver lining or double rainbow in all things. I envied her this.

"Awesome. I really need tonight, ladies," I said.

"Count me in. I've been at home, binge watching reruns for the last two weeks. I could use some time away from my TV," Liz stated, an edge of disappointment in her words. I'm certain she was upset at herself for being such a couch potato.

"Yes!" I wrapped an arm around each of their shoulders, drawing their warmth into my sides and absorbing their positivity. This was the exact piece of reality I needed. A night out with my favorite people. To forget everything that threatened to steal my happiness. A night of the carefree, spirited Sarah.

"Babe, you almost ready? We're supposed to meet everyone in twenty."

I rounded the corner, my fingers fumbling to fasten my necklace as I walked toward Jackson. My limbs had trembled for the last hour, nervous and excited for the evening, and my dexterity had left the building. "Can you help me with this?" I asked.

Spinning around, I faced away from Jackson and swept my honey locks over one shoulder. He eased the eye and clasp from my hands, his nimble fingers hooking the necklace in place. A second later, a warm breath painted my bare shoulder. His feverish, calloused fingers lingering at the base of my neck before he traced a line down my spine. A shiver rippled throughout my body and sparked goose-flesh along my skin.

His lips danced up the curve of my neck, stopping at the sensitive flesh below my ear. "You're lucky I'm seeing you in this top now. If I saw this ten minutes ago, you'd need to get dressed again," he said, a growl ripping from his throat. Jackson nipped at my earlobe before licking and biting his way down my neck and shoulder, a new wave of shivers erupting and converging at my core.

"So you like what I'm wearing?" I squeaked out as I bit my lower lip. My desire alive for the first time in a week.

"Like doesn't even cover what this top is exposing."

He outlined the fabric of my top. The shimmery material edge started at the front of my shoulder, ran down my side, and stopped level with my navel. It only covered my breasts and a fraction of my abdomen. The back was open, with exception to the thin strands which ran across the back and neck and held it in place. A short denim skirt sat low on my hips, the bottom hemline exposing the majority of my long legs.

"I'm glad you more than like it. Maybe later, you can show me how much you more than like it," I teased.

Jackson spun me to face him. His smoldering sapphires locked onto me as he drew me closer, the hunger in his gaze lit my flesh on fire. He ate me alive with his inspection and, for a split-second, I gave serious thought to ditching our friends. If he let me, I'd rip the clothes off his perfect, chiseled body and take him on the floor where we stood.

"If you keep looking at me like that, we won't make it

out the door. We should at least show up, seeing as the entire evening was our idea," he taunted with a wink.

"Okay, okay. Fine," I huffed as Jackson chuckled at my pity party. "But mark my words, sir." I tapped a finger on his chest. "This is far from over tonight."

"Yes, ma'am." His face beamed with promise and wonder at what the rest of the night would entail.

People crowded every bar we explored during our adventure. We went from place to place in search of the perfect atmosphere that played good music but with a decent crowd. We wandered in and out of a few places before finally locating one that satisfied us all.

It ended up only being six of us — Rick unable to ditch work. We sent our love to him in the form of goofy, kissy-faced text messages. He responded with pouty-faced texts and a promise to tag along next time.

The six of us stood around a tall table with our drink of choice. Jackson caged me in with his front deliciously close to my back. My body buzzed as the music pulsated around us. Everyone enjoyed a great night out as all dreadful thoughts drifted into the ether.

Christy and I chatted about how fun our next outing would be. "I hope Rick can join us," I said. Just as I asked Christy when Rick finished work, Jackson's fingers traced down my sides. My eyes rolled and slipped shut as his fingers danced over my skin. A moment later, he laced his fingers with mine and towed me onto the dance floor. Jackson walked backwards into the throng of bodies, his eyes locked on mine. A wicked, sexy grin brightened his face in the darkened space.

Before he escorted me to the dance floor, I hadn't paid attention to the song playing. It wasn't until we reached the center of the floor, sweaty bodies gyrating against one another everywhere, that I listened. A sultry bass vibe bounced off the walls and resonated in my bones. Every cell in my body ached to have Jackson's body flush against mine. The tempo flowed like molten lava and seeped into my pores like liquid sex. He spun me and pressed my back against his front, his fingertips igniting a trail of sparks along my skin as he guided us to the seductive beat.

The music pulsated as I stared at other couples giving themselves over to the beat. Voyeurism never interested me, but I gave into the visual stimuli as Jackson lit my body on fire. Calloused fingers roamed and kneaded my stark flesh, from hip to midriff, as he pressed his erection harder into my ass and I melted into him. His breath ghosted the nape of my neck a beat before his lips and tongue bruised my skin. An energy exploded inside me at the contact and flowed through every nerve ending in my body like an electrical grid, pooling at my core. I traced my hands over his forearms and imprisoned his splayed hands near my naval. His mouth continued to assault my flesh as I pressed my ass against his straining erection.

Anyone observing might say we were fucking, right there, in the middle of the nightclub. But I gave no fucks. Freedom surrounded me. An invisible weight lifted away when I was myself, in my element, surrounded by people I cared about. Jackson provided me with the perfect remedy, and I was so thankful.

Turning me to face him, he slid one leg between mine. His jeans rubbed rough on my panties in a delicious rhythm. With each circle and thrust of his hips, my body trembled against his thigh. My breasts smashed to his torso, his hands traced down my bare back and palmed my ass, keeping me upright as we put on a show for hundreds of patrons.

The attention would intimidate some people, but we only saw each other. In this moment, we were completely lost to the world around us. Arms slung around his neck, face buried in his chest, I clutched onto him as he drove the pressure further between my legs. I tipped my head back and Jackson pressed his forehead to mine as our bodies became one, with each other and the music. My hair a veil around us, it shrouded my slacked jaw from onlookers.

"So fucking hot, babe. You're close, aren't you?"

I nodded, and he licked a line over my upper lip, tingles left in his wake. Without shame, I panted against

Jackson's lax lips. My fingers dove into his hair and tugged at the strands. The tension in my core wound tighter than a virgin on prom night.

The song edged higher, seconds away from its peak. Jackson drove his hips into me harder and faster as he sucked at the tender spot beneath my ear. In a lucky twist of fate, my orgasm detonated as the song climaxed. As realization dawned and I remembered where we were, I was thankful the music masked my screams.

Bliss and a tinge of embarrassment flooded me as my orgasm dissipated. We just shared one of the most intense and intimate moments while surrounded by hundreds of strangers. No one glanced our way or cared we just dry fucked in the middle of the club. And with that, my embarrassment faded. In its place, a foreign yet desirable thrill took hold.

He sucked on my earlobe, then licked the shell of my ear. "That was the hottest fucking thing I've ever seen," he said, his breath hot and heavy on my ear. "I need to be inside you. Now."

Jackson's hunger a direct line to the saturated flesh between my thighs. Without hesitation, I snatched his hand and led us off the dance floor toward our friends. A brief round of goodbyes to everyone and, in less than five minutes, we were out the door and in the car.

Halfway to my apartment, my body still vibrated from my orgasm. I itched for more. Of him. Of us. My body is bursting with pent up energy as I fidget in the passenger seat. A distraction is necessary. Only one thing popped into my head.

A moment later, I reached across the console and unbuttoned his jeans, the teeth of his fly separated with ease. My mouth watered as I scraped my nails over his erection and slipped my hand beneath his boxer briefs. One stroke, then another, before I removed my hand.

Jackson gasped as he white-knuckled the steering wheel. "I am still driving, you know," he stated. But there was no attempt to stop me.

"I'm aware. But I'm bored. And horny. Don't you think it's time to repay you?" I asked, licking my lips.

His eyes averted from the road a second as my hand kneaded his upper thigh and traced a line up his erection, pausing at the waistband of his briefs. Jackson made no attempt to stop me. Eager to taste him, I tucked my fingers beneath the elastic band and exposed his hard cock. I sheathed him with my hand and stroked his length. The velvety soft skin a juxtaposition to the firm stone of his erection. Arousal slickened my panties again at the thought of him inside me.

I ached for him.

As I stroked him, Jackson's jaw slackened. A harsh pant passed between his lips. A minute later, he drove past the entry gate of my complex, parked next to my car and cut the engine.

Jackson all but ripped my seatbelt off as he yanked me over him and slid his seat back. His pants shifted underneath me and dropped to his knees. I fumbled in the confined space to hike my skirt up and shove the skimpy fabric of my panties aside.

My head slumped forward as the tip of his cock glided between my folds and taunted me. He lifted his chin and our lips met as I seated myself on him. As he slid deep inside me, I dug my nails into his shoulders and clutched him as if my life depended on it. Jackson hissed as I gasped. The air abuzz with static electricity, our bodies statues as we adjusted to our surroundings.

And then Jackson bucked his hips. My body ricocheted up, then plummeted down. I gripped the seat as my eyes rolled back. Jackson inside me was a delicacy. Nothing compared to the way Jackson fit my body. As if we were cut from the same pattern. As if he'd memorized my body before we met, and I'd done the same. In fantasies or a past life.

His hands squeezed my hips, certain to leave bruises by morning. They served as reminders of tonight. Reminders I enjoyed the sight of. He bucked again and sent a ripple of heat throughout my abdomen.

I clawed the seat and rode his cock. My body flickered and ignited as each live wire inside me zapped with current. The world around me disappeared as I orbited earth in the mesosphere. Sex with Jackson an out-of-body experience.

"*Oh god. Oh god. Oh my fucking god. Fuck me.*" The chant rolled off my tongue like a litany. "I'm so close. *Oh god, yes... Fuck me, Jackson.*" My plea guttural. A lust-driven command foreign to my own ears.

The car filled with slaps and moans and the undiluted scent of sex. Raw and pure and I never wanted it to end.

"Come for me, baby. Milk me." His direction gruff as his teeth sunk into my shoulder. The bite a sharp sting of lightning that electrified every nerve ending in my body. Another pump of his hips and he knocked me into the abyss, his name vociferated on my lips.

As my climax faded, his cock pulsed inside me. My name a growl deep in his throat. We stayed in his Jeep a while longer, arms locked in an embrace. After several minutes passed, our breaths and hearts returned to their normal patterns while a light sheen of sweat coated our bodies.

Right here. Right now. The growing affection we shared encased us in our own little bubble. All my worries drifted away. All my fears absent. In this place—our world—everything was absolutely perfect.

Sunlight slithered through the blinds and woke me far too early. I rolled onto my back and stretched my arm across the bed to discover the space beside me empty. In its place, an indentation of Jackson's body.

Propped up on my elbows, I noticed the bedroom door had been closed. A sizzle crackled outside the room, followed by a muffled *shit*. I reached for a tank top and pajama shorts and slipped them on, then shuffled out the door in search of my guy.

From the moment I opened the door, pure deliciousness assaulted me. My mouth watered and my stomach grumbled with a vengeance. I stumbled toward the kitchen, my feet less sluggish with each step. Maple syrup, coffee, potatoes, and the aroma of citrus surrounded me like an invisible force field. My stomach grumbled again, as if I needed a reminder.

I rounded the corner and paused as Jackson stirred something on the stove. With his back to me, I ogled as he alternated between pans and the cutting board. Clad in black boxer briefs that hugged his sculpted ass, an apron string tied at his neck and waist protected his bare torso. What made my mouth water more? The steamy scent of breakfast or the sight of Jackson practically naked in an apron? A tough decision to make this early in the morning. I bit my lip, leaned against the closest wall, and gawked.

A moment later, Jackson went back to the cutting board and busted me. His lips curved up into my favorite smile, the one which made women weak in the knees. "Hey, gorgeous. I didn't hear you. I wanted to surprise you with breakfast in bed," he said as he walked over and placed a soft kiss on my cheek.

"The sun wouldn't let me sleep anymore. Maybe it

wanted me to witness this spectacle. I should grab my camera. Because this..." I gestured the length of his body. "This should be a keepsake."

"Picture worthy moment, huh? Better hurry then because it's almost ready. Then the apron disappears."

I bolted from the kitchen and prayed I'd be back in time. Digging through my purse, I snagged my dying phone. A second later, I grabbed a digital camera from the shelf in my closet. Two are better than one. Plus, the camera would capture the visual better than my phone.

I ran back to the kitchen too fast. My feet skid across the tile as I raised my cell and opened the camera. Once my momentum stopped, I tapped the screen twice. Jackson smiled at me in the photo as he waved a wooden spoon my way. Pleased with the image, I set the phone down and brought the camera to my eye. Jackson posed and teased and made goofy faces at the lens.

I snapped a few shots before pulling the camera away from my eye. "Go back to what you were doing. I'm not really into posed photography."

"I didn't know you were such a shutterbug. Just so you know, breakfast will be ready in two minutes."

He went back to focusing on his task. I brought the camera back to my eye and pressed the shutter button over and over. Jackson's body is a rare piece of art. I captured the thick muscles railing his spine, the strength in his broad shoulders, the magnitude of his biceps and triceps, and damn... those glutes. The photos wouldn't need manipulation, only some lighting adjustments.

Just in time, I snapped one last photo before he removed the apron from his chest. "I hope you got what you wanted because breakfast is ready."

Setting the camera on the countertop, I stepped up to his side and rested my chin on his arm. My eyes wandered over the buffet he had assembled. "I did. Let's eat."

He took our plates and headed for the living room. I gathered the coffee pot, mugs, cream and sugar and placed them on a small serving tray. As I sat beside him, I set the tray between us on the coffee table.

"Everything looks and smells amazing. Thank you," I said as I leaned into him and pressed a kiss to his cheek.

"You're welcome, babe. Eat up, before it gets cold."

Buffet a polite term for the mountain of food on my plate. I had difficulty deciding what to eat first. Maple turkey bacon, scrambled egg whites, home fries or the berries and orange wedges drizzled with honey and mint.

Breakfast was orgasmic. And if anyone else would've been present, they'd swear—by the moans and groans—Jackson and I were having sex. No meal is better than sex with Jackson. But his cooking ran neck-and-neck with second place.

And then perversion kicked in. I wondered what it'd be like to eat Jackson's cooking during sex? The food in my mouth all but spewed across the room. My chest heaved as I inhaled food and my body launched into the worst coughing fit. For the best reason.

Jackson dropped his plate on the table and slapped my back with gentle force. "You okay?" I nodded. "Lift your arms up, hands over your head. Did you swallow wrong?" I followed his instruction and nodded again. My face and chest bloomed a brilliant shade of red with each forceful cough of my lungs. "I'm grabbing you some water." He bolted off the couch faster than lightning and returned just as quick with water.

When I gained control of my lungs, I chugged half the water. The cool liquid soothed some of the irritation. "Sorry. Didn't mean to scare you," I said, all harsh and scratchy.

"I know you like my cooking, but please don't inhale it," he teased. His booming laughter bounced off the walls as his hand painted circles over my ribcage.

"It wasn't that. I guess I got lost in thought and wasn't paying much attention to chewing or swallowing. I won't do that again," I murmured as heat pinked my cheeks.

A brow arched as his eyes pinned me. "What exactly were you thinking about?"

Me and my big fat mouth. Oh well, guess it was out in the open. But, hey! Maybe it would be a good thing. Maybe I would actually get the fantasy. "Just day dreaming about eating your orgasmic meals while we had sex. I got a little distracted by the whole idea."

"*Really?* Huh. I may just have to bookmark the idea." A wicked grin highlighted his beautiful face.

God, I hoped so.

ELEVEN

WEEKENDS SPENT with Jackson were comparable to heaven and ended far too soon. Since our second date, we've spent every non-working moment of the weekend together. Our plans determined whose bed we slept in. After the infamous letter, Jackson slept beside me every night. And I had zero complaints.

Once we exhausted ourselves between the sheets, Jackson curled his frame to my back and clutched me tight to his chest. A different warmth spread through my veins. Not arousal. But more akin to snuggles and hot cocoa and unrelenting hugs. Pure comfort. And there was no other place I wanted to be. In such a short span of time, Jackson became my home. A home I never imagined my life without. The sweetest place in existence.

The elevator dinged, disturbing my morning daydream. I walked the short distance to my desk in a haze. Yesterday morning's breakfast feast looped in my memory like an old black and white film. We'd spent hours in my bed entranced with each other. I clamped my thighs tight as I passed my coworkers. An insatiable connection thrived between me and Jackson. A connection I prayed never fizzled.

"Ugh, it's going to be a long day," I muttered to myself.

As I entered my cubicle, I snapped myself back to reality. Before I spoke with any clients today, clarity was needed. Although we weren't a customer-facing business, Monday was always busy. It was also the time of year when northerners traveled home. And like every year prior, travel plans included questions regarding benefits.

By the time my lunch hour arrived, my stomach was ready to eat me whole. The grumbles certain to alert everyone nearby. I dialed Liz's desk—then Christy's—and whined about my hunger pangs. A minute later, we agreed to meet downstairs at Carol's.

Is it sad that lunch was the best part of the workday? Nothing paralleled to sitting with my besties at a small, metal table with uneven legs. We talked about life and love and whatever the hell floated in our heads.

We discussed our weekends. Each of us enthralled with the other's story. Between the three of us, we exploded with happiness. Our lives full and fun and blissful.

Christy and Rick started to plan their summer vacation. They hadn't decided where, but narrowed it down to two places—the Bahamas or Virgin Islands. Either way, they intended to do a seven-day cruise and forget about everything except themselves.

Liz confessed she'd met someone when we were out the other night. They exchanged numbers and had texted and talked throughout the weekend. "He's super, fucking hot. We're planning to hang out this weekend, maybe grab a bite," she said. Her face lit up like a toddler on Christmas morning. Seeing her like this made my pulse skip. I worried about her once Jackson and I started dating. But her exuberance melted away any residual concern.

Nothing made my heart sing more than these two women and all the wonderful things happening in our lives. A few months ago, this moment would've been a remote fantasy. But now, my heart constricted and my eyes pooled. All of us happy and fulfilled.

"Sometime soon, with your new mister hottie, the six of us should go to dinner. Oooorr..." I said. My hips wriggled in the wooden chair. "Maybe I should ask my personal chef to cook. Who, by the way, looks mighty fine in an apron and his drawers. His mama taught him well." At the mention of Jackson and his culinary skills, memories of how he looked in my kitchen pinked my skin.

"Sounds like a great idea." Christy tapped her chin as her eyes darted between us. "We could each bring something, so Jackson doesn't have to cook everything."

I aimed a finger at her with my thumb up and clucked my tongue. "Smart thinking. Let's wait till next week, after

Liz has a smoking hot weekend, and then sort out the details. Good plan?"

"Yes," they said in unison. Without warning, the three of us burst into a fit of laughter and every pair of eyes locked on us. And we gave no fucks. I loved our terrific trio.

A few minutes later, lunch ended. We shuffled back to the elevator and our floor of cubicles. Our hesitance to exit the car when it arrived was comical. But after a unified huff, we meandered back to our desks.

I leaned into the lumbar support on my chair and inhaled. After two deep breaths, my mind slipped back into work mode. *Only a few more hours to go.* Wrapping the phone's handsfree earpiece around the shell of my ear, I jostled the mouse to wake my computer and entered my password. F1n3@S$mF—if anyone took the time to hack my password, they'd keel over from hysterics.

I clicked on the weekly reports and retrieved my client and prospect lists. After I printed them off for outbound calls, I opened my email inbox and saw a few unread messages.

The first message was from a client sending me thanks for helping them update their policy. I typed out a quick reply and hit send.

The second email was from Marco—carbon copied to Bob in human resources. A congratulations on hitting my sales goal with three weeks left in the quarter. I sent a quick thank you and printed the email, stashing it in my *Go Me!* file in my desk.

The third message had no name or subject line, just a weird blend of letters and numbers.

From: 21LT993YW200054JFQ02399
To: Sarh.Bradley@hammondlife.com
Subject:

My beautiful Sarah,

Under the light of the moon, your skin shimmers like a million flecks of glitter painted across the sky.
In the center of the club, your body moves like no one is watching.
No one but me.
I'm always watching. Always listening.
Like when your pussy came all over that guy's leg the other night.
I saw the fire in your eyes. Heard the sound of your release, even over the sex inducing music.
And when you fucked him in front of your apartment, your tight little cunt riding his tiny dick like you were at a rodeo, I jacked off in the bushes next to your window.
One day, when you're tired of sir steroids, I'll be the one ramming your juicy cunt with my fat cock. You'll be screaming my name for days. No other name except mine.
I attached a few pictures for your viewing pleasure.

I shoved away from my desk with trembling hands. Tears streamed down my cheeks as my lungs begged me to breathe. I needed to get out of here. Get away from my computer. In the narrow aisle of cubicles, I all but sprinted toward Liz's desk, darting past coworkers on the way. As I stepped into Liz's small space, I clutched my knees and bent at the waist, heaving.

"Sarah?! What the hell's going on? Are you okay?" A bang disrupted the monotony in the office as Liz's chair slammed into her credenza. She bolted to my side and gripped my shoulders.

"Can't. Breathe." I wheezed as my stomach rolled.

Liz guided me to a chair opposite hers. "Sit, sit, sit. Tell me what I can do." Squatting down beside me, she placed a hand on my knee, the other on my shoulder. Her eyes widened with panic as she watched me have a total meltdown.

"I don't know. Maybe call Jackson. I got an email. Tell him I got an email. Like the letter, only worse." My wheezing morphed into slow, methodical gasps.

"What letter? What email? Talk to me." Her brows pinched together as she silently pleaded for answers.

"Can you just call Jackson for me? He'll explain. Please..." The request faded on my lips.

"Do you know his number? Where's your phone?"

I patted the pockets of my black dress slacks, relieved to find my phone there. I handed the lifeline to Liz with a trembling hand. After she unlocked it, Liz scrolled through my contacts and called Jackson.

Liz's eyes refused to leave mine while my phone was

glued to her ear. A flash lit up Liz's face. Shock registered as Jackson greeted her, assuming it was me.

"Hey, Jackson, it's Liz. Sorry to bother you at work. Sarah wanted me to call you," she paused, listening to Jackson's response. "She's okay, I think. She stumbled into my office a minute ago, out of breath. Asked me to call you. Something about an email she got. Said it's worse than the letter."

A moment later, Liz's face transformed from worried to fearful. This did nothing to settle the angst bubbling inside me. The hole in my chest expanded as unease ate away my sanity. My stomach churned again and I begged my lunch to stay down. I assumed Jackson explained the letter I'd received, and let her know that we filed a police report. That he'd been with me during every moment, minus work.

My emotional state registered with Liz. She tried to maintain control and keep me calm. "Sarah, Jackson wants to know what the email says," Liz said in a soothing tone.

I shook my head, unwilling to say the words. Not wanting to see them again, let alone speak them. My fingers quivered as I shoved a loose strand of hair behind my ear. "It's still open on my computer. I can't look at it again. Please, Liz."

She nodded. "Let's walk down there together. Okay?"

Liz stood with my phone still glued to her ear and took my hand in hers. She told Jackson to wait as we headed back to my desk, dropping the phone to her side and hiding it. The closer we got to my tiny square footage of office space, the more nausea churned in my gut. My limbs trembled as bile rose in my throat. A shiver rippled from head to toe as the urge to vomit became inevitable.

Deep breaths, Sarah. DO NOT throw up at work. You'll never hear the end of it.

When we reached my cubicle, I remained rooted at the entryway. Liz glanced to me as understanding washed over her face and she dropped my hand. She stepped around the corner of my desk and sat in my chair. Her eyes darted side-to-side as she scanned the words plastered across the screen.

Her eyes magnified in horror as she peeked up at me, concern etched in the lines on her forehead. I sat down in one of the chairs in front of my desk and dropped my head into my hands. Liz whisper-read the email to Jackson and I forced my fingers in my ears.

Something passed by in my periphery. I chanced a look up as Liz walked to the printer and grabbed a page from the tray before handing me the phone.

I dragged in a breath before I spoke, but still had trouble finding my voice. "Hey." It's all I said. The only word my mouth formed.

"Babe," Jackson said, his voice a soothing metronome. "I'm leaving work in a minute. Liz will stay with you until I get there. Whoever you need to talk to at work, tell them you're sick and need to leave early."

"Okay." My fingers fumbled with the hem of my shirt.

"I'll be there soon. Stay with Liz," he reiterated.

"I will," I whispered.

I disconnected the call and glanced up at Liz. After relaying Jackson's directions, I rose from the chair. I had to leave, but didn't know how. Liz clung to my side and held my hand as we walked to Marco's office. With each step, I considered what to tell Marco. Something that wouldn't prompt endless questions.

Unfortunately, women dealing with premenstrual symptoms had been overused in the office. Some women called off an entire day and tanned their skin by the pool, saying the hot sun was therapy.

Cold symptoms? Maybe. But I'm not sure Marco would buy it considering I was rainbows and sunshine an hour ago. Think, think, think. What else is there?

"Liz. What the hell do I tell Marco? Can't say it's a cold. He won't buy it. I was fine until after lunch. Help me, please," I begged.

Her hand rubbed soothing circles on my back. "Uh… Maybe you can pass it off as food poisoning. Say lunch didn't agree with you and now you're nauseous. That should work."

Food poisoning is a better idea than anything I came up with. My mind started to shut down and run only necessary functions until Jackson arrived. "Thanks, Liz. That'll work perfectly."

We reached Marco's office, his heavy wooden door was cracked open a few inches. I sucked in a breath and straightened my spine as much as possible. Hesitantly, I rapped my knuckles next to the nameplate—*Marco Meyers, Senior Sales Manager.*

"Come in." Authority rang strong in those two words.

"I'll wait out here for you." Liz pivoted to the side, out of Marco's view when I opened the door.

Marco glanced up from a stack of papers in his hands, a pair of reading glasses rested low on his nose. "What can I do for you, Sarah?" He leaned back in his chair, setting the papers on top of his keyboard.

"Hey, Marco. I'm not feeling so hot. Must've eaten something bad at lunch." As if on cue, my stomach grumbled so loud Marco heard it. "Is it okay if I leave early? I'll have someone pick me up."

His sharp eyes assessed me, raking up and down my body to validate my statement. *God, I hope I appeared as sick as I felt.* His fingers tapped the arms of his oak chair, cogs spinning. Second-by-second, I fidgeted in front of him as he accepted my half-truth.

"Yeah, no problem, Sarah," he said, finally. "You don't look so good. Kind of pale actually. Go home, eat some chicken noodle soup, get some rest. If you're not well in the morning, call me. You can afford to miss a day or two."

"Thanks, Marco. I'll let you know." I gave him a tight smile and he told me to get well soon.

I stepped outside his office and gave Liz a thumbs up, relieved I could leave. She yanked me back to her side and hooked her arm in mine as we walked back to my desk.

"Let's grab your stuff and I'll walk you down to the lobby. Want me or Christy to bring your car home later?"

I reached into my bottom desk drawer and retrieved my purse, giving Liz my keys. "That would be a huge help. Thanks, Liz. You really are the best." My hand squeezed her forearm a little tighter.

"Anything for you, girl. I'll let Jackson get you out of here, but soon we're all sitting down and having a *family meeting*. You need to fill us in." Concern poured out of her and the worry line from earlier reappeared.

"Soon, I promise. Just give me a day. Maybe come over tomorrow for dinner and we can all talk."

"Keep me in the loop. I'll talk with Christy when I get upstairs, tell her what you told Marco. That way the story jives. We can let her in on everything later. Okay?"

"Okay."

We stepped off the elevator and walked to the lobby and parked ourselves on a bench. I leaned into Liz and rested my head on her shoulder. A deep inhalation later, I shut my eyes, closed out the world, and whispered to the darkness. "Why is this happening to me?"

I meant it more as a rhetorical question, not really expecting Liz to answer. She didn't have answers. No one had them. "Don't know, sweetheart. But between all of us, we'll figure it out. We'll keep you safe. Swear." I hugged myself harder and moved closer to Liz as her words comforted me.

"Babe, I'm here," Jackson said. His hand splayed over

my thigh, but I refused to open my eyes. The dark was safer right now.

After a moment, I lifted my head and squinted at the brightness. The receptionist stared at us from her marble-topped desk. "Hey," I croaked. "I gave Liz my keys so they can bring my car home later."

He took my hands in his, stood me upright and pinned me to his chest. "Let's get you out of here." I nodded as he shifted toward Liz. "See you later."

Liz handed a creased piece of paper to Jackson. "In case you need to show it to them." The email. A monster clawed inside my gut.

"Thanks, Liz. I'll let you know what they say."

Jackson steered me to the exit. As we passed through the glass doors, I glanced up. "Let Liz know *who* says what?"

Jackson opened the passenger door to his Jeep and helped me inside. He shut the door and jogged to the driver's side and slid in. "Let Liz know what the police say after we update them."

Jackson maneuvered into traffic and drove past hundreds of people. People not being stalked by some unknown lunatic. Who had normal lives. People not scared to go places or exist outside the walls of their home. Who could be themselves.

People not like me.

I laid on my bed, curled into a fetal position. My work clothes stripped off and replaced with pajama pants and a tank top, courtesy of the best boyfriend in the world. He brushed his fingers over my hair, tucking a fallen group of strands behind my ear.

"What can I get for you, babe? Water? Food?"

He showered me with love like no other. How did I get so damn lucky? "Maybe some water."

"Okay. I'll be back. Then I'll call Liz." He left the bedroom, his stride quick and purposeful. Clinking rang out as ice dropped into the glass, followed by the quieter swish of water dispensing from the fridge door.

He strode back in and settled beside me, offering me the glass. I shook my head and curled tighter into my body as he set the water on the bedside table. "Be back in a minute. I'll just be in the living room." His hand cupped my face and traced the line of my jaw before he stepped out of the room.

A small creak grated from the other room. The same creak I'd heard hundreds of times, but tuned out. As Jackson sat on the couch, I heard every shift of his weight on the weathered springs. I locked onto the glass of water and watched the ice cubes bob. A small pearl of moisture bubbled on the outside of the glass. A moment later, my eyes were stinging and my throat was clogged.

How did I get here? What got me to this point?

This whole situation reflected an unfathomable nightmare. How did a person—who wouldn't harm a bug in her home—happen to have some crazed person following her every move? Sending her 'gifts' and 'love letters' meant to scare her into their 'rescuing arms'. When in actuality, it created the opposite effect. All I wanted was to stay in my apartment with Jackson and never leave until the police captured this nutjob.

Maybe leave occasionally—a trip to the grocery store, perhaps a quick trip to the gym. After all, the gym in my gated community should be safe. With the gate and guard, it wasn't easily accessible. All the stores I shopped at within a mile or two. Which was manageable. I'd be a temporary recluse. At least until an arrest happened.

Jackson's soft rumble carried from the couch to my ear. "I know, Liz. Not leaving her side. I cancelled my appointments tomorrow and I'll have her call off work in the morning." He went quiet a moment—Liz must have been speaking. "We'll be here all night. Just let me know when you're here and I'll let you in."

The room silenced another moment. "We added it all to the police report. The officer said they'll contact the IT department at Hammond. See if the email can be traced." He gave a small *mmhmm* and another *I know*. "Let's shoot for dinner here, tomorrow night at six-thirty. Tell Christy and Rick and I'll get everything else done on this end." Another brief pause. "Thanks, Liz. Talk to you later."

And then nothing but silence. Silence and fear. I needed him here with me. Needed him pressed against me. Needed his embrace to hold me close, to never let go. To soothe my anxiety and promise everything would be okay.

Jackson's bare feet padded across the wood floor, growing louder with each step. I turned my head as he tugged his shirt over his head. A second later, he swathed me in warmth under the protection of my fluffy comforter. His arm slid over my midsection and dragged me into him. His front to my back. Our limbs a snuggled pretzel.

Jackson whispered sweet words in my ear. He vowed to keep me safe. Promised to do everything within his power to end this nightmare. And then his lips pressed a tender kiss below my ear.

My heart fluttered at the unrelenting nature of his tenderness. As I drifted off to sleep in his arms, my hands secured him tighter to me. My mind half awake-half asleep, three infamous words slipped from my lips. *I love you.* And then I drifted off to a place where it was him and me and no one else. A place where monsters didn't exist.

TWELVE

I LAID AWAKE IN BED, wishing for the millionth time to fall asleep. Twisting, I glanced at the clock and groaned. In an hour, the alarm would go off. So much for sleep. Rigid as stone, I tried not to disturb Jackson. I envied his deep, even breaths and occasional snore while he slumbered. As I stared up at the ceiling, a muted amber luminescence from the clock highlighted the room. My eyes lost focus as they gazed at the dusty white paint.

Closing my eyes, I begged the heavens to let me fall asleep. To escape the craziness which currently held my reality captive. To drift off to a happier place. I should be dreaming about Jackson and hiking and mountains. About secluded meadows and picnics and laughter. In this dream, the sun shone high in the sky, its rays bouncing off puffy, white clouds and warming our skin. Flowers and grass and streams perfumed the air. Birds chirped and squirrels scavenged for nuts. No place compared to here.

Our happy place. The perfect escape. Too bad it's not reality.

Hot tears pricked my eyes. I held them at bay a moment before the first salty drop leaked out and rolled down to my ear. As best I could, I restrained my sobbing and smothered the whimpers desperate to escape. The droplets continued their unrelenting stream and puddled in my ear. Before much longer, I'd be full-on bawling.

Jackson stirred beside me and he shifted to haul me closer to his chest. My solo crying session hit full speed as my nasal passages clogged and blocked my ability to breathe. Any moment, I would wake Jackson with my sniffles and tears. But not if I slipped out of the bed grace-fully and grabbed tissues. In both scenarios, I'd disturb him and the day would be miserable.

I peeled the comforter and top sheet back and inched my legs to the edge of the bed. With slow precision, I clamped his wrist in my fingers and gently lifted his fore-arm. Scooting my body inch by inch, I slid out from under his hold.

"You okay?" Jackson mumbled groggy with sleep. Even in my current state of misery, the sex appeal of his morning voice called out to me. I peered over my shoul-der; a pair of tired sapphire eyes laser-focused on me.

"Yeah. Just need to use the bathroom." His arm shifted and freed me.

Jackson's fingers skirted over my palm as I stood, a fresh batch of tears activated by his tender touch. The mattress squeaked behind me, followed by a faint thump on the floor. In a heartbeat, Jackson's hands cradled my face as his thumbs swiped the cascading tears away. "Talk to me." Warm lips pressed mine, the lightest of pressure, before he leaned away to study me. "I'm here. Whatever you need. No matter what."

I inhaled deep, barely a molecule of oxygen made it to my lungs, my sinus cavities clogged and complaining. In a very unladylike fashion, I reached up and swiped the length of my hand underneath my nose. It was a disgusting sight, and I was in desperate need of a tissue.

"Come with me. I've got you." Jackson tucked me into his side and walked me to the bathroom.

"I'm sorry." Another snotty inhalation, followed by a river of tears. I'm so pathetic. "I didn't want to wake you. Just couldn't fall back asleep. And then I kept thinking about everything. It's like a rat race in my head. And then, the adrenaline that stopped my crying earlier vanished. Everything crashed down on me all at once. Sorry, I tried hard to be quiet. You looked so peaceful and I didn't want to disturb you."

Word vomit spewed from my lips like bad seafood. It wouldn't stay down, morphing into a vicious cycle of endless words. As much as I didn't want this to burden Jackson, he should know where my head was at. And how I needed his strength since I was utterly weak.

"Don't apologize, babe." He spun me to face him. "I'm here for you. Whatever you need. No matter what time it is. If you need me, even if it's to brush your hair, I'm here."

I nodded as my body relaxed more. "I'll try." He

helped me into the bathroom, then stepped away and gave me privacy. I blew my nose; quite an effort on my part. I used the toilet, washed my hands, and snatched the box of tissues on my way out.

Jackson laid under the covers. The down-turned corner exposed him from the waist up. He beckoned me with a curled finger and I crawled back into the bed, and molded my front to his chest as he swathed me in warmth and comfort.

Ear pressed to his sternum, I regulated my breath to the steady rhythm of his heartbeat. His chest rose and fell steadily. His strong arms embraced me as his spicy scent infiltrated and soothed every atom in my soul. This was exactly where I belonged. Beside Jackson. My fortitude. And then I remembered... The three little words that escaped as I drifted off to sleep earlier.

My body became as rigid as stone. My arms curled in closer, tighter to my chest as I closed in on myself. "What's wrong?" he asked, concerned.

Should I tell him? I don't want lies between us. Maybe it was all a dream. Did I really say those three words aloud? "Nothing. Just remembered part of a dream. At least I think it was a dream. It's difficult to know the difference anymore."

Jackson's hand rubbed the length of my back and calmed me, washing away some of the worry. "Tell me. I'll let you know if it was real or not."

I dug deep and mustered up the courage to confess. Perhaps, for the second time. *What if I didn't say it before and*

I say it now and I scare him away? I can't lose him. I'd splinter without his strength. But I had to know if I left that sentiment floating in the air.

Dragging in a methodical breath, I spoke on the exhale. "It's all a bit foggy... but I remember telling you something." My pulse throbbed in my ears, a whoosh of blood with each pump of the fast-beating organ. Jackson laid patient and waited for me to continue. "I think I told you I love you."

I cringed. My head and heart ready for the blow of pain and hurt. Prepared for rejection or denial. Seconds mimicked hours as I waited for a response. But Jackson didn't utter a word as his hand continually stroked the length of my spine. Absolute silence. Any second, I'd lose my mind. Time crept. Why wasn't he answering? I blinked to relieve the stinging sensation in the backs of my eyes. A lump lodged in my throat. I had zero expectation of Jackson returning the sentiment. All I wanted was confirmation on reality versus fantasy. Especially now, when much of my life imitated one huge nightmare.

Drawing his arm back, he wedged it between us as he lifted my chin. His sapphires stunned me with their radiance. Jackson guided my lips to his for a blip of time, resting his forehead on mine once our lips parted. "It wasn't a dream," he whispered. One little sentence. Four words strung together. My heart fluttered and my stomach twisted as I waited.

Jackson didn't appear put off, but he wasn't saying anything either. He didn't need to repeat it, not unless he reciprocated. But there was one thing I needed. For him to admit he cared about me. It didn't have to be the infamous *L* word. I accepted that. And respected it.

We laid face to face, Jackson's eyes closed, his forehead rested on mine. His chest pressed mine as he inhaled deep and held it a few heartbeats. Slowly, he exhaled. When his eyes reopened and focused on me, something hypnotic captured me. Sapphire blues scorched my emeralds. The windows to his soul revealed truths without a word spoken. Spellbound and bewitched, I was a slave to him.

We laid there—blue to green—still; soundless. A soft, pink hue outlined his jaw as dawn ascended and the tinge of daybreak emphasized his rugged features. I sighed into the quiet as my emotions skyrocketed toward the peak of my internal roller coaster.

Jackson tilted his chin, and we exchanged a set of small kisses. The kisses morphed, flourished, became impassioned and unstoppable. Hidden meanings bloomed with each pass. Heat blossomed as his tongue brushed my lower lip. My lips parted and I gasped. Labored breaths and frenzied lips. His tongue stroked mine and I lost it.

We were all hands. Tearing clothes from each other as our frantic kisses drifted to necks and curves and dips. Fuck, I needed him. And this was his way of showing me he adored me. Maybe he wasn't ready to say the words yet, but he could show me. That's the funny thing about love. Some people ached to hear a four-letter word. Begged it be spoken to reassure them. To others, love was an unspoken devotion. Displayed in touch or gestures or the willingness to be present. Right now, Jackson was showing me his unspeakable love.

He rolled me onto my back and hovered inches above me. Our eyes locked as Jackson's erection pressed into me. His cock caressed the slickness between my thighs, but didn't move any farther. He paused. His gaze focused on me as he waited for confirmation. Never wanting to take advantage.

I lifted my hips and the tip of his cock dipped into my wetness before I fell back onto the sheets. That simple reassurance was all he needed from me. A second later, he dipped down and kissed me again. Jackson kissed me slow and sweet as he poured his soul into mine. My fingers weaved through his hair as I held him to me. Slowly, my body stirred back to life and simmered for more. Of him. His taste. His touch.

Jackson bucked his hips, and I gasped as his length filled me. I dug my head into the pillow as he slid out and pushed back in. Jackson's rhythm unhurried as he cradled me to him. We weren't fucking. Or having sex. This… it was making love. We consumed each other from the inside out. And nothing compared.

"Oh, god," I panted.

In a subtle, measured stroke, he glided in and out as he trailed kisses down my neck and licked along my collarbone. A hurricane brewed inside my body. My skin on fire as my heart swelled and punched at my ribcage. Jackson was everywhere—caressing my flesh and branding my soul. And then his forehead pressed against mine and we locked eyes. On the cusp of orgasm, Jackson kissed me like I was his last breath.

I gasped with ferocity as his lips skirted my jawline. A sweltering heat exploded between my legs and scattered like lightning as my body tightened. He pumped his hips feverishly. Heat prickled every layer of my flesh. Desire and love fused my core. Grunts and pants and moans echoed in the room as our bodies ravaged each other. Both chasing release.

The intensity too much. I buried my nails in his ass as my body free fell off a cliff and into an abyss of euphoria. Jackson leaned into the crook of my neck as his hips surged with force. Deep, labored grunts vibrated in my ear, his moans closer together. And then he was there... diving off the cliff into euphoria beside me.

Jackson's breath beat hot below my ear. A moment later, he trailed kisses up my neck, stopping when he reached my temple, resting his cheek on mine. His scruffy jaw scraped as he whispered. Soft words escaped his lips. They reverberated in my marrow, and it took my brain half a minute to put two and two together. He pulled back and searched my eyes.

"Say it again," I lilted.

"I love you." Three. Little. Words. My chest flooded with helium as the organ beneath my sternum hammered uncontrollably and soared to the heavens.

"Do you need help with dinner?" I walked up behind Jackson, wrapped my arms around his midsection, and rested my chin on his shoulder.

He swiveled his head and kissed me quick before returning his attention to the stove. "I'm good, babe. I've got the food if you want to set the table."

"Okay." Reluctantly, I removed my arms from him. After pressing a kiss on his bicep, I opened the cabinet and grabbed plates, then utensils, and set the table.

An unfortunate side effect to my little apartment was the lack of dining room space. I rearranged the living room a smidge and put my two-person breakfast table near the couch and coffee table. It wasn't the ideal setup, but it would work for tonight's dinner. Plus, I'm sure no one cared about the furniture arrangement, as long as we were all together.

Everything in place as the savory scent of garlic, oregano, and basil wafted through the air. Fifteen minutes and everyone would be here, a cloud of curiosity and questions hovering above them. And no matter how hard I tried, I couldn't keep my eyes off the clock. Nervous energy a virus in my belly. Clammy palms. Bouncing knees. I bit down on my stubby thumbnail.

The living room blurred around me as I listened to Jackson stir and strain. A whoosh of the oven's convection as Jackson opened the door. *Clang-clang*. The sheet pan set on the trivets. *Pfft, pfft*. More oil and garlic spread on the bread. Another whoosh from the oven. Hundreds of thoughts hurtled through my head. Thoughts I didn't want to tackle alone. I needed a distraction. So, I walked back into the kitchen and gawked at Jackson as he added a creamy herb pasta to a large bowl.

"Give me something to do," I blurted, clipped and abrupt.

Jackson glanced up, brows furrowed and eyes pinched, and honed in on my nail biting. With a quick nod, he pointed to the counter next to the sink. "Finish cutting vegetables for the salad?"

I nodded and inhaled deep, relieved to have a task to divert my attention. Sidling next to Jackson, I started to chop. The spring mix already in the wide, wooden bowl. Carrots—sliced thin and on an angle. Done. Tomatoes—cut into wedges. Done. Cucumber—peeled and sliced into rounds and then halves. Done. Avocado—seed and skin removed, cut into chunks. Done.

I placed the veggies on top of the greens and decorated the salad like a floral arrangement. With all the toppings in place, I grabbed two heaping handfuls of blueberries and sprinkled them over the top. Then, I dumped a healthy portion of walnuts onto the cutting board, rough chopping them before scattering them over everything.

A knock at the door startled me from my salad brain. Jackson glanced my way and asked, "Want me to get the door?"

Tracing my fingers over his forearm, I kissed his cheek. "No, I've got it." He nodded, grabbed a pair of hot mitts, and pulled the garlic baguette slices out of the oven. It smelled divine.

Approaching the door, I pushed up on my toes and peeked through the small peephole. My friends stood on the other side of the door, chatting in hushed tones. I stepped back and reached for the knob with trembling fingers.

Taking a deep breath, I plastered a smile on my face. A second later, I twisted the cool metal and opened the door, welcoming my friends in as if nothing was wrong. We exchanged hugs and pecks on the cheek. *Hello's* and *how are you's* passed back and forth. The whole situation reflected a staged show, an air of caution gobbling the energy in the room.

Us ladies went to sit in the living room while Rick headed for the kitchen to shoot the shit with Jackson. Just as we sat on the couch, the guys rounded the corner, both carried serving dishes. The delicious aroma of Jackson's cooking had my stomach growling.

I had eaten little since lunch yesterday. Crazy how an email held so much power over me. Earlier today, Jackson convinced me to drink a nutritional shake. He'd said *At least get something in your system. Maybe if it isn't solid, it won't upset your stomach.* Good call on his part.

Everyone took a seat and loaded up their plates. Fettuccine with a creamy pesto, olive oil and garlic baguettes, sautéed bell peppers and onions, and a salad with balsamic vinaigrette dressing. I picked up my plate, brought it to my nose and inhaled deeply. My eyes closed and Jackson shook with laughter beside me. It was obvious I loved his cooking.

"You better eat." I opened my eyes, caught in his smoldering stare as he zeroed in on me. He leaned into me and whispered in my ear. "Or we'll appear rude to our guests when I haul you to the bedroom."

My breath hitched before I resumed my previous position. I pressed my thighs together and begged for relief, but the polite hostess in me stayed put. I picked up my fork and started to eat my dinner. A twirl of pasta wrapped around the tines, strands of pasta dangled from my fork when I peeked up at my friends, eyes on their plates and shit-eating grins plastered from ear to ear. Slightly embarrassed, I smiled with them.

Jackson squeezed my knee—our signal—and I glanced at him. His eyes asked if I was ready to talk with my closest friends. Share the story of how some unknown, sick and twisted pervert watched me and sent me creepy messages. My eyes averted, dropping to his Adam's apple as it bobbed, as my head bobbed up and down. One last, stronger squeeze to my knee before splaying it flat.

"Thank you all for coming over tonight. We wish it

could be under happier circumstances, but we're still grateful." Jackson held my gaze and steeled himself for what he'd say next. Discussed earlier today, we decided he'd tell them everything. It concerned me I wouldn't be able to say anything because of tears or fear or nervousness, and we had no plan to dance around the subject.

"We need to share some things that've happened to Sarah recently. After it's out in the open, plans will be put in place. With all of us." Three sets of eyes landed on us, hooked on every word. "Liz. Christy. Sarah needs you right now. As much as she needs me. We're not sure for how long, but someone is stalking Sarah. Based on the notes she's received, we—and the police—assume it's a man."

Christy slapped a hand over her mouth and sucked in an audible gasp. "Oh my god, Sarah! I don't know what to say. It doesn't seem right, but I'm so sorry." I nodded and stared down at Jackson's hand on my knee. His thumb drew circles on the inside of my leg.

"I want to let you know what kind of person the police think we're dealing with. That being said, some of what I'm about to share is vulgar." Almost as if a master puppeteer controlled them, the three of them nodded in unison. Jackson's calm tone continued. "A few days after Liz's party, Sarah received a bouquet of sunflowers at work. The card attached had a message telling her how beautiful she was. But whoever sent them indicated they saw her regularly. As in, every day. She had no idea who sent them and asked me because she'd mentioned her favorite flower to me at Liz's party. When I'd told her I wasn't the sender, she gave the flowers away."

Jackson paused a moment, drinking a couple large gulps of water. Everyone ate a bite or two while waiting for Jackson to continue.

"A few more weeks passed and nothing else happened. We started dating and nothing out of the ordinary occurred. Then, about a week and a half ago, Sarah found a letter in her mailbox. Whoever it is typed the letter on an old-fashioned typewriter, and meant for it to read like a love letter. But it followed the same connotation as the card with the flowers. Emphasizing he saw her daily, even smelled her often, and one day she would belong to him. No one mailed her the letter. The envelope only had her first name on it. Somehow, it got into her locked mailbox. After reading the note, Sarah called me for help. We took the letter to the police department and filed a report. Since that day, I've stayed with Sarah after work and on the weekends. The police told us to act normal. Go about our lives. That most of these situations pass without further activity. So that's what we did. We wanted everyone to go out last weekend. We wanted to have fun, forget about everything and just be ourselves with our friends."

Jackson picked up his glass and finished the water before taking a quick bite of garlic bread. Christy and Rick sat hooked on every word. Liz's attention focused on me, since most of this wasn't new to her. After he swallowed the last bit of his bread, he continued.

"Yesterday, Sarah got back to her desk after lunch and

checked her email. An email from a strange sender showed up in her unread messages. She opened it and read the beginning, which was somewhat sweet like the previous notes. But as she continued reading, it became lewd and vulgar. The man told her he'd been watching her. Saw us all at the club. Watched us having sex later that night, getting himself off at the same time. And reminded her she'd be his one day. He attached photos, which Sarah hadn't looked at when she'd read the email. When I came to pick her up from work, I had Liz print the email and images off for me, as I planned to file another police report. The pictures contained images of all of us, drinking and dancing at the club over the weekend. The majority of the pictures are of Sarah. Some are close up, catching different expressions on her face. We filed a new report with the police and they're working with security at the office to determine where the email came from."

A low shriek ripped from Christy's lips, her eyes watering and on the verge of letting go. "Holy shit, Sarah! Oh my god! I can't believe this is happening. I wish I could help."

Rick wrapped his arm around her mid-section and tugged her into his side. "Sarah. Jackson. Whatever I can do to help, tell me. If we need to run shifts, so be it. We need to keep these ladies safe." Rick's brow furrowed as his forehead creased.

"Agreed. No one should be uncomfortable or vulnerable, but let's be vigilant and watch out for each other. This guy seems to have all his focus on Sarah, but the police said that could change if he feels threatened. I'd like us to come up with a game plan. I know we can't always be everywhere together, seeing as we don't all work together or have the same schedule. It'll be easier for the girls, since they work the same hours at the same place. I'd like to set up a group chat, one we use to check in with each other. Thoughts?"

Jackson had so much of this sorted out, and it made my shoulders fifty pounds lighter. My brain fogged more and more as the story went on and everyone pitched in their two cents worth. I sat back in my chair, stared at the pasta as my fork tines twirled the noodles clockwise. I realized, a minute later, the room was suddenly still and silent. I peered up to see everyone's eyes on me, waiting for me to speak.

"I'm sorry, what?" How embarrassing.

Jackson rubbed his hand back and forth over my knee. "We were just asking if you'd be okay with carpooling to work for the rest of the week. Liz offered to pick you both up. Okay?"

Carpooling? Would that really stop this maniac? I doubted it. Giving a non-committal shrug, I said, "Sure, carpooling is fine."

"All right. I'm the only one who doesn't have everyone's numbers. Let's take care of that now, set up the group chat, and dismiss this topic for the evening." I listened as Jackson added everyone's contact information to his phone. A moment later, four cell phones chimed and alerted us to the first group chat message. My brain returned to its foggy state.

Would life be like this going forward? Carpools and group chat check-ins?

The rest of the night flew by. Liz told me she'd be here by eight-thirty to pick me up. I shuffled to the door with everyone, expressing my gratitude and love, then bid them good night.

When the door closed, I launched myself into Jackson as tears poured out of me. I wanted it all to vanish. He held me there, shushing me and telling me it would be okay. He wasn't sure how it would end, but he kept assuring me he would keep me safe. I stayed there crushed against his chest, my only thought...

I hope you're right.

I stared out the passenger window of Liz's Prius as the city passed by in a blur. No idea how I would get any work accomplished today, but I had to try. When I called into work yesterday and told Marco I wouldn't be in, he asked me to stop by his office the next day. He didn't disclose any details, but I suspected security talked with him and he wanted to talk to me.

The drive from my apartment to the office was short. My eyes scanned the sidewalks and every car. I mentally questioned every man who looked my direction. Wondered if the man in the blue windbreaker was him. Or maybe the guy in the dingy button-down and khaki pants. It could be anyone. We parked in the lot, Liz giddy when she parked in a spot next to a tree. I wish something so simple made me better.

Liz cut the engine, and the three of us stayed put a moment longer. My eyes lost focus. Christy touched my shoulder and snapped me back to the present. "You know we've got your back, bitch, right?"

Laughter bubbled in my chest. Something as simple as using her favorite word lifted some of the tension clouding me. "I love you, Chicky. You and that mouth. I needed a laugh. Thank you." I laid my hand over hers a second, took a deep breath, and opened the door.

As we walked toward the main entrance, Liz said, "If you need us today, for anything, shoot one of us a text. Don't use our group chat. Unless you need Jackson and Rick to know." Liz wrapped her arm around my shoulders and rubbed my upper bicep.

My eyes bounced between the two. "I will. Hopefully, the day goes by and nothing else happens. It'd be nice to have a normal day."

Walking into the building, the three of us waved good morning to Holly. My face practiced its *I'm perfectly fine* smile as we boarded the elevator. "When the doors open, I'm plastering on the fakest smile. You two go to your desks, I'll go see Marco. He needs to speak with me. We need to pretend everything is normal."

The weight of their stares is like gravity times ten, and my shoulders lock up. Liz nodded and said, "Sure, sweetie. Whatever you want. Just keep us posted."

"Normal. Okay, bitch. If that's what you want, normal it is." Christy shot me a wink, and I shook my head.

A ding signaled our arrival, the doors slid open, and the three of us parted ways. My face screamed happiness and enthusiasm, but my heart shriveled and withered into a dark corner. I walked down the hallway, stopped at Marco's open door, and poked my head inside. "Hey, good morning."

"Morning, Sarah. Come in. Close the door, please." The handle clicked into place, the sound louder than expected and I jumped. "Have a seat. I wanted to speak with you about the other day."

Marco's monotone voice gave nothing away, and I had no clue whether it upset or worried him or neither. "Okay." I sat down in a chair adjacent his and shoved my hands into my lap.

"I had a conversation with Edwin in security." With one line, I knew exactly why he summoned me. "He informed me he received a call from the police department. Regarding an email you received the other day. I won't speak of the content of the email as I'm sure you're aware and don't want to discuss it."

"Thank you." I gave him an impish smile.

"I wanted to share that we plan to investigate this further and to keep an eye on personnel." I scrunched my brow. *Keeping an eye on other personnel? Did they think it was an employee?* He registered my confusion and followed up. "When Edwin did some digging, it would appear someone sent the email from a Hammond IP address. We're still narrowing it down, but are determined to get this sorted out quickly."

Holy shit! It's a *co-worker?* That flew in out of nowhere —complete left field—and slapped me across the face. "What am I supposed to do? Liz, Christy, and I have safeguards in place while here. We've got others when we leave. But I guess I never really considered it being someone here."

A sympathetic smile touched his face. "Good. I'm glad to hear you have friends here. You'll most likely see more management perusing the sales floor. We'll pass it off as goals not being met and the end of the quarter approaching. We'll keep it low key."

"Okay. Do you mind if I keep my cell phone handy? I'll put it on silent. I just want it in case I need to reach Liz or Christy. Can they have theirs close by, too? I would feel better." I rambled, but needed Marco's approval. I wanted him to know that, with everything going on, this was a minor favor I needed him to grant.

"Certainly. You haven't seen it yet, but we sent an email late yesterday. Our floor will have a meeting at nine-thirty today. At the meeting, we plan to mention the whole goals scenario and management stopping by everyone's desk to see what they're doing to stay on track. I would like for you, Ms. Warren, and Ms. Nolan to sit in the front, center table. This will allow myself and Bob to scan the room a little easier, see if anyone on our floor gives any tells. The other floors, two and four, are having similar meetings at ten and ten-thirty. We'll get everything sorted out."

"When I get to my desk, I'll let Liz and Christy know about the table. I really want to get back to work today, but I worry I won't be able to focus. As always, I'll do my best. I just want to let you know where I'm at with this whole situation."

"Thank you, Sarah. If you need to, spend today doing follow-up calls or letters to clients. You're welcome to do emails, also. We've taken the liberty to monitor all incoming and outgoing emails more stringently until they resolve this matter. You will not be receiving another email like that while you're here."

His words brought relief, the knot in my stomach unraveling a little. I closed my eyes and sighed. "Thank you, Marco. You don't know how much this means. Your support is priceless."

"Of course. Now, head out to your desk and try to do your best. If anyone asks why you were in my office, tell them I was checking up on you and your food poisoning, okay?" It seemed as if he had it all mapped out. Perfect explanations for every shift from the office's normal routine of things. My heart swelled and my eyes stung but

I held it together. It astounded me I had so many people standing in my corner, willing to do whatever it took to put everything back into its rightful place.

I nodded, stood from the chair, and left Marco's office. As soon as I got to my desk, I typed out a message to Liz and Christy, passing along the meeting table info and that I'd received permission for them to keep their phones nearby. We would have to talk more later, but not in the office.

THIRTEEN

BY THE END of the week, being at work was a hardship. I had zero focus. Especially after learning one of my coworkers sent the flowers, letter, and email. Although it may not be someone on my floor, the idea had me sick to my stomach.

After lunch on Friday, I spoke with Marco and requested to work from home the following week. In the past, other employees worked from home due to accidents, surgery, or a sick family member and it wasn't a hassle. When I asked Marco, he quickly approved the request.

Before leaving the office, I visited Bob in human resources and received a secure laptop and company cell phone. Marco suggested I stay home until the situation remedied. But he delegated one new task. "Sarah, please keep me up to date on any changes. We will do the same," Marco requested. A small favor to ask in exchange for being allowed to work in a safer environment? No problem.

I shared my new work status in the group chat with everyone. By the reply texts, it was evident everyone agreed with the idea. A huge weight lifted from my shoulders when I walked out the doors of Hammond Life. Hopefully, between the police and Hammond security, the person would be apprehended soon. I couldn't afford to take time off, so this was the next best solution.

The only downfall... long stretches of time alone. Being locked inside my apartment wasn't safe enough in Jackson's mind. He wanted a physical body near me at all times. Honestly, no one in our little family was fond of my eight-hour seclusion. Yes, I'd be working. But no one would be around if something happened. This spooked everyone, including me.

Over the weekend, I planned to speak with the apartment complex management and explain my situation. I'm hoping they'll reassure us the gated community was secure. Because if they said otherwise, I'm lost.

"Yes, ma'am, Ms. Bradley. Thank you for bringing this

information to our attention. We'll be sure a guard is at the gate and do regular walk-throughs around the complex. The only reason we're missing a guard is because we let someone go. It's tough finding good help these days."

The owner of the apartment complex, Gerald Chang, smiled while folding in on himself. Apology etched lines in his forehead and bleak expression. I didn't blame Mr. Chang, or the complex, for my stalker problems. Mr. Chang wasn't the reason some lunatic watched my every move. But he assured me and Jackson the situation was a top priority.

"Thank you. I appreciate it, Mr. Chang. The complex's security features were the main reason I became a resident. I'll feel safer knowing extra measures will be taken. Again, thank you."

"It's our pleasure. Everyone should feel safe, regardless of where they are on the property. I apologize for the current lack of a guard, but I assure you I'll have it corrected within twenty-four hours. We have a couple candidates lined up. Perhaps we need both." Mr. Chang smiled then chuckled.

I understood he laughed at hiring two guards, but I wanted to tell him to shut the fuck up. This wasn't a laughing matter. Far from it. Did this creep stalk other women in the complex also? God, I hoped not.

Pushing up from my chair, I shook my landlord's hand, as did Jackson. We left his office and thanked him one last time.

My anxiety lessened with each passing minute. My home would still be a safe place. A place I could sit alone all day and not worry if someone watched me through the blinds. A place I could breathe and shut out all the bullshit. My safe place.

"I'm heading out, babe. I'll be back for lunch, if that's cool?" Jackson asked as he slung a duffle bag over his shoulder. Clad in a black t-shirt and loose-fitting, black workout pants, he grabbed his keys and kissed the top of my head.

"Yeah, that'll be perfect. It'll keep my workday somewhat normal," I mused. I leaned against a pillow and powered on the laptop. The new work cell on the comforter beside me, on and ready. My *Miso Awesome* pajama set today's work attire.

"I'll see you around twelve-thirty." A kiss on the lips, and then he left for work.

The laptop's operating system loaded and I entered the password Bob wrote down. Less than a minute later, I logged onto my desktop remotely. The connection rivaled the dial-up internet days. But that was probably because the laptop was older than dirt, hence the archaic load speed. Good thing I started it up early.

I walked to the kitchen, made a cup of hot tea and a bagel with peanut butter, then headed back to my makeshift desk. Plopping down on the bed, I crossed my legs in a variation of a yoga lotus pose. I opened my work email and several messages loaded from the weekend which looked safe to view.

I bit into my bagel, chomped away, and responded to the emails. My work flow ran smooth due to the light workload. Although my current office setting wasn't traditional, I breathed easy and got my work accomplished. Being home is a balm for my soul. For a split-second, I closed my eyes and reveled in the peace.

These working conditions just might grow on me.

I snapped out of my work daydream and dove head-first into the nitty-gritty. Time flew by quick—emails came and went, calls dialed, reports completed. Before I realized the time, Jackson unlocked the door with the key I'd given him after the first letter.

Some people would say giving Jackson a key after a month was too soon, but who cared what other people thought. I loved and trusted him. With my life. He cared for me and kept me safe. Things I'd never experienced with anyone else. Not to this degree. Sometimes you just know. Sometimes it's better to listen to your heart and ignore the crowd.

I heard a thud as his duffle hit the couch. A second later, Jackson popped his head around the doorjamb.

"Sorry. Don't want to interrupt if you're with a client," he stated. After he noticed I wasn't on the phone, he stepped into the room and kissed me. He tugged on my pajamas and smiled. "You're too cute right now. Working in your pj's. Do they help your productivity?"

I leaned into him. "It seems so. I may have to speak with HR about the dress code policy. Who knew wearing comfortable attire and working from bed could make you so productive," I joked, cocking my head and giving him a silly smile.

Loud and throaty laughter spilled out of Jackson. In turn, I smiled bigger than I had in days. "For you, I'm sure they'll take it into consideration. You ready to eat?"

"Yeah. Let me mark myself as away, lock the computer, and I'll be right there."

Jackson walked out of the room and went straight to the kitchen. A couple dishes clanked on the counter before I heard the cutting board come out. I missed lunchtime with Liz and Christy, but a girl could get used to this.

What's better than working from home in your favorite pajamas? When your boyfriend stopped at your place for lunch, made you an amazing salad, and you still had twenty minutes left. So, what do you do with your remaining lunch hour? Sex, of course.

With a few minutes to spare, Jackson gave me one last kiss. "I should be done around four-thirty or five. Be back after."

"Go, go, go. Before I make you stay," I said as I shoved at his chest. His lips brushed against my knuckles. Then he headed for the door. A second later, a low thump echoed through the apartment as he shut the door, followed by the click of the deadbolt.

Best. Lunch. Ever. But alas, back to work.

The only sucky part about working from home was my inability to print reports. At one point, I had six different files open and toggled between them as I worked. It made work a challenge, and tasks took longer to finish, but was doable.

An unfamiliar noise chimed in the room. I unlocked my phone, but I had no notifications. The chime sounded again. I picked up the work cell phone on my bed and noticed two text notifications.

Initially, I thought it might be a client I called earlier. When I unlocked the phone and opened the messages, I learned how wrong I was. The message came from a six-digit number—616263.

I pursed my lips as my lungs singed. How do I breathe? My heart beat a vicious rhythm as I opened the messages.

Unknown: You stupid cunt. You thought you could get away from me. Just because you're not here, doesn't mean a fucking thing.

Unknown: That pretty boy toy you've been playing with, that ends now. If I see him anywhere near you starting tomorrow... Let's just say there will be blood. Yours, his, maybe both.

In a flash, I threw the phone on the bed, jumped to my feet and grabbed my phone, dialing Jackson. I wasn't sure if he was with a client, nor did I care. I had to talk to him now. In less than twenty-four hours, my haven away from the office was no longer sacred.

"Babe, I can't talk. I'm with a client right now," Jackson said when he answered.

He tried to hang up the phone, my shriek stopped him. "Jackson, I need you. Something happened."

"Tell me." His voiced, clipped and urgent.

"Work gave me a cell phone, so I could call clients. Somehow, whoever this is, they got the number. They sent me messages. Threatening me." My chest heaved as I spoke. "Threatening you."

"Fuck! Okay, we got this. Let me make a couple calls real quick. I'll call you back in a few, okay?"

"What do I do till then?" My brain started to shut down, all over again. I needed him to tell me what to do. Because all I wanted was to find a dark alcove and hide until this nightmare ended.

"Call your work. Tell them about the messages. Maybe they can trace them. See if they'll offer a different phone."

"Okay, I will."

"I'll call back soon, babe. Just make sure everything's locked up and the blinds are closed. I love you."

"I love you, too."

And then he was gone. I called Marco, explained the entire situation. He put me on hold a few minutes. When he returned, I heard Bob and Edwin mumbling in the background.

"Sarah, you still there?"

"I'm still here," I said as I paced semi-circles in my darkened bedroom.

"I know this may be difficult for you, but can you read the messages to us? Bob from HR and Edwin from security are with me. We'd like to record it, then come retrieve the device and give you a new one. Also, just as a precaution, can you screenshot the messages and send them to your personal phone and then to my number?"

"Sure," I said, reluctant. I had no desire to read the texts aloud. Having to read them was one time too many. I walked over to the menacing device and picked it up. It burned a hole in my hand as I held it. Unlocking the screen, the message popped up, and I took a quick screenshot and sent it to myself.

When my phone chimed the incoming text, I opened the image and forwarded it to Marco. "I just sent it. If you don't mind, I'd prefer not to have to read it aloud."

Marco's phone pinged on the other end. "Hang on one

second, Sarah." The three men talked in jumbled tones, most likely the hands-free microphone covered with one of their hands. "Okay, I've got it. I understand your reasoning and we all accept that. If you don't mind, Bob and I would like to come by, within the hour, and pick up the phone."

"Yes, please. When you get to the gate, the guard will have to call me to let you in."

"We understand. We'll see you soon."

The call disconnected. I walked to my computer, set my work profile to 'away' and logged off the computer. I brought the phone and laptop out to the living room, setting up a new work area. If it were my phone, I'd crush it and throw the tainted device out a window.

Walking through every room, I checked all the window and door locks, as well as the blinds. All secured and closed. I paused in the bedroom and my body shook from head to toe. I tried to calm myself with slow, methodical breaths.

After settling as much as possible, I went to my closet and found something else to wear. It wouldn't be long before I had company. I grabbed the first things I saw—a navy, cotton shirt and a pair of jeans. I stepped into the bathroom, the only room I deemed safe and changed.

My phone rang and Jackson told me he'd be here soon, and that the police were headed to my apartment. The semi-calm state I had obtained from my short meditation... gone. Within the hour, people would swarm my apartment. None of them bad people, but I only wanted one of them here.

As uncomfortable as I was, it would only get worse once everyone sat in the same room. It seemed as if everyone who visited recently, besides Jackson, came here to discuss this crazed lunatic.

Water bottles sat on various surfaces of my living room—some unopened, others empty. From my spot on the center of the couch, my eyes darted from one person to the next. Jackson's hand rested on my knee, his thumb stroking the edge.

My apartment currently occupied six people, excluding Jackson and myself. Marco, Bob, and Edwin from Hammond Life. Mr. Chang from the apartment complex. The two police officers we'd spoken with since the beginning—Sheila Hawks and Shawn Richardson. The six of them discussed the various aspects they were involved in and where things stood on their end.

How was this my life? Sending one last cry to the heavens to wake up from this nightmare, I closed my eyes and attempted to shut out my surroundings.

All these people in one room. The reason they were here. The walls closed in on me as the air thickened, their voices a collection of white noise. I couldn't take it anymore. A victim in my own life. I rushed to my feet and all eyes instantly zoomed in on me. A second later, I went to the kitchen, needing to be farther away from the chaos that was my current life.

I braced myself by placing my hands on the cool,

granite countertop as my head hung low between my shoulders. I inhaled deep and rhythmically, trying to collect myself. When I opened my eyes, I spotted Jackson's shoes. He stood near the kitchen entrance, watching and waiting.

I sucked in another deep breath before I backed away and stood more upright. He closed the short distance between us and bundled me in his embrace. Right here, this was where I wanted to be. But this serenity had been threatened and there's no way I'd let anything happen to Jackson. I wouldn't be able to live with myself if he got hurt because of me. Everything good in my world crumbled at my feet. All because of someone who was too chickenshit to come out of the shadows.

"Jackson," I whispered. "We need to listen to whoever this madman is. So no one gets hurt."

He held me at arm's length as his hands rested on my biceps. Rich blue sapphires zeroed in on me and questioned my logic. "We can't let him win, babe. He wants us apart, so he *can* hurt us. Physically and emotionally."

My eyes stung, tears threatened for the umteenth time in the last couple of weeks. "I wouldn't be able to live with myself if something happened to you." My throat clogged with emotion. But I couldn't let anything happen to him. It would kill me.

His thumb brushed over my cheekbone, wiping away an escaped tear. "Nothing will happen to me. I'm more worried about what he'll do to you if no one else is here." I leaned against his chest and rested my head on his shoulder. Jackson locked his arms tight around me.

Officer Hawks stepped into the kitchen, her demeanor authoritative yet soothing. "Ms. Bradley, if you and Mr. Ember wouldn't mind returning to the other room. We'd all like to discuss our plan of attack in this situation."

Plan of attack? God, I hoped it was a good one.

"Yeah. Sure." Jackson and I walked back to the room of chaos and I resumed my position on the couch.

Officer Hawks scanned the room, everyone focused on her. "We all decided the best course of action right now is to follow the demands of the perpetrator. Mr. Ember, for the time being, you are to not have physical contact with Ms. Bradley. We believe it is in everyone's best interest you remain in contact, but only through phone calls, text messages, or via computer. We will establish an undercover presence wherever Ms. Bradley goes, making her aware of who the officer will be. Since the perpetrator does not appear to have an issue with Ms. Bradley's female friends, we suggest they spend more time together. Preferably here or one of their homes. No public establishments, with exception to acquiring necessities. Our undercover detective may pose as an old friend who just moved back to the area. Hence why they will be around you more often and perhaps in the same *career field* as you. Ms. Bradley, we'd also like for you, later this evening, to make a *scene* outside with Mr. Ember. If this person works for the same company as you, he most likely wouldn't be nearby for another hour or so. Everyone, including Mr.

Ember, will leave here when we're done talking. Mr. Ember, we would like you to go do something, anything, and then return between six and six-thirty. Spend time together, have dinner, whatever you need to do. Around seven-thirty, we'd like the *scene* to go down. We will have an unmarked car close by, watching the building. Although neither of you will mean what is said, you need to convince any onlookers. Make whoever it is believe you're angry with each other and you're breaking up. Remember, we all have a role to play. It is important your role is believable, otherwise things could go from bad to worse in a split-second."

Not ten minutes ago, I told Jackson this very thing. That we needed to do what this maniac wanted. To spend time apart. But hearing the words. Hearing someone else tell me I needed to fake a breakup with the man I'd give my life for. The only person I'd ever been in love with... I couldn't breathe. My chest constricted, and I wrapped my arms tight around my mid-section.

He tilted my chin toward him. "Breathe, babe. Please breathe." I took a few cleansing breaths, his sapphires the only thing in my tunnel vision as my body shook. "This sucks. Big time. But we have to catch this guy. If this is how we do it, then we have to try. Whatever is said later, we know..." He placed my hand on his heart and his over mine. "We know how we truly feel. I love you and I won't let him hurt you."

I closed the space between us, linked my arms behind his neck, and smothered him in kisses. "I love you, too." I also wanted to say *this person had already hurt me because he stole you from me.* But I kept my lips sealed and enjoyed the short time I had in Jackson's arms.

We sat on the couch, my body draped over Jackson's lap and I clung to his frame. "I don't think I can do this," I whined while I picked at the chipping polish on my nail.

He slid me off of his lap and rose from the couch, extending his hand to help me up. "I know you can. We've gone over everything. We know how everything has to look. Most importantly, we know it's not real and *very* temporary." Jackson took both my hands between his and rubbed his thumbs over my knuckles. "Neither of us have dealt with anything remotely close to this, but we have to believe the professionals know what they're doing. I'm just thankful for FaceTime and texting. We just need to be discreet when we're not home."

His words rang true in my head, but I still wasn't certain this was the best way. I wanted to believe they'd made the best decision under the circumstances, especially considering I had no idea what to do. "I know. It's just that this is the most difficult thing I've ever had to do." I don't know if I can handle this. Any of it. That is what I wanted to tell him, but kept it to myself, knowing it won't change anything.

"Me too, babe. Let's keep the group chats going. I brought everyone else up to speed before I got back. They all understand everything needs to be as if we broke up."

Ugh, god! Hearing those words, even though it was all show, made me nauseous. "Okay."

We stood at the door, Jackson's duffle bag in his hand, my phone in mine. Our eyes glued to each other, our lips melding one last time in the most passionate kiss, not knowing when we'd actually be face-to-face again. "God, I love you so much, babe." His thumbs stroked my cheeks.

"I love you, too." Giving him one last kiss, I drew in a deep breath, closed my eyes and said silent prayers to all the gods of the universe. *Please let this be over soon.* I twisted the knob on the handle, my eyes laden with tears. Yanking the door wide open, my voice not my own as I yelled at Jackson like I never wanted to see him again.

When the whole scene ended, I shut my front door, turned the bolt, dropped to the floor, and curled into the fetal position. It wasn't real, but it was the worst feeling in the world. I laid there, crying, and waited for Liz and Christy to come console me. But their comfort wouldn't be enough because... half of my soul just got in a car and drove away.

FOURTEEN

JACKSON

"I LOVE YOU, TOO." She took a deep breath and closed her eyes, my way to her soul closing as her lashes painted her cheeks. Her hand on the doorknob as her eyes popped open, red and tear-stained. The door jerked open, her voice boomed—foreign to my ears. "Leave! Get the hell out of here!"

It's not real. It's not real. "You crazy ass bitch! Don't have to tell me twice! Trying to play off your ex as a stalker. I don't need this bullshit! I can replace you in a heartbeat," I belted out as I tugged my duffel behind me, walking away from the love of my life. Tears ran down her face, and I headed for my Wrangler.

God, this fucking hurts.

"I'm sure you have plenty of lady friends to keep your bed warm!" She yelled to my back, and her voice stuttered a fraction. A stutter only I would notice. A stutter which made my heart ache.

"Right back at ya! I seem to remember you love the ladies, too! Good riddance!" I jumped in my Jeep, cranked the engine and peeled out of the parking lot, speeding toward the front gate. In my rearview mirror, I saw her go back inside, the light in her window displayed her shadow as her body collapsed to the floor.

Fuck!

I drove out of the complex and headed to my house, the only place I would rather be was with her. The roads seemed quieter than normal, cars sparse as I turned onto my street. The sky darker as I stepped onto the path leading to my front door. And the moon absent in the night sky.

Void. The same as my heart. And soul. Which I left with her for safe keeping.

I finished putting away the load of laundry I'd washed to pass time. Glancing at my watch, I realized it was close to ten-thirty. Liz and Christy should have left her place by now. By now, she'd be changing into her pajamas and getting ready for bed.

Over dinner, we'd agreed to FaceTime at ten-thirty

before going to bed, and again at eight-thirty to say good morning. Between those hours, we'd send texts or random pictures. Although she had the worst part in this whole situation, we both struggled with being separated.

The night she started drifting off, and she mumbled *I love you*, I was scared. Terrified. Fear halted me dead in my tracks. I had been in several relationships, most of them not too serious, none of them ever involving those three words. No use in denying I had strong feelings for Sarah. Stronger than I'd had for any woman. *But love?* In the moment, I had no inkling if it was love.

When she woke the next morning, tears stained her cheeks and she was so adorable with her nose stopped up. Right then and there, all I wanted to do was take care of her. Hold her. Make her feel safe. *Love her.* She'd slid back into my arms, talked about remembering something but not positive if it was real or a dream. I had a sneaking suspicion what she referred to, but wanted to hear her say it.

She recounted her story, telling me how she thought she remembered telling me she loved me. I laid still as a corpse, except for my hand, which was on auto-pilot caressing her back. I didn't want to lie to her or make her believe it wasn't real. She handed me everything. And I had wanted to do the same. But I wasn't sure I could say the words. Not yet.

"*It wasn't a dream.*" I'd told her.

If I wasn't ready to say the words, maybe showing her was a more viable option. So, I gave her every part of me in other ways. With her, it was never just sex. Sure, some occasions were a lot raunchier than others, but there was always meaning behind every touch. Every taste. Every groan of pleasure.

I poured every drop of myself into that morning with her—making love with her, our connection more powerful than anything science dared try to explain. The bond between us incomparable to any prior—our bodies synchronized, and our passion constructed into a living, breathing entity. No doubt about it, I was absolutely lost in her. Still am. And I couldn't contain it any longer. I refused to restrain the fire she'd lit inside me. Her love fueled my soul. Those three potent words passed from my lips to her ears with ease.

It's a heady emotion. Love. I would obliterate heaven and earth to be with Sarah. And I was willing to suffer and not be by her side if it meant she'd remain safe. Life no longer had a purpose if she ceased to exist. Sarah was worth everything and I would do whatever it took to keep her forever.

My phone vibrated and a picture of me and Sarah kissing flashed on the screen. I pressed the button to answer and a live feed of Sarah lying in bed popped up. "Hey, babe. How are you? I miss you already," I confessed.

She yanked the blanket up to her neck. "I miss you, too. This sucks. I hope they figure this all out soon. I'm not going to be able to live like this." Her hand slid up to her cheek and tucked a cluster of loose hair behind her ear. Strands I wanted to tuck.

"I hope so, too. I've gotten accustomed to falling asleep and waking up with you in my arms."

Her face transformed from elation to sorrow, the shift in expression reminded me of theater masks. "There's no possible way I'm getting decent sleep. Not being alone. Not with that creep still lurking outside somewhere."

God, I wanted to hold her right now. Comfort her. Take away her anguish. It angered me that this asshole was able to go about his shithole existence while we suffered on the sidelines. I tried to not let her see my frustration, it wouldn't do either of us any good. But fuck... this was frustrating as hell.

"All we can do right now is hope the police find this asshole soon and lock him away. Then we can get back to you and me," I cajoled as I traced a finger over her face on the screen, trying to soothe her fears.

It wasn't the same. Not by a long shot.

I saw her, spoke with her, told her how much I yearned for her. It was nowhere near enough though. Being miles away from her in a crowded city... I forgot which way was up.

If someone told me months ago, I'd be one of those guys—the guy desperate to be with his girl—I would've laughed in their face. I never pictured myself falling madly and deeply in love with someone. Before her, life just did its thing. I woke up, went to work, had drinks with the guys, hooked up here and there. A simple life. Easy. No one ever made me want more. Not until Sarah.

When I wasn't with her, I wanted to be. Every waking thought I had included her. She gave my monotonous existence purpose and meaning. I hadn't told her—and I intended to keep it secret—but I planned to help the police catch this piece of shit. The sooner, the better.

I didn't care what actions needed to be taken. This fucker would pay.

"Jackson? Did you hear me?" she asked, a little edgy.

"I'm sorry, babe. I spaced out a second. What'd you say?"

"Think I'm gonna go take a bath. I wish you were here. Not because I'm about to strip down." A hint of a smile lined her mouth. "I just..."

"Me, too. Go. Take a bath. Try to relax a little. If you want to call or text or video call again, I'm sitting on the other end waiting," I encouraged her.

Her eyes pooled at the corners as her bottom lip trembled the slightest bit. "I love you." A tear rolled down and fell from her chin.

If this didn't kill me, I'd consider myself a lucky man. I desperately wanted to say fuck it, drive back to her apartment, and soothe her. Provide her with the protection she begged for. Hold her close and whisper it'll all work out.

"I love you, too. Let me know when you're headed to bed."

She blew me a kiss and restrained her lingering tears. I returned the sentiment, and then the screen went black.

This shit needed to be over and done with. NOW.

"Have you gotten any updates? I asked Hawks and Richardson, but they didn't say much."

Her forehead and brows scrunched. "I talked to Hawks this morning, she told me there might've been someone ducking in the bushes under my window a couple nights ago. By the time they got there, all they found was an empty potato chip bag. They took it as evidence and are trying to get prints off of it."

Damnit!

Five days blended into one long nightmare. Not that this hadn't been a nightmare from the get-go. Neither of us slept well. Sarah hadn't gotten much done at work. I'd worked, but nowhere near full capacity. I wanted to be easily available if something happened.

"Have they suggested anything? Asked you to do anything different? See if you can lure this prick out. Safely."

Sarah hung her head, hid behind a wall of hair, and spoke with dread. "No, they want me to do things the same as usual. I don't understand how me sitting in my apartment, like a goddamn prisoner, is going to catch this guy," she fumed. Anger saturated every word as her life flipped upside down for someone else's sick pleasure. She had every right to be angry. As did I.

"This is bullshit! Tomorrow, we're doing something. Together. We can figure out a way, coordinate with everyone else if we have to. We can't live like this. We can't let him win."

Her eyes widened and a smile stretched her face tight. Hope glowed on her face for the first time in days. "How? He's watching every move I make."

"Every move *you* make. Not every move *I* make. He can't be in two places at once. I'll put it in the group chat and maybe we can get together at Christy's or Liz's. Have dinner, a game night or movie night. Whatever. And I'll ask Rick to pick me up, so my car isn't there. Rick and I will be there before you. What do you think?"

A glassy haze covered Sarah's eyes as she contemplated the idea over and over. Running through scenarios and how they'd play out. "Yes... we can make this work."

I wanted to throw my hands in the air in victory. Lift her off the ground, press her supple body against mine, and spin round and round. Soon, I would see her again. Hopefully tomorrow night.

"Yes we can, babe. I'll throw it in the chat when we're done. Tomorrow night..."

"Tomorrow, yes..." Her sigh lingered in the electronic energy between us. We sat quiet a moment and absorbed our jubilation. "I won't make it past this weekend without you. Without your touch. It's like part of me is missing."

"I miss you, too. I haven't breathed since we've been apart. My chest is barren without your heart next to mine. Tomorrow…"

"Tomorrow," she repeated. "I love you." Her eyes locked on mine.

"I love you more." And I wasn't afraid to own it.

Mozzarella and garlic perfumed the air as lasagna baked in Christy and Rick's oven. A large, black box containing all the expansion packs of Cards Against Humanity sat in the middle of the dining room table. The only thing missing was my girl. I counted the minutes — seven to go — until Sarah walked through Christy and Rick's door.

Static electricity buzzed my skin at the idea of seeing and touching my girl again. *Fuck.* I more than missed her. Deprivation doesn't even touch the level of loss consuming me. Although our sex life was killer, it was the last thing on my mind.

I sat on a barstool in the kitchen, a foot propped on the

lowest peg, and bounced my knee like a hyper child. Checked my watch—two minutes. Why the hell does time move so damn slow when you're waiting for something good to happen?

"Quit looking at the time, man. It's only going to make it worse," Rick said as he passed me a beer.

"I know, but I can't seem to restrain myself. This whole situation is doing a number on us all. I don't know how much longer we'll be able to keep up the charade." Being physically away from each other for almost a week wrecked us. Our relationship is as strong as ever, and our feelings amplified each second we were apart, but as humans... we crumbled to pieces.

It's taking a toll on her that was noticeable in her eyes and when she spoke. Every time we were on the phone, the purple half-moons below her eyes were darker. I wondered if she'd slept at all. When we talked, her voice rasped—and not in the come hither sexy sort of way.

God, I needed her in my arms. Needed that connection with her again. Needed to reassure her we would get past this mountain-sized obstacle. Together.

A low thump sounded as the deadbolt unlocked. I snapped my head toward the door and saw Liz and Sarah walking into the room. All the air sucked from my chest. My stool scraped against the tile as I rose. I stumbled an inch as I set my bottle on the counter. Everything passed in slow motion as I closed the space between us and hauled her into my arms.

I clutched her tight against my chest and relished in

her warmth as it vanquished the chill of her absence. A second later, her feet dangled above the floor as I lifted her high and crushed my lips to hers. I didn't give a shit if everyone watched our public display. She was here. In my arms. Where she should be.

Her golden locks shielded us as we made up for lost time. My arms pinned her securely to my chest, but it wasn't enough. She wrapped her legs around my waist and tried to pull me closer.

If our friends weren't here, clothes would've been on the floor already as our bodies rediscovered one another. I hadn't gotten my fill of her, but she stopped the kiss as her soft hands skimmed my stubble. Her face brightened. Eyes glimmered, lips plumped from our kiss, and a smile that fizzled the ache in my chest. God, I fucking missed her smile.

"Hey," she whispered an inch from my lips.

"Hey." I brushed her hair away and exposed us.

Her feet unhooked behind me and slowly lowered to the tile as our eyes magnetized. Sarah leaned in as her arm hooked mine. She laid the side of her face in the crook of my neck and inhaled. A beat later, her body relaxed and the world realigned a little more. We both needed this. And for this momentary blip in time, Sarah and I were whole.

Until tonight, I'd never played Cards Against Humanity. But I decided within minutes, this game would be in our regular rotation. I never laughed so hard or gasped in shock so many times in such a short span. If you played the perfect combination, you either had the hottest, raunchiest, nastiest or most distasteful phrase. I'm officially addicted.

We played our last round of cards and the black card stated ending a romantic dinner with... I glossed over the white cards in my hand—a celebrity name, penis size, incest, superheroes. But my prize-winning choice sat on the right in my hand.

I laid the card upside down for Rick to read, drew another white card, and waited for everyone to choose. Rick picked the handful of cards up, read the black card again and filled the blank with each white card answer. When he read my card, I laughed like an idiot. A romantic date ending with phallic-shaped dessert. To say I was easily amused would one-hundred percent accurate.

We ended the game and Christy won by a landslide, her girly, victory giggle cracked us up. But I didn't want the night to end yet. Not ready to let my girl go back to her apartment. Without me. Alone.

As if reading my mind, Christy announced, "Everyone is more than welcome to stay. Some of us may be more sober than others, but it's also late. There's a bed in the guest room and the couch isn't the most uncomfortable in the world."

I glanced down at Sarah, her arm hooked in mine, as my eyes plead with her to say yes. She squeezed her arm tighter around mine, and I shifted closer to her. Our lips met somewhere in the middle and a bomb triggered inside me. Her lips wordlessly communicated with mine and begged for us to stay.

When the kiss broke, I clasped her chin in my fingers and stroked her soft bottom lip with my thumb. My eyes locked on hers. "We're staying."

Christy slipped into hostess mode and directed us. "Okay, you guys take the spare room. Liz, you staying?"

"Yeah. That way everything seems the same when we leave tomorrow." Liz flashed Sarah a gentle smile.

She made a valid point though. Everything needed to be in sync, and we couldn't leave anything to chance. This creep probably followed Liz here after she picked up Sarah. They should leave together, too.

We helped clean up the game and remaining dishes. When Christy was content, we walked down the hall and headed for the bedroom, fingers intertwined.

Faint moonlight illuminated the room as beams leaked through the thin blind slats. Closing the door, we stood stock still and memorized each other in the darkness. My hands gripped her soft, curvaceous hips as I stepped into her and dipped my mouth to hers, taking what I'd missed over the last week.

Her warm, supple lips molded to mine, sucking and tugging. The rush that faded in her absence flooded my veins. I traced the lines of her body—an arm slid around her waist while the other caressed between her shoulder blades—and pressed her to me. Her mouth bloomed like a flower and opened up for me. Our tongues teased and taunted, only pausing to taste and suck and nip. Heat scalded my solar plexus and fanned out like wildfire.

Sarah stroked the muscles along my spine and up my shoulders before yanking off my shirt. We separated long enough for our shirts to hit the floor. As we stumbled back, her legs hit the mattress, and I lay her down.

She crawled back, and I followed, hovering over her. Slipping my hands under her, I unhooked her bra, yanked it off, and tossed it to the floor. Nimble fingers unbuttoned my shorts as her feet came to my hips and shoved the cotton down.

Every second heated. Every touch memorized. No idea when we'd be together again and not taking any part of tonight for granted.

Her heels dug into my ass as she thrust up and rocked roughly against my cock. "Fuck," I whisper-moaned, sucking her bottom lip. Her nails clawed down my back and bit my flesh. A thin layer of sweat flared over my body as the painful pleasure swallowed me whole and woke the animal inside. On the next stroke, I slid back further and positioned my cock at her entrance and traced her folds.

"You're so fucking wet, babe," I growled.

Her hunger was a powerful force that beckoned me. A second later, she bowed off the bed in the hopes that I'd pivot forward. As much as I wanted to prolong the moment, my willpower crumbled. As her ass hit the sheets, I jolted forward and hissed when her walls hugged me like a glove.

I froze and absorbed every sensation skyrocketing through me. Hovering as bliss flitted across her face. My cock heavy and to the hilt inside her. A beat later, her head tipped back and pressed into the pillow as an audible gasp escaped her lips. Captivated, I studied the lines of her throat and the pulse below her ear. Leaning down, I sucked the base of her throat and tasted her salty skin, nipping and sucking my way to the sensitive spot beneath her ear. Her breasts pressed firm to my pecs as she muttered, "Oh god…"

When she collapsed against the sheets, her nails bit my skin and carved lines from my ass to my shoulders. As she marked me as hers, the beast inside me clawed up and surfaced. I bucked my hips as a low growl rumbled in my throat. Fervor glowed in her eyes as our bodies synchronized in the dim moonlight.

Her legs clutched my hips as she hooked her ankles. I slid a knee up for more leverage and rammed into her over and over. Before long, her walls clamped me like a vice. As she milked my cock, I fought the urge to come. I wasn't ready for this to be over. Not yet.

I picked up the tempo and pumped in and out of her as I bit her shoulder. She shuddered as her body convulsed around me, screaming loud enough for the neighbors to hear.

But neither of us fucking cared.

I paced my strokes and gave her a minute to come down. The second she opened her eyes, I kissed her hard and told her to wrap her arms around my neck. When she obeyed, I flipped us over and she straddled my thighs as she lifted herself and then slammed back down on my cock.

Sarah pressed her hands to my chest and clawed my pecs as she circled her hips. She rode me like a bull as I bucked my hips. Fully seated inside her, I hit every tender spot. Her jaw slack as she panted and cried out into the darkness.

I gripped her hips as she clawed me with ferocity unlike any other time. Her hips circled faster and harder. Face tipped skyward. Breath in short bursts. Soft cries on her lips. My hands slid up her sweat-slickened abdomen. When the pads of my fingers clamped onto her nipples, I pinched and twisted and lit a bonfire inside her. Instantly, she pumped her hips wild and feral and met me thrust for thrust. She dropped her head and blonde hairs tickled my abs and lit a new level of intensity.

Almost there, her orgasm on the cusp of explosion. I bucked my hips harder each time she rocked forward and her walls slowly closed in on me. One last thrust forward and she detonated around me, her body shaking uncontrollably. A red flush danced up her chest as she heaved.

Before she caught her breath, I sat up, flipped us over, pulled out of her, and pressed her face into the mattress. She was exhausted, no doubt, but knew she'd let me get one last orgasm out of her. I wanted us in tranquility together.

I gripped her hips, yanked them up and savored her magnificent ass. I bent forward, pressed my cock to her entrance, and whispered into her ear. "One more, babe. Together." She reached between her legs and grabbed my balls and rolled them like a pair of Japanese Baoding balls.

Fuck!

I needed to come, and she edged me. I wanted to go slow and relish every inch of her body, mark what's mine. My hips plunged forward and I sunk inside heaven. My hand flattened between her shoulder blades and pinned her shoulders to the mattress. Her profile slack jawed as she gasped and clawed the sheets. Pure magnificence.

I glanced down at our joined bodies and stared as my dick slid in and out of her wet pussy. Fuck, she ravaged me. I traced her spine to her tailbone then crushed her hips in my grip, pumping in and out her frantically.

God, I fucking loved this woman. Our relationship would never be solely about sex—an added bonus. I loved every part of her. Her beauty. Her charisma. And her desire to see goodness in everyone.

Truthfully, I was the lucky one. The one she chose. Someone she couldn't live without. *Me.* The notion seared my skin with a newly discovered desire.

My skin painted in moisture, electricity fired inside of me, rippled from my limbs to my abdomen and converged in my balls. She mewled as her pussy milked my dick, and I finally let go, fiery and explosive. I grunted loud and guttural, offsetting her whimpers. I collapsed beside her as she dropped her hips and wheezed.

Our eyes locked as we reveled in what just happened. Ten rapid heartbeats later, she whispered, "Holy fuck!"

Goddamn, I loved her.

FIFTEEN

THE OTHER NIGHT at Christy's ran vicious circles in my head. Not just the sex—although it was pretty fucking phenomenal—but how close Jackson and I were for hours. Arms brushing, fingers laced, bodies inches apart, a sweet hum buzzing between us. His arms cocooned me while we slept. It was the first time in almost a week we'd slept through the night.

I don't welcome danger, but how could I not spend time with him. When we woke Sunday morning and the faint light of day replaced the moon, we cuddled and talked for hours.

We devised a plan to see each other, not every day, but three or four times a week. In our plan, we orchestrated other get-togethers with everyone, rotating where we'd hang out so a pattern didn't form. Sleeping in each other's arms a dream, but a tough pill to swallow knowing it wouldn't happen often.

After hours of master-minding, we dressed and joined everyone for a late breakfast, sharing our idea. My heart skipped a beat when everyone agreed. Their smiles of encouragement made this whole situation a little less scary.

In the early hours of the afternoon, we parted ways. The promise of time together in two days put me in a jovial mood. When Liz dropped me at my apartment, I called Marco and said I'd be back in the office the next day. Honestly, I'd probably be just as safe at work as I am at home. Maybe safer.

Either way, this creep still lurked in the shadows. Harassed me. Tried to rule my life. I refused to hide in the dark like a defenseless, frightened girl. This was my life and I would fight for it. Brave. Strong. Courageous.

I slid into Liz's backseat—Christy rode shotgun—and greeted my favorite ladies. Carpooling now the new norm, which grew on me faster than expected. Catching up with Liz and Christy before work one of my new favorite activities. Yesterday, I spent my first day back at my desk, re-acclimating to my workspace and the office noise.

The workday went by without interruption. At lunchtime, the three of us unanimously agreed to eat somewhere besides Carol's since the assumed admirer/stalker worked at Hammond. Later, everyone hung out at Liz's place. Rick brought Jackson over before Christy, Liz, and I arrived. As planned, the guys left after Liz took us home.

The dynamic weird, but if I got to see Jackson, I didn't care. However long, Jackson and I agreed to put up with this crazy routine until an arrest happened. I refused to have my life stolen.

"We aren't at work yet, but where should we go for lunch?" Liz asked, her eyes glued to the road.

"I'm game for whatever," I eluded. Where we went didn't matter as long as it was outside the office.

"Ooh, ooh. What about that new place a couple of blocks from the office? Shelly raved about it. It's Tex-Mex with flair." Christy's hands animated as she painted us a picture.

"I'm good with that. Liz?"

"Good with me."

The day came and went; the colorful Tex-Mex restaurant the highlight of our workday. That night, I told Jackson about the amazing fajitas I ordered and suggested we go there in the future.

Talking about food morphed into a conversation about how much I missed his cooking. How I longed to see him in boxer briefs and an apron again. Our discussion transitioned from my lunch to his cooking to him in an apron to sex in the blink of an eye.

Before long, I stripped bare in front of the live feed. He mimicked my actions, our hands groping our own flesh at the encouragement of the other. I shuddered as he jerked his hand up and down his hard shaft, each rise and fall stirred an ache between my legs. The burn hotter and wetter with each stroke. Jackson tugged faster as he watched my fingers dip and emerge.

Masturbation not foreign to me, but something I'd always done alone. This voyeurism… unexpectedly turned me on. Pure and raw intimacy. Although we'd been completely exposed to each other before, this vulnerability tipped the scales and took us to a new plateau.

My body trembled as I climaxed, not as powerful as when Jackson and I came together, but more potent than any previous time alone. Jackson came seconds later, his sticky seed coating his taut abs and pecs, his muscles taut. And I hungered to lick him clean.

I glanced at the time—eleven-eleven. My superstitious heart begged to make a wish. So, I closed my eyes for a moment and sent a wish out to the universe. *Please let this person get caught. Please let my life go back to normal.*

"You tired, babe? I can let you go."

I was tired. Tired of living in fear. Tired of being a victim. Of being isolated. Of being without Jackson by my side. "Yeah."

"I'll let you go. Try to get some sleep. I'll see you tomorrow." His tone a soft lullaby.

"Love you."

"Love you, too, babe."

Another week and a half had passed and nothing eventful happened.

No calls or texts. No emails or letters. No unexpected gifts. Nothing.

I wondered if the police arrested the creepster and forgot to mention it. One could only hope.

The sun brightened the sky more than usual. Warmer temperatures prickled my skin as a light breeze ruffled my hair. Exultation coursed through me now that it was Friday afternoon and only four hours of work remained.

Liz, Christy, and I perched on barstools at a tall wooden table. Women in tight, short-shorts and barely-covering-their-breasts tops carried trays, weaving between the tables. The smell of fried foods wafted in the air and my stomach growled in delight.

A tray lowered next to us and was set on a stand as the waitress delivered our lunch. The buffalo chicken Caesar wrap I ordered mouth-watering, and I moaned.

"You ladies need anything else?" the server asked. Her

auburn hair secured in a ponytail that swayed as she bounced side to side.

"No, I think we're good," Liz answered with a smile and a wink. They eyed one another a moment. Liz's smile slipped to a wicked gleam as her eyes scanned the woman's curves. I'd be an idiot to miss the sexual tension passing between them.

"All right, ladies. Holler if you need me," Tiffany, her name tag read, beamed. As she walked away, Liz scanned the rest of her body.

Playfully, I smacked her arm. "Could you be more obvious?"

"What?" Her pitch an octave higher. "I can't help myself. She's cute. And fuckable." The megawatt smile on her face lit a city.

"Oh my god!" Christy's hand smacked Liz's opposite arm. "Shut the hell up, bitch! People can hear you."

"So what," she retorted. "She's hot. I'm available. Who knows?"

I laughed at my best friend, and former fuck buddy. How I loved her. She lived a carefree life, something I envied her right now.

"Single? What happened to mister hottie?" I asked.

Liz rolled her eyes. "Let's just say, not all men are as great as Jackson or Rick."

"Ouch. His loss. I say, if you think Tiffany's hot, go for it. You never know. Maybe she swings that way. Or both. Either way, you'll never know if you don't ask," I comment.

Liz stared at the grouper tacos on her plate. A smile brightened her expression as she turned to look at me.

"Thanks. That means more than you know." Her eyes alight with the bond we shared.

I'd said it because the relevance meant the same when she gave me her blessing with Jackson. Oftentimes, I wondered if Liz didn't date because of me. In case things changed between me and Jackson and I needed her again.

The bond Liz and I shared would never change. Our connection always stronger than most friendships. But I didn't want her life limited because of our bond. My future with Jackson wasn't set in stone, but instinct told me—deep in my bones—we would be together years. And Liz should have the same happiness.

Over lunch, we talked about our weekend plans. Christy suggested another game night. Liz mentioned us all ordering an obscene amount of guilty pleasure foods and spending a day doing a movie marathon. I listened to them prattle on, running down a list of options, all indoors and at one of their homes.

Anger flooded me and everything went red. This bullshit had to end. Ugh, I was sick and tired of living according to someone else's desires. I hated feeling like a frightened child, essentially locked away in a closet. I stopped listening. This fucker didn't own me and I should be able to go out with my friends. Be out in the world. Live my life. The threshold of my patience officially maxed out.

"Enough!" I belted out louder than expected. It felt exhilarating.

Both their eyes widened at my exuberance, lips in a tight line. "What?" Liz asked, confused.

"Enough," I said. "I'm tired of this. I'm tired of being a prisoner because of some asshole lunatic. It's been almost two weeks since anything happened. Maybe he got arrested. Or maybe something happened to him. Either way, I don't care anymore. This is my life, damnit. And I want to do something outside the confines of my home, and yours."

"Sarah..." Christy warned. "I don't know if that's really the best idea. We don't know this guy has been caught. Don't you think Marco would've mentioned if someone suddenly stopped showing up?" Although she made a valid point, I didn't care. Why should I be forced to live like this? This creep wasn't stealing my life from me.

"You're probably right, but I don't care. I'm over being held captive. This weekend, we're going out. This weekend, I'm taking my life back," I told them, my mind set.

They stared at me, deer in the headlights, my bold statement rendered them speechless. Surprisingly, Liz spoke first, methodical and orchestrated. "All right, Sarah. Why don't we run this past the guys? See what they think."

Her concern valid. Liz worried about me. But like it or not, this was happening. "Sure, I'll put it in the group text right now. But I'm telling you, regardless, I'm going out this weekend. With or without everyone. I'd prefer it if I had company."

My fingers tapped out the message, and their phones chimed after I hit send. I slipped my phone back in my purse and finished my lunch. They wanted me safe. I got it. But enough was enough.

We finished our lunch in silence. When the waitress came back to clear the table, Liz pulled her to the side.

Tiffany's face transitioned from concerned to someone being seduced by an attractive woman. Her body loosened, her shoulders relaxed, and a crinkle formed at the corners of her eyes as she smiled. Whatever Liz said, it intrigued Tiffany. Liz took out her phone, her fingers raced across the keyboard as she tucked Tiffany's phone number away in her contacts.

When Liz returned to the table, her skin glowed and her cheeks were flushed. It delighted me to see my best friend like this. Happy, excited, giddy over the possibilities. Who knew where things would go with Liz and Tiffany, but at least she took the first step. Sometimes, a single step was all it took to find happiness.

"Babe, I really don't think this is a great idea. It's not that I don't want to go out. I just don't want anything to happen to you. Or anyone else, for that matter." Concern etched Jackson's voice as his brow scrunched inward.

"Nothing will happen. Everything has been quiet for weeks now. I'm tired of sitting on my couch and twiddling my thumbs, meanwhile the world continues to move forward. Please..." I beg, the word heavy on my tongue. "Come over. Pick me up. Take me out of this place before I lose my fucking mind. Everyone will be there. We can keep an eye out for each other. Please..."

My request didn't sit well with him. He told me so last night. But I begged and pleaded with him. He caved after fifteen minutes and some tears. He understood, as much as I did, how this whole situation wore on me. What it did to my heart. To us. To our sanity.

I stared back at him as we FaceTime talked, and his expression morphed from concern to defeat. All he wanted was to keep me out of harm's way, but accepted he couldn't keep me home tonight. No matter how hard he tried.

"I'll be over soon. Are we meeting everyone at the bar?" he asked, defeat in his voice and posture.

Tempted to jump up and down, I resisted. My enthusiasm on cloud nine. "Yeah. Liz is bringing a date, so there will be six of us."

"Be there in a few, babe," he answered more tender.

"Yay!" My excitement burst at the seams. "I'll see you soon. Love you."

"Love you, too, babe."

The bar was packed with patrons sipping beers and fruity drinks as a sea of bodies danced on the floor. A typical Saturday night, but energy surged in my bones. We managed to snag a table, ordered a couple pitchers of beer and some appetizers, and slipped into old times.

Much of our conversation revolved around Tiffany — the newest person in our tight-knit circle. Christy asked the questions most of us wouldn't dare ask, and her lack of intimidation never ceased to amaze me. Tiffany rolled with it, not cowering once during her spotlight inquisition.

Throughout the night, we learned Tiffany attended college to earn her master's in clinical psychology. She worked at the bar-and-grill because tips were great and it kept her head above water. Tiffany wasn't lesbian — yes, Christy straight up asked the question — but she didn't discriminate when it came to dating. Male, female, race, religion. None of those factors influenced her reason behind dating. All she cared about was the person's vibe. Being a psychology major, she vetted most people within seconds.

Jackson and I stayed at the table. His arm slung over my shoulders pinned me to his side, and I loved it. Rick hauled Christy off to dance a couple times. Liz did the same with Tiffany. I curled into Jackson, elated to see my friends smile and laugh and enjoy themselves.

A few glasses of beer later, we were ready to call it a night. Christy and Rick right behind us. Liz and Tiffany hung all over each other and planned to stay until last call.

I hugged Liz and whispered in her ear. "Let me know how everything goes. Talk to you tomorrow."

We parted, and she nodded as we said good night. Tiffany and I exchanged a warm hug. I secretly hoped she and Liz hit it off. Tiffany was so affectionate and honest, and my intuition told me they would be a good match. The group loved her, too. "It was so nice to meet you. Take care of my girl."

"Nice meeting you, too. And don't worry, I will." Her smile genuine. Her heart open. And just like that, I knew she wouldn't hurt my friend. Knew she had an equal interest in her. The thought soothed my soul, and my fondness of Tiffany grew tenfold.

We stepped onto the sidewalk outside the bar, the cool early April air blew strands across my face and the crispness was invigorating. I tilted my chin up and met Jackson's eyes, a soft glow behind his sapphires. "Take me home," I ordered, the sultry demand rolled off my tongue.

I stood stock-still as the soft glow flipped to fiery passion. I may not of said the words, but my tone insinuated what I wanted.

"Yes, ma'am," he replied without hesitation.

We hopped into the Jeep and he drove me home. Stripped me out of my clothes, and he made love to me until dawn. When the sun came up, we fell asleep. His arms embraced me like never before, and we stayed that way until Monday arrived.

SIXTEEN

TWO WEEKS LATER

I woke to pans clanging in the kitchen. Something sizzled and the smell of garlic and bell peppers filled the air. I walked into the kitchen and wrapped my arms around Jackson's waist and kissed the back of his shoulder. "Good morning."

He turned and pressed his lips to my forehead. "Morning, babe."

Turning back to the stove, he moved food around the pan to prevent it from burning. "Whatcha making?"

"Western omelets, home fries, and juice."

"Mmm... Can't wait." I scraped my nails over his abdomen before removing my arms and letting him know I would be back after brushing my teeth.

When I walked back into the kitchen, he slid the omelet onto a plate, and carried both plates to the table. I poured us both a glass of orange juice and brought them to the table. We sat in peace-filled silence, his food giving me a foodgasm per usual.

With only a few bites left on my plate, his already cleared, he glanced at me and waited until I finished chewing. "It's supposed to be nice out today. Anything you want to do?"

"Lemme think." I pierced a few squares of potato and shoved them in my mouth. Over the last two weeks, Jackson and I eased back into where we were before the whole stalker situation started.

In the last month, nothing new occurred. No appearances made. No indications the guy hung around. The police backed off a little and told us maybe the guy got his jollies by scaring people and that ship sailed. They asked us to inform them if anything else came up, but until then everything should return to normal.

Normal. I have never loved that word until now. Many people thought normalcy was overrated and boring. They did not understand how great it actually was. To be able to do what you want, whenever you want.

"Let's go hiking. Maybe out at the wildlife refuge. It's been a long time since I've been out there." I scooped up the last bit of my omelet and savored the last bite as it hit my tongue.

"Great idea. You get ready, then we'll head to my place so I can change. Maybe stop and grab something for lunch and make a day of it."

I loved the idea. The refuge along the Atlantic coast had trails and wildlife everywhere in the park. We'd easily spend hours out there and not see the same view twice. Nature was my playground and hiking in the refuge with Jackson was bound to be seventh heaven.

"Awesome," I said and grinned. I stood and bolted for the bedroom. "I'll be ready in ten." His laughter echoed from the kitchen to the bedroom as clothes flew from the closet to the bed.

A long day of hiking equaled no cooking dinner. Both of us spent. I set a bag of food on top of the coffee table, took out to-go boxes, and spread them out. Jackson walked in from the kitchen with spoons in hand. He handed one to me as I gave him a set of chopsticks.

"Bon appétit."

We clinked spoons before slurping miso soup. Bite after bite, my stomach grew into a beach ball, blown to full capacity. Sushi the perfect way to end our day. And as much as I wanted to eat more, I stopped myself.

I slumped against the couch, unbuttoned my shorts, and slid my hand in front the waistband. Jackson noticed and belted out a hearty laugh, making me smile. Probably thought this was my best impression of an overindulged, old man on Thanksgiving. But whatever. I loved sushi and always stuffed my face.

We flipped on the tv and watched a show about the galaxy on a science channel. Hours later, I woke in Jackson's arms with my body pressed close to his chest. He laid me on the bed, fully clothed, and curled up behind me as we both drifted off.

Seven-forty-seven. Too damn early to be awake on a Sunday. I wrapped Jackson's arm tighter around my midsection, closed my eyes, and tried to force myself back to sleep. Twenty minutes later, I remained wide awake.

I carefully slid from under Jackson's arm—his soft snores adorable—and headed for the kitchen, deciding to make breakfast for him for a change. Nowhere near as creative as Jackson, I whipped up a few of my favorite things.

By the time he walked in the kitchen, I'd cooked a batch of maple, steel-cut oats, sliced up bananas and apples, and topped it with crushed walnuts. Coffee brewed and the tea kettle softly whistled.

He folded me into his arms and inhaled me, planting a kiss on top of my head. "I would've made breakfast."

"Not that I don't love it when you make me breakfast, but now it's my turn. It's nothing fancy, but it tastes great."

He tightened his arms and kissed me once more before letting go. "It smells fantastic. Let me grab coffee."

We ate breakfast, then talked about getting together with everyone else. After breakfast, I sent a quick message to the group chat, which now included Tiffany. Liz and Tiffany converged into a regular duo over the last few weeks and we'd all grown to love her. I texted the group and asked if anyone wanted to hang out.

I peeked up from my phone to Jackson's nude body, his rippled back faced me as he tested the shower's water temperature. I dropped the phone to the bed, peeled away my clothes, and headed for Jackson.

As I stepped into the shower, I marveled at the sight of him as water cascaded down the lines of his neck to his strong pecs and rippled over the ridges of his abdomen. With his eyes closed and his face under the spray, Jackson hadn't realized I had snuck in with him. I reached out, placed my hands on his chest, and stepped into him. Just the heat of his skin on mine stirred the ache between my thighs.

Jackson's chin dropped and a waterfall trickled from his inky hair. A pair of rich sapphires smoldered as they raked over me. Two months together and shower sex, surprisingly, had not happened yet. The idea of him fucking me against the wall lit me on fire. I imagined the slaps echoing off the walls as he rammed into me and I slid up and down the tile. The guttural groan from his lips as I clamped down on his cock. Our moans of pleasure as we climaxed together.

He pinched my chin and tipped it up. For three weighted breaths, Jackson devoured me with his eyes. Then, his lips crushed mine—starved for my taste. A moment later, he nipped from my jawline to my neck, sucked the sensitive spot beneath my ear, and nibbled his way to the base of my throat. I gasped as he bit the line above my collarbone and dropped to my breast, sucking my nipple and biting at the bud between his teeth. An inferno blazed with fury as every nerve ending exploded. When he released my nipple and brought his lips back to mine, I scraped the V leading to heaven and gripped his erection as if my life depended on it.

"Fuck me against the wall," I demanded in a low growl.

My command sent Jackson into overdrive as he clutched my hips and hoisted me against the wall. I wrapped my legs around him and locked my ankles as his cock rammed into me. I gasped as he thrust his cock to the hilt inside me. The fullness and stretch of my body around his girth overwhelmed me in this new position. Delicious and ravishing. He peeled my hands away from his neck and pinned them to the tile above me, holding me in place as he pumped his hips. An insatiable hunger whirled in his eyes and made me whimper.

"You feel so fucking good like this, babe," he said before crushing his lips to mine.

He let my hands go, and I snaked them back around his neck. One of his hands gripped my ass as the other fisted my hair and yanked hard. My body was sparking like a live wire as Jackson dominated every inch of me. Everything new and heated and raw. The passion. The hunger. Undiluted. Insatiable.

"Oh, god. So good, Jackson," I moaned, practically unintelligible.

My breath came out in jagged pants as I begged him to fuck me harder. To make me see stars. In a heartbeat, he yanked my head back, bruised my ass, and thrust in and out of me as if we'd never see each other again. "God, I fucking love you," Jackson grunted between thrusts. The words bled from his lips and I came alive.

I combed my fingers through his hair and balled my hands into fists and tugged. Jackson hissed, and I bit the spot where his shoulder and neck met. Pure carnality unleashed as he fucked me harder, my back burning as the tile rubbed my skin raw.

"Close. So close…" I panted out as my body edged. Jackson growled in my ear as heat shot from every pore of my body and fused in my core. He nipped and kissed his way down and up my neck, sucking when he reached the spot that always sent me over the edge. So. Fucking. Close.

"Let go, babe," he growled, letting go of my hair and clamping my ass with both hands.

One pump, then another, and I erupted around him. My walls closed in and milked every drop of his orgasm as we screamed loud enough to frighten the neighbors. Neither of us cared. It wasn't the first time, and certainly wouldn't be the last.

Jackson pressed his forehead to mine as we worked to catch our breath. "That…" he huffed out. "That was fucking glorious." He pressed a chaste kiss to my nose. "Have I expressed my undying love to you recently?"

I laughed, then nipped along his jawline. "Hmm, I don't know. Maybe you should again, just in case," I teased.

"I love you beyond comprehension, Sarah Bradley." Then Jackson peppered my mouth and neck and body in kisses, and each stamped my skin for a lifetime.

Something as simple as waking up next to the person you love can make your entire world a better place. I woke before the alarm this morning with the sun barely tinting the sky. I flipped onto my side and faced Jackson and watched his chest rise and fall.

I watched him for close to an hour, completely mesmerized and unable to believe that this strikingly handsome man belonged to me. Jackson Ember could have any woman he desired, yet he chose me. A simple woman with hints of wild and hippie flowing in her veins. Not that I didn't believe we belonged together, it just astounded me how I managed to be the one.

After studying every line and lash and lock, I itched to

sweep my fingers through his short, black hair. As he slept, it laid soft against his scalp, free from the product he added to spike it. So soft. So alluring. I tucked my hands under my cheek and resisted the urge.

As I continued my visual perusal, I locked onto the squared angle of his jaw and was spellbound. Stubble dusted his jawline and I yearned to reach out and feel the small hairs scratch my palm, but I resisted and averted my gaze to his lips. Those lips... A girl could get lost for days in his kiss. Full lips highlighted his bone structure, but didn't steal the show from his other features.

But my favorite... I propped myself on an elbow and stared down at this statuesque man. Unfortunately, his eyelids shielded me from his magnificent sapphires. If someone presented me with one option, and I was only able to see one part of him, it would be his staggering eyes. Hands down.

The first time I saw him—walking into the gym and holding the door open—he hadn't noticed me, but he had captivated me. Those magical, alluring blue sapphires. In that moment, a minor blip in time, I caught a glimpse of him. One potent enough to ingrain his soul in mine. The night of the party—the first time he truly captivated me— it was as if two souls found their way back to one another and fused into one.

The story of soul mates has various perceptions. Some said we each have more than one, that soul mates were not limited to just lovers but also friends we held dear in our heart. Other stories showed we have multiple soul mates in the same lifetime, souls who met and shared part of their life, and taught us lessons to lead us to our one true soul mate. Our twin flame.

Jackson was that to me... my twin flame. My joy was his joy. My sorrow was his sorrow. And my pain was his pain. Once we found each other, one couldn't live without the other. A strange concept to explain, but Jackson is the breath oxygenating my blood. Stumbling upon your twin flame compared to locating a person you never realized was missing your entire life. And once you found him or her, being apart was unfathomable.

His body stirred as muscles came to life. Eyes squinting and adjusting to the bright sunlight. He tilted his head toward me—my face casting a shadow over his profile—as he drew me closer to him and painted a sweet kiss across my lips.

"How long have you been watching me?" His shy smile brightened the room more.

"Not long. You looked so peaceful. I didn't want to wake you."

The wailing buzz of the alarm clock jolted us from our sweet moment, the small black box squealed at us to get up and face the world. I drew back the covers, reached over and slapped the disrupting device, rendering it silent.

Reluctantly, we vacated the warm, cozy sheets and dressed for our day. I'd never paid close attention until now, but Jackson and I moved fluidly around each other. The energy surrounding us emulated a human form of synergy as our individual movements complemented the other. There was never any awkward bumping. Never an undesirable touch.

We were one soul, separated by two bodies, moving in harmony. We didn't have to speak a word, we simply knew.

Our morning routine ended with a kiss—I slid into my car, Jackson in his—and we headed to work. Life beyond perfect. My and Jackson's relationship spectacular. Work had been great, too. Being back in a normal routine relieved all of us, seeing as I no longer required an escort everywhere.

When I reached my desk, two larger than life smiles greeted me. Two pairs of eyes shone brighter than the summer sun. "Hey, ladies. What's up?" Their behavior not completely out of the ordinary, but it was early, and I hadn't caffeinated enough to handle their perkiness.

"Since everything is to be back to old times, Christy and I discussed getting back to the gym. All of us put it on the back burner when all that crazy shit happened. What'-daya think?"

I missed my old morning routine with Christy and Liz. My body certainly missed the rigorous workouts. Although, Jackson kept me active and my body in shape. But that stayed between the two of us. "Yeah. That'd be great. Just the three of us? Or anyone tagging along?"

"Ooh, ooh. Great idea." Christy wiggled side-to-side in her chair. "Rick needs to get out more. Maybe if Jackson joins, the two of them can do manly gym things. And we can watch." If her giggle were visible to the human eye, it'd look like pink cotton candy.

"Let's put it out there, in the group chat, and see what everyone says. I love it! I've missed working out with you guys."

"Me, too." Liz nodded. "Just glad we can get back to it."

I tossed the idea into the group chat and everyone jumped on board. We chose a couple days everyone could meet up and a couple days when it'd be 'girls only' or 'guys only'. Another piece of my life given back to me. Halle-fricking-lujah.

I cut the steering wheel to the right and parked my Beetle two spots down from my front door. Florence and the Machine blared from my speakers, and I belted out the chorus before cutting the engine. A gust of wind caught my ponytail and whipped it in my face as I exited the car, essentially blinding me. I shoved the wayward locks aside and turned back to the car.

Reaching down, I grabbed my purse and the brown bag loaded with groceries, and headed for my apartment.

Tonight, I would try my hand at cooking eggplant parmesan. Jackson almost always cooked for us. My culinary skills no match for his, but it was time I stepped up and cooked something.

Variety wasn't in my repertoire, but the few things I cooked, I mastered. Luckily, eggplant parmesan made it on the list.

I reached the stepping stones that branched off of the sidewalk and trailed to my door. A teal, wooden chair and a circular table large enough to hold a glass and a book sat on my front porch. Nothing lavish, but I loved the cozy vibe.

A few steps from the porch, a long, narrow box sitting on the chair stole my attention. The outside of the box was decorated in generic images of roses and tulips with a wide blue ribbon wrapped around the center.

My feet sunk into the earth as I kept distance between me and the box. Was it more flowers? By now, if Jackson planned to gift me flowers, he would deliver them in person. Especially after everything that happened.

I set the brown bag down at my feet, peered over my shoulder and scanned the parking lot. With sunglass-shielded eyes, I scanned every nook and cranny. No one loitered in the lot. No clapping footsteps or rustling bushes or birds chirping. I focused on the trees and studied them longer than usual. Nothing.

I faced my front door and the box that flashed bright neon warning signs. I forced my unwilling legs to move — taking two steps, one foot in front of the other—and picked up the box. A label on the front of the box from a delivery service. But if memory served me correct, the first flower delivery arrived from a florist.

With the box in my hand, I stepped away from the chair and purposely exposed myself, in case I needed help. Clutching a corner of the blue ribbon, I slowly tugged the bow free and watched the satin fall to the ground. As one hand gripped the bottom of the box, the other grabbed hold of the top. With precision, I removed the lid and saw a mountain of tissue paper inside. Hesitant, I peeled back the layers and something slimy slithered over my finger. I screamed and threw the box in the grass.

Clutching my chest, I stepped back until I bumped into the wall. In the box, hidden behind folds of tissue, laid a bundle of dead flowers. More specifically, sunflowers and daisies. Roaches, worms, beetles and other insects crawled and squirmed through the flowers. Bile rose in my throat and I pinched my lips tight.

As I stared at the box, a piece of paper flapped with the breeze. I tip-toed through the grass, standing back far enough nothing crawled on me, and quickly tugged on the page.

Hopping back to the porch, I hung my head and flipped the paper over in my hands. As badly as I wanted to read the note, I also wanted to light it on fire and yell at the top of my lungs. My life just returned to normal. Happiness returned to my world. Why was I being forced back into this hellacious fear? Again.

The note felt like a lead weight in my hands. But

avoiding it helped no one. I needed to read it and be done with it. The only person who ruled my life, my world, was me. My blood pressure spiked as anger surged in my bloodstream. "How dare you!" I screamed to the heavens, hoping this obsessed, batshit fucker heard me. I was so over the crazed lunatic who threatened my livelihood.

I unfolded the edges of the paper and exposed another typewritten letter. Instantly, my pulse flew off the charts.

Tsk, tsk beautiful little Sarah,
I thought we went over this. I explained myself well enough for you to understand.
I thought you were intelligent. I thought you knew the rules.
But I guess I was wrong. That won't happen again.
Don't think I haven't been watching you. Not a day passes where I don't see you. I have eyes everywhere. You thought you could fool me. Well guess what, my beautiful Sarah. I'm no FUCKING FOOL!
I gave you a chance.
Told you to stop seeing the pretty boy.
Did you listen to me? Not one fucking word was heard, obviously. I know about the little meetings at your friends' houses. I listened, outside that little guest bedroom window, while mister muscles fucked your brains out.
Maybe I didn't make myself clear before.
YOU BELONG TO ME! YOUR CUNT IS MINE!
Tick, tock little Sarah. Before you know it, there will be blood.
Eenie, meenie, miney, mo…
Who will I pick…

You won't fucking know...

I grabbed the brown bag, unlocked my door and threw the keys on the foyer table. With fumbling hands, I yanked out my phone. *This cannot be happening again.* Please, whatever higher power existed in the universe, don't let this happen again.

SEVENTEEN

"HEY, babe. I'm finishing with a client. Should be done with my last one in about an hour, give or take. Then I'll be over."

I wheezed, my lungs unable to draw in enough air as I desperately gasped for oxygen. Jackson was frantic on the other end of the line, shouting my name and pleading with me to answer. After several deep breaths and counting to ten, I located my voice.

"It's happening again! Oh my god, it's fucking happening again!" I shrieked.

"What are you talking about? What happened?!"

Unstable on my feet, the room tilted beneath me. *Why? Why was this happening?* "There was another delivery. A box at my door when I got home."

"You have got to be *fucking* kidding me," he bellowed, his anger evident. Not aimed at me, but to the asshole instigating this. "I'll be there as soon as possible. Call the police. Have them come out and update the case." I nodded as my vision blurred. "Babe, can you hear me? Call the cops."

"Yeah, sorry. I'll call as soon as we get off the phone. I'll let you know what they say," I stammered.

"Please. I'll be there as quick as possible. Lock the doors. I love you."

"I love you, too," I mumbled.

Our call disconnected and my mind drifted into the ether, wishing Jackson and I somewhere far from here. Why was this happening?

My mind blank. Limbs numb. I heaved and reminded myself to breathe. Everything suddenly surreal. I should call the police, but what good has it done? From where I stood, not a goddamn thing.

With each passing minute, my desire to care lessened more and more. Why not throw in the towel? This madman was determined to ruin my life. I retrieved the officer's business card from my wallet and dialed the number. After three ridiculously long rings, I almost disconnected the call when a woman's voice answered.

"Officer Sheila Hawks, you're on a recorded line."

"Officer Hawks, this is Sarah Bradley. I'm calling to update the police report I've filed. I received another delivery today. With a letter," I sputtered.

"Ms. Bradley, I'm sorry to hear that. We keep hitting dead ends with this guy. I wish I had better news." Silence rang loud and clear. I sat shell-shocked and waited for her to continue. "Would you be able to bring the letter and delivery down to the station now? Best if we dust if for prints as soon as possible. Maybe we'll get something off this new evidence."

"Now?" I asked. I bit my fingernail as sanity slipped from my consciousness. Not sure if driving is such a hot idea right now. But sitting here and doing nothing until the morning was the most absurd idea. She understood the urgency. Officer Hawks didn't have some whack job following her every move and dictating her life. Crushing her soul. But she wanted to do everything in her power to help me and I appreciated that.

"Ma'am, maybe you should wait. It's not a good idea for you to drive right now. You're distraught, and seeing as you called me instead of Mr. Ember, I'll assume you are alone. Perhaps it's best for you not to drive. Take some deep breaths, lock your doors, and try to relax until Mr. Ember can safely drive you. We'll get everything sorted out then."

I understood what she told me and acquiesced. She continued to speak, but I stopped listening. Her voice white noise on the other end. When she finished, we exchanged our goodbyes, and I told her I'd come by later.

Did the police give two shits about my problem? Maybe they had more involved and dangerous cases on their desks. Cases with leads. Cases with a possible resolution. Either way, I refused to be the poor, helpless victim. To sit in my apartment and wait. Desperate to escape and blow off steam, I paced the living room. Ideas whooshed like a hurricane as I contemplated ways to gain my life back.

Heading to my dresser, I grabbed a sports bra and a pair of yoga pants. I changed from my work clothes into the exercise gear and picked up my gym bag. More than likely, I had another forty-five minutes to an hour before Jackson arrived. My nerves firing on hypersonic speed, I needed to center myself. Needed to feel something, anything, besides the numbness. And if I sat in my apartment another minute, I'd lose my shit.

Sarah: Called the police, they said to come down in the morning. Going to the gym for a few. I'll be back before you get here.

Jackson: Babe, that's not a good idea. Stay inside. I'll be there soon. We can go together if you want. I don't want you to go alone.

Sarah: It'll be fine. The gym is usually packed right now. No one will do anything to me. Plus, I'm not leaving the complex. It's a 3 minute walk, tops.

Jackson: Please. Don't go. I have a bad feeling about this. I'm begging you.

This is why I didn't call him. I knew he would disagree with me leaving my apartment. But he didn't understand. This affected me more than him. I refused to just sit idle and wait for the shit to hit the fan. Or stop living because some creepy asshole tried his damnedest to ruin my life.

Sarah: I'll be back before you know it.

I set my phone to silent and tossed it in my bag alongside a bottle of water and walked out the door. Twenty minutes—thirty tops—and then I'd return home. Show him everything was fine. That nothing would happen to me.

That I was safe.

EIGHTEEN

THE DOOR to the gym whooshed open. My ponytail brushed the exposed skin of my back as the air above the doorframe gusted. The gym not as packed as I'd thought it would be, ten plus people spread out amongst the machines. This place resembled my form of sanctuary, and my body relaxed with each passing minute. It was crazy how something so simple brought so much comfort.

I wound my way through the equipment and headed to the treadmills, only one of ten occupied. Setting my bag down, I took out my phone, headphones and water. I left the bag on the bench as I always did and my water parked beside it.

My feet straddled the treadmill belt as I scanned the music playlist on my phone. I searched for something loud and screamy to help me escape reality. After a moment of scrolling, I landed on one and tapped the first song, closing my eyes and breathing deep as the music drowned out everything. "Thank you," I whispered to the music gods.

My fingers jabbed the treadmill buttons as I selected my pace, incline, and time. Seconds later, I was warming up and on my way to a fast-paced walk. Within minutes, my mind would wander away from everything torturous.

Ten minutes into my high-paced walk/light jog, my lungs opened up and drew in more air than I'd breathed in weeks, almost months. The sensation liberated me.

I cranked up the speed a couple notches and eased into a slow-paced run. Working out always provided more clarity and helped me see things in a different perspective. It made me stronger and more capable.

Empowered.

Fearless.

Music blared in my ears as my feet pounded the tread-mill. Mileage ticked away as I pushed myself and bumped up the speed again. The treadmill wasn't as enjoyable as running or walking outdoors, but my body kept pace and I forget about the world around me.

Far too soon, the treadmill slowed for the cool down cycle and my pace is now a brisk walk. My pulse hammered in my veins and gave me the adrenaline boost I sought. Confidence inflated my chest and I felt invincible. More optimistic than earlier when I saw the box on my porch. I was ready to tackle anything and everything. Assured I would get through this. *We'd get through this.*

The machine slowed to a stop as my body acclimated to the lack of forward momentum. I stepped off the belt, pulled the towel from my bag, and wiped my brow before taking a huge gulp of my water. I stood next to the bench, drank more water and caught my breath before I picked my bag up and headed back to my apartment.

The gym exit was ten feet away when my head started to spin. The room tilted and spun more with each step. It's like I was on a Tilt-A-Whirl at the county fair. Maybe I overexerted myself. Pushed too hard. *When was the last time I ate?* Hours ago. Shit. As soon as I reached my apartment, I'd eat something.

I slowed my pace, reached for the wall next to me, and put all my effort into staying upright. The room spun a little faster. When I made it back to my apartment, I'd crash on the couch a minute, then eat something. Although, if Jackson saw me passed out on the couch, he might flip out. I don't know.

Don't focus on that now. Focus on getting back to the apartment. One foot in front of the other. You've got this.

I pushed the door open and air rushed around me. The sensation amplified the spinning, and I felt more dizzy with each passing second. I stepped outside and made it a few feet across the sidewalk. What the hell was happening to me? This wasn't overexertion. No matter how much effort I utilized, I wobbled.

Fear coated the blood in my veins. I shielded my eyes as the sunlight blinded me. *What the fuck was this?* Right now, I was scared shitless. Of being out in the open. Of being completely exposed. And *him.*

One minute, I overflowed with confidence. And the next, I drowned in terror.

Forcing all my strength to surface, I attempted to step forward. *Just let me make it home. Please, I'm begging. All I want is to be safe and in my home.*

I took another step forward, my balance shifted beneath me, and my vision blurred. Too late to scream for help, I prayed someone would rescue me.

And then everything faded away as the world turned black. Vanished. No sight. No sound. Total, utter darkness.

NINETEEN

HIM

THE DOOR to the gym opened and there she was. My beautiful Sarah. She stepped inside and paused briefly, scanned the equipment, and noted the small crowd. A wide, purple elastic band trapped her long, soft, golden hair in a ponytail. A few free strands grazed her face and she swiped them behind her ear.

I should be the one tucking those strands away. The one running my fingers through her hair.

Sarah wore my favorite sports bra. The charcoal and peach number. The one that pushed her tits up. Her cleavage more predominant and on display for me. And although they sat snug in place, they still bounced when she walked. Her nipples pebbled beneath the fabric. Nipples I'd soon wrap my lips around. Most of the leggings she wore were similar, but today she'd slipped on a black pair. Mesh slashed across portions of the leg and exposed her skin slightly. And her ass... round and plump and delicious beneath the spandex.

Her fucking curves made me hard. Given the opportunity, I'd stare her down all day. Twenty-four-seven. Three-sixty-five. So fuckable in everything she wore.

On the stationary bikes, opposite the entrance, I tugged the hood on my jacket over my head. Her head was so focused, she never even saw me. But I sure as fuck saw her. I reached between my thighs and adjusted my cock as it lengthened in my shorts. I'd jerk it right here if no one else was around.

Just the sight of her made my dick scream. A drop of pre-cum smeared my lower abdomen. As if she controlled the blood flow to my favorite appendage. Able to get me off without even touching me.

I visually trailed her as she walked to the treadmills. Her go to spot when she came to the gym alone. Always away from other people, if possible. She set down her bag and delivered a fantastic view of her ass. A second later, she placed her water beside the bag and popped earbuds in her ears as she searched for music on her phone.

I pedaled vigorously and psyched myself up for the moment to come. Adrenaline dumped into my veins. The high circulated and jump started my heart into fifth gear.

The treadmill belt started and her shoulders relaxed as she walked. At first, she fast-pace walked until the machine picked up speed. Completely entranced with her curves, my eyes magnetized to every inch of her body.

Her ponytail swung side to side and lightly brushed

the exposed skin between her shoulder blades. Her tits bounced in time with her stride. Nipples taut, they begged for my teeth and tongue to clamp and lick. Her ass jiggled as her feet pounded the belt. The curve where her ass met her thigh tightened with each step, and my dick jerked.

Observing her like this—fucking sweet as sin body sweating and bouncing and begging to be fucked—had me on the verge of jumping off this bike, yanking out my dick, and jacking off in front of her. I gave no fucks who witnessed. Hell, I wouldn't be surprised if the other guys here joined in on the action. Every time my hand slid up and down my cock, Sarah flashed in my vision. Goddamn, she was so fucking beautiful.

She'd be more glorious on her knees in front of me, sucking me off as I shoved my cock down her throat. Tears spilling from her eyes as mascara stained her cheeks from the pleasure. Sarah sucked cock like a pro. I witnessed her prowess a time or two.

Maybe bent over in front of me, plump ass in the air, pussy pleading for my fat cock. With her hands pinned behind her back, and in my grip as I pile-drove her cunt.

Or better yet, cuffed to the four corners of my bed, blindfolded and screaming in pleasure as I fucked every orifice of her body. She'd beg for more. Scream my name. Wish she'd known sooner how much I desired her. Craving me as if it were her last breath.

Soon, she would see. Once I had her in my clutches, she would see. See what she missed all these years. That everything I offered was better than what the muscled pussy she dated gave her. That she should have had me sooner.

Sarah had jogged eight minutes. My guess, she'd be there another ten. Before she finished, the swap needed to happen. Then to the men's room, where my blue balls became a little less blue.

I pedaled slower and eventually stopped before rising from the seat. I grabbed my towel, wiped my brow and neck, then picked up my water bottle. Glancing in her direction, I checked to see if she noticed me get up. Her eyes are forward and zoned out on something not there.

Perfect.

Absolutely perfect.

I walked around the back of the bikes and headed for the row of benches behind the treadmills. My stride swift and eager. I stopped behind her and stood next to her belongings. The sweet scent of her skin blended with sweat and radiated off her in waves as her feet pounded on the machine. The exquisite perfume penetrated my nose and prickled over my flesh.

Fucking delicious. My cock twitched in approval. Implored me to haul her off the treadmill and flaunt what she did to me.

I wiped my towel over my face as a distraction to anyone watching me. I set my water bottle down next to hers, messed with my shoelaces, and picked up her water. After watching her eight hundred and forty-six days, I had plenty of insight on her life. Water was a main staple in her life. This brand the only one she drank.

I glanced over her shoulder and noticed she has nine minutes left. Enough time for me to bust a load and wait for her outside. Rising from the bench, I stepped away and bolted for the men's room.

The locker room is empty and clinical with its white tiled walls. I stepped into a shower stall, yanked down my shorts, spit in my palm, imagined her juicy pussy, and tugged on my cock. Before long, I blew my load. Not a challenge after recalling all the moans I'd heard outside her window. Exploding in my palm, I sprayed my jizz across the stall walls and floor. I reveled in how soon it'd be when I doused her face with my seed.

I wrenched my shorts up, stepped out of the stall, and exited the bathroom. Still on the treadmill, Sarah walked slower as the machine ran the cool down cycle. Another minute or two.

I walked out the gym door, strolled ten feet down the path, and stepped into the tall shrubs and trees decorating the entrance. She would be out here any minute and I had to be ready. My excuse on the tip of my tongue, in case anyone saw me with her. The speech practiced countless times. I reached down and grabbed the duffle I stashed here. A bag too large to carry in the gym.

The door opened and her frame came into view as she stepped out. She stopped moving and tried to get her bearings. I glanced down at the water bottle in her hand. More than half the water missing. She'd collapse any second now.

After a moment, she took a few steps and her knees

buckled. A second later, her eyes rolled back as she fell to the ground.

Down for the count.

The time had finally arrived.

I ran toward her, no one nearby to worry over why this woman just collapsed. I opened her bag, threw the bottle inside, and fished out her keys. I scooped her into my arms and walked toward her apartment. Everything would finally come to fruition.

Her front door was in sight when someone strolled past us, clad in basketball shorts, a tank, and running shoes. He paused and asked, "Hey man, she all right?"

I ground my jaw before answering with one of the many lines I'd rehearsed before today. "Yeah, yeah. Too much exertion, not enough food. Not the first time. I'm taking her home," I stated, not halting my stride.

"Need help?"

His concern and eagerness to help is warranted, but he needs to back the fuck up. Did it *look* like I needed any fucking help? *If you left me the fuck alone, she'd already be inside.*

"Nah, man. I got this. Thanks, though." I plastered on a fake smile and hoped it appeased him.

Finally satisfied, the man walked off. *Thank fuck.*

I reached her door and unlocked it, carrying her inside and locking it behind us. Carrying her into her bedroom, I set her on the bed and stared at her body a moment. She should be out for a little longer. The pills I crushed and added to the water were meant to knock her out quick.

I started peeling her clothes away from her body. Slipping my fingers under the waistband of her leggings, I tugged them down to her ankles and deposited them on the floor. The black lace thong hidden underneath stirred at something primal inside me and I couldn't wait to slide them off and run my fingers over the flesh they protected.

I'd save that for last.

I shoved the tight sports bra up and zeroed in on her breasts. Soft pillows of heaven I anxiously waited to sink my teeth in. The bra pinned her limp arms up and I fondled and pinched her nipples. Tweaking them with the edge of my nails.

She laid still as a mannequin.

My balls ached and I reached below my cock and rubbed them.

Lastly, I slipped off the black triangle of lace. Once the scrap landed on the floor, I grazed my fingertips over the sweet mound of flesh below. *Sweet fucking Christ.* Bringing my hand to my nose, I inhaled deep and memorized her sweet, floral fragrance.

Opening my duffle, I drew out four lengths of cord and fastened each of her limbs to a corner of the bed. After they're in place, I tugged them a few times and checked their strength. Once satisfied they restrained her properly, I stood back and ogled every lock of hair, every dip and curve, every line and orifice. My cock saluted in appreciation.

Ravishing.

I lit candles in her room, then retrieved more items

from my bag. A thick stack of photos. Images of her at work, in the park, eating lunch with friends, sleeping, fucking. I scattered them beside her on the bed.

Next, I took out two bundles of fresh sunflowers. I removed the wrapping and placed a few beside her before scattering the others all over the bedroom. Glancing down at my watch, I picked up the pace.

She already called lover boy. *Fucking asshole. Always in my fucking way.* It wouldn't be long before he arrived— fifteen to twenty minutes tops.

Taking the small bottle out of my pocket, I cracked open the lid and waved the smelling salts under her nose. She lied still a minute—no reaction. But then a slight change. Her lashes twitched and her eyes pinched tighter. Her body shifted in discomfort as she tried escaping from the restraints. Her breaths pushed and pulled in short bursts of air. Her chest rose and fell rapidly.

Her eyes fluttered open—barely an inch—blinked slowly and repeatedly, and then attempted to focus. A moment later, her head swiveled left to right. More than likely, she figured out where she was.

But how did the drugs affect her vision? Was the room fuzzy?

Did she see me?

Had she figured out it's me in the room with her?

Answers only she knew. But if she hadn't determined it yet… she would soon.

TWENTY

WHAT THE HELL HAPPENED? Was I in some cavernous, sealed off room without walls or windows? Everywhere I looked, it's pitch black. As if I'd fallen off the earth and got sucked into a void.

Surrounded by nothingness. Absent of light or noise. Lost in my own head with no one to help me find my way out. Pressure pierced me from every angle, closed in on me and pulled me under like gravity. Pinned me down and depleted me of life. I've never experienced claustrophobia, but this must be what it felt like. A boulder crushing my bones and stealing my breath.

Wherever this hell was, I had to escape.

Locked in place, my arms refused to respond when I willed them to move. I tugged at my upper limbs again, miffed when nothing happened. As if anchored in place. Exasperated with my arms' inability to function, I willed my legs to walk, to graze the earth below my feet, and learn where I was. But my legs and feet remained rooted in place.

Like a piece of sculpted marble, I was a statue frozen in time. Gravity the strength of Jupiter immobilized me.

Where the hell am I? Eerily quiet. Darkness for miles... Chills surged through my veins and lungs.

Terrified is an inadequate term for the dread consuming me.

Somehow, I got sucked into purgatory. A place packed with nothing and existence had no expiration. Absent of life, sound, sight, time. Absolutely nothing. Except me.

Alone.

Panic-stricken.

Unsure of what happened to me.

A pungent odor pierced my nasal cavities. Lungs burned from the source. Mouth salivated to rid the new taste. Alveoli worked double time to draw oxygen in and expel the scent. I tried moving my head to one side, then the other, to escape the rancid smell. But it lingered.

As I swiveled side to side, the pervasive stench continuously invaded. No matter how hard I tried, I couldn't escape the odor.

My lids are like weighted balloons, I worked to open them. With each passing attempt, I squeezed them tighter, wetness pooling at the corners. My head thrashed from side to side, propelled backward, tucked into my chest. No matter the effort I exerted, I couldn't break free from the excruciating smell.

The dark veil prohibiting my sight thinned and faded.

My eyes fluttered with blurred vision. In a flash, the foul odor instantly disappeared, and my nasal passages and lungs gained immediate relief.

I tested my limbs. Sore, aching, and weak. A sting burned my torso. Exhaustion consumed me. But all I wanted was to shift myself out of this uncomfortable position.

I went to stretch my limbs, roll onto my side, but determined that my body won't budge. My head is a bit groggy, I tugged harder and used every ounce of strength I possessed. But nothing happened. Glancing to my wrists... *shit, shit, shit*. Rope hugged my wrists and bound me to the frame.

Adrenaline spiked my bloodstream. I glanced around the room and my vision sharpened. As awareness set in, I realized I was in *my* bedroom. My hands were bound with a thick, brown rope—the harsh threads chafed my skin with every jerk—connected to the frame of *my* bed.

I thrashed harder and the rope cut my skin deeper. Mind over matter, I ignored the pain from the wounds now forming at my wrists. Panic and fear bubbled to the surface with every breath and consumed me. Dragging in several deep breaths, I closed my eyes and tried to recall my last memory.

The last thing I remembered was walking toward the gym exit. Dizziness hit me in waves, but I thought I'd be able to make it back to my apartment. Then, darkness. As if a machine switched off. Nothing except black.

I lifted my head off the mattress and glanced toward

the foot of the bed. Bare, exposed, and one hundred percent vulnerable. I yanked at the restraints again, refusing to be a prisoner in my own home. But my efforts go unrewarded.

When my body settled back against the sheets, I wondered how I would get out of my current predicament. Before any brilliant ideas sparked, I glanced around the room and froze when my line of sight hit the corner. A hooded figure stood absolutely still. His build a little pudgy, stocky, and grotesquely masculine. I closed my eyes tightly, tried to refocus, and implored my eyes to work properly. Like an old digital format buffering, the room sharpened and my sight became crystal clear. The man's face was masked by the hood, his hand feverishly stroking his naked erection.

I attempted to scoot farther away from him, but I was stuck. Bile gurgled in my throat.

Holy fucking shit. I needed to get the fuck out of here. Someone needed to help me. *NOW!*

Speech evaded me as I opened and closed my mouth a couple times to speak. But I swallowed back my fear and rediscovered my voice—my only hope. I parted my lips again and turned my volume to maximum level. *"Help me! Please somebody fucking help —"*

A second later, his hand slapped against my mouth. Hard. He grabbed my sports bra from somewhere next to me and shoved it into my mouth as he removed his hand.

"Shut the fuck up, whore!"

I continued to scream through the material, my voice

too muffled to carry. My eyes burned and pooled with tears, the onslaught a river streaming down my face.

The faint sound of a zipper broke the silence, and I watched my attacker as his hands unfastened the front of his hooded sweatshirt. When the pull tab reached the bottom, he shoved the hoodie open, and dropped the hood from his head.

Alan? You have got to be *fucking* kidding me.

The hoodie fell to the floor before he worked the cotton shirt over his head and discarded it. He stood completely nude, less than five feet away from my vulnerable body, spit on his hand, and returned it to his erection.

My stomach churned as acid crept up my throat, inch by inch. Nausea infiltrated every molecule inside me, and the desire to vomit grew tenfold. *I needed to get away from him. From this situation. Whatever I had to do, I needed to get out of here.*

I thrashed harder. Screamed louder. My endeavors rendered pointless. A chill spread throughout my body, down to the bone, as I faced the sick possibility of this piece of shit raping and/or killing me.

"Hush now, my beautiful Sarah." His voice thick with menace, and his sick and twisted version of sweetness. "We don't have much time. Shouldn't we make the best of it?"

He stalked closer to me, stroked himself faster, jaw clenched. The bed dipped, his weight shifting the mattress as he crawled up and rested his knees between my legs.

It was imperative I got the fuck away from him. Who

knew what this sick fuck was capable of, and I sure as shit didn't want to find out.

I struggled against the restraints. Jerked my wrists within the binds. Wrenched my ankles, hoping to free myself. Another thrash, another failed attempt. The flesh at my wrists bled. My face was saturated with sweat—the moisture blurring and obstructing my view.

He held up a photo, then another, and then another. Pieces of glossy paper surrounded my body, the edges scraping my skin as he picked them up and tossed them when finished.

"Look at you. You're so fucking beautiful. *Too fucking beautiful.* Don't even know a good man when you see one."

He paused and I assumed he referred to himself. I wanted to scream *"What good fucking man would stalk women and hold them captive!"* His fingers ran along the contours of my face and I tried to jerk my head away from his touch. But he clamped his fingers tight around my chin.

"If only you knew how much I love you, my sweet, beautiful Sarah." His fingers left my face and glided down my neck, down my chest, and then groped my breasts. He hissed his approval of my body and rubbed himself harder with his other hand.

I screamed, *"Don't fucking touch me!"*, but my packed mouth muffled the cries. Intuition yelled at me to quit fighting. It turned him on and egged him further. I refused to give up, but was lost. Inhaling deep, I closed my eyes, shut him out, and prayed to whoever heard me.

Please. Someone. Anyone. Help me. I don't want to die. Please don't let me die. Please help me.

His mouth latched onto my throat, and a growl of excitement ripped from his lips as he tasted my flesh. I was dying, and this was hell. His mouth crept down my body, licked and sucked my breasts, and bit my nipples so hard he probably broke the skin. I cried out, my eyes drained of tears as the ducts ached to produce more. Burning. Singeing.

Someone... please... help me. I didn't want to give up hope, but I wasn't sure how much more of this my body would handle.

He inched down my body, toward my navel. His tongue lapped my skin. His teeth biting with force and piercing my flesh. A moment later, his hands landed on my knees, the skin of his palms rough and scratchy, their weight sliding up my thighs and toward my apex.

Please, god, no. Please don't let him do this to me. I'm begging. Please don't allow this asshole to steal my soul.

He lifted his head to look me in the eyes. A gnarled sneer on his lips, eyes loaded with vicious lust. "This pussy belongs to me. You hear me?!"

My only response was to cry. My body convulsed with each passing second.

My life some twisted version of hell.

He lowered his head and licked me above the small sliver of pubic hair on my mound, his hands roaming closer. He sunk his teeth into my flesh, bit the hair-layered mound with fierce aggression with his fingers millimeters from my most sacred place. I screamed, over and over, and prayed someone heard.

A bang on the door had him upright on his haunches. Jackson bellowed my name from the front door, a snippet of relief exploded inside me. I tried to force the material from my mouth with my tongue, but the fabric only budged a fraction. I screamed at the top of my lungs nonstop, thrashed my body and banged the bed frame against the wall. Jackson's voice boomed louder by the second.

As I continued my efforts, I glanced toward my attacker. His smile stretched his face like the Joker in a Batman movie—as if moments like this were his bread-and-butter. One of his hands furiously pumped up and down on his erection, the other hand reached for the junction of my thighs.

My tongue moved every direction and finally pushed the fabric from my mouth. "*Jackson! Help me!*" The words repeated over and over as Alan's fingers ran up and down the folds between my legs. I thrashed in every direction, exerting every ounce of effort I could to clamp my legs shut and thwart his fingers.

Jackson screamed for me and Alan laughed maniacally as he molested me. "*Jackson! Help me!*" I screamed. Because I won't survive much longer.

TWENTY-ONE

JACKSON

Still no response.

Fuck!

Dizziness consumed me over the number of texts I've sent in the last fifteen minutes. They started out as me letting her know I'd left work and was on my way to her place. When she didn't answer the first after a couple minutes, I sent another.

Then another.

Nothing.

The more I sent, the more frantic my texts became. Still, I got no response from her.

When I called, her phone went straight to voicemail.

She told me she planned to work out at the complex gym for a few—which was not a good idea, especially after another note and delivery—but she wouldn't deliberately ignore me. Not like this. Not after everything that's happened. She definitely would not have turned off her phone.

Fuck! Fuck! Fuck!

I called the police, told them I was headed to her apartment, she wasn't responding to calls or texts, and my concern that something had happened to her. They told me they'd send a unit out to meet me and to wait to enter until they arrived.

Less than a mile from her apartment, and every traffic light turned red as I approached it. I slammed my fists against the steering wheel, yelled at no one, and screamed to the gods for not letting me get to her faster.

The second the light turned green, my tires squealed against the blacktop as the sign for her complex came into sight. I turned into the entrance; the guard giving me a once over and opening the gate. The metal barrier crept at a snail's pace as my need to yell escalated. As soon as there was enough room for me to pass, I hauled ass to her building, flying over numerous speed bumps, and not giving a damn about my car or surroundings.

I spotted her car, parked a few spaces from her apartment, and parked my Jeep a couple spaces farther down. Jumping out, I jog to her door, looking down to see her watch on the porch, the face cracked.

Shit!

I clenched my fist and brought it up to the door, banging hard. "Sarah! It's me. Open up."

No response.

I bang on the door again, louder this time. I put my ear

against the painted metal and hear faint muffled screams on the other side.

Fuuuuuuuck!

I yanked out my key to her apartment, slid it in the keyhole, and cranked the deadbolt free from the frame. Turning the handle, the door cracked open, but was halted by the security chain. In the open space of the doorway, I yelled for her. "Sarah! Can you hear me? I'm here." A man's laughter rang loud in my ears.

Son of a bitch!

I stepped back, positioned my footing, then hauled all my weight into my foot as it pummeled into the center of the door. The frame budged slightly. Giving the door another kick, the wood splintered, and the door opened an inch more. One more solid kick and the door crippled under the pressure, allowing me access.

I ran inside, the living room empty. Ran down the small hall and into her bedroom, and everything flickered in slow motion as I entered. Sarah was on the bed, tied to the frame, screaming at the top of her lungs for me to help her. An overweight man sat between her knees and ejaculated onto her body as his fingers moved between her legs.

Everything in my vision went red. *I'm going to kill this piece of shit!*

I bolted to the bed, tackled him away from her, and the two of us hit the floor on the other side. I pinned his body under mine as my fists met his face and pummeled until he no longer moved. Once satisfied he'd stay put a minute or two, I jumped to my feet.

I dashed to Sarah's side and carefully untied the binds from her wrists and ankles, noting the raw skin at each point. She bolted upright, scooted herself off the bed as quickly as possible, grabbed a towel and tightly concealed her body.

Coming to stand in front of her, I slowly reached forward, hesitant to touch her. After a minute, she didn't shrink away from me, and I dragged her to my chest and stroked her hair. I sucked in a deep breath and withdrew from the embrace. My fingers brushed over her cheekbones and cupped her face as I took inventory of her appearance. Eyes red and swollen. Cheeks puffy and stained from her tears. Skin pale and chilled.

I rested my hands on her shoulders, my grip soft yet firm as I controlled my voice, making it as gentle as possible. "I need you to go into another room, I don't care which. Wherever you feel safe. I need to take care of him until the police arrive. Can you do that?"

Her eyes darted back and forth, from me to her assailant. I waited for her to answer, not wanting to rush her. She nodded as her chin quivered. "Yes." That single word loaded with too many emotions. She turned from me and slowly walked into her bathroom and closed the door except for an inch.

Unfastening the ropes from the footboard, I walked over to the psychopath on the floor, flipped him onto his stomach, and wrapped the rope around his ankles and wrists, hog-tying him. He grunted, and I kicked him in the leg. "You don't get to speak!"

"Ms. Bradley. Mr. Ember. Hello?" A man's voice echoed from the front of the apartment. "It's Officer Richardson. I'm not alone and we have our weapons drawn. Can you hear me?"

"We're back here," I yelled.

The police rounded the doorway, guns drawn, and ready to fire if necessary. I held my hands up in surrender and tipped my head toward the bathroom door. "Sarah is in there."

Officer Richardson stepped closer in my direction while Officer Hawks walked toward the bathroom and three other officers entered the bedroom behind them. "I assume this is the guy."

I lowered my hands and peered down to the form at my feet, who was definitely no man. "When I ran in, he had her tied to the bed while he molested her and masturbated over her. I knocked him out and tied him up with some of the ropes."

"We'll need to gather statements from both of you. After we get those, and photographs of the crime scene, you can take Ms. Bradley to the hospital for further examination."

My head bobbed in acknowledgement as I grew speechless. The adrenaline rush I had minutes ago faded away as reality settled in and flooded my heart with dread. After a minute, I coughed and spoke up. "Can I see Sarah?"

Richardson looked over at Hawks, their eyes met and spoke in a silent language only the two of them shared, a minor tilt of her head and I was granted permission. I walked slower than desirable toward Sarah, not wanting to cause her any further panic after everything she'd endured. When I reached her, I brought my hands up to her cheeks and let my palms hover.

Although I had held her just moments ago, I was suddenly scared to touch her now. I didn't know if she'd want any form of touch after what happened. After she'd been separated from the situation and her own adrenaline rush tapered off. I stared into her eyes, her emeralds more translucent than usual, the whites of her eyes webbed with red.

She stepped an inch closer to me, tilted her head to the side, and rested her cheek in my palm. Her eyes closed and a deep sigh left her body as her arms wound around my waist. I wrapped my arms around her mid-section, and pressed her towel-covered body to mine as hundreds of guilty thoughts weighed me down.

"Ms. Bradley?" Officer Hawks's voice soft and kind. "We'd like for you and Mr. Ember to step more into the bathroom." We both glanced at her, confused. "We need to remove the perpetrator from the room. We'd rather you didn't have to watch."

We both grasped the gravity of her words at the same time and inched farther into the tiled safe haven. Once alone, I peered down at her and tipped her chin up. "I'm sorry I didn't get here sooner. I'm so sorry, babe."

A fresh wave of tears rolled down her cheeks as her lower lip trembled. "I should've listened to you. I shouldn't have been so stubborn. None of this would've happened if I'd only stayed here and waited, like you asked."

"No, no, no." I shushed her and ran my thumb over her trembling lip. "You do *not* get to shoulder the blame for this. This was *not* your fault. Do you hear me? This is *not. Your. Fault.*"

Her arms snaked around me and squeezed hard, knocking the breath from my lungs. I kept one arm around her waist while the other stroked the back of her hair. We stood like that, unmoving, until Officer Hawks reentered the room.

"Ms. Bradley. Mr. Ember. We'd like to escort you to the hospital. Can we help you find some clothing? Be sure not to discard the towel. We'll need to confiscate it for evidence."

"Jackson, can you please grab me something to wear? I don't care what."

"Sure, babe."

I headed out of the bathroom with Officer Hawks on my heel. "You may want to grab whatever else she may need for a few more days and any special, belongings she'd like to remain safe. The apartment won't be accessible until the crime scene is cleared. It could be two to four days."

"Of course. I'll grab clothes and see if there's anything else she'd like to bring."

Pulling down the suitcase in her closet, I packed several undergarments, tops, and bottoms. I grabbed a few things off her dresser I'd seen her wear on previous occasions and placed them inside. I brought clothes to her in the bathroom, passed along what Officer Hawks said, and asked her what to grab from the bathroom.

After we gathered everything, I grabbed her purse and we headed out the door. Both of us ready to leave her tainted apartment behind.

TWENTY-TWO

FROM THE DARKNESS of the bathroom, I heard Jackson yell. "You don't get to speak!" His voice followed by a grunt. I wrapped the towel tighter around my body, the terry cloth scraping under my arms. The shield of the fabric nowhere near what I needed.

"Ms. Bradley. Mr. Ember. Hello?" A familiar voice snuck through the crack of the door. "It's Officer Richardson. I'm not alone and we have our weapons drawn. Can you hear me?"

The desire to shout consumed me. I wanted them to know I heard them, but my mouth wouldn't move. My lips unable to form the words. My throat dry and voice hollow.

"We're back here." Jackson's voice bounced off the walls.

Footsteps entered the room as I peeked through the

thin line. Jackson held his hands up next to his face as he gestured toward the door. "Sarah is in there."

I spotted Officer Hawks just before her body cast a shadow on the door and blocked my view. Her voice barely a whisper. "Sarah. It's Sheila Hawks. Can I open the door?"

I nod and the door doesn't move. After a breath, it dawned on me she can't see me. I cleared my throat in an effort to speak. With a scratchy voice, I garbled, "Yes. You can open the door."

The door slowly pushed open as her eyes assessed me. I clutched the towel tighter. "I'm not going to hurt you. Is there anything I can do to help?"

I shook my head. *I don't think anyone can help me. What could she possibly do? Comfort me?* Not sure anyone could fill those shoes right now.

"I know this is difficult, but we'll need to get a statement from you. It can wait until after you get examined at the hospital."

I shook my head vigorously. "I don't want to go to the hospital." The words escaped like rapid fire. No way would some random stranger poke and prod my body. I'd already been invaded and violated enough to last a lifetime.

"I know, sweetie, but it's important we make sure your wounds get cleaned up and we get you the proper medications. I know it's scary, but you can have whoever you want in the room while everything happens."

Her final words granted a little relief. At least Jackson could sit with me while the doctors did their evaluation.

"Can I see Sarah?" Jackson asked. After a silent exchange between the two officers, Hawks granted Jackson permission.

Jackson took measured steps in my direction, the way an intimidated child would approach an upset parent. He stopped in front of me as his hands lifted to the sides of my face, but not touching me. His darkened sapphires glassy and on the verge of tears. Not sure I could handle him crying.

I stepped closer to him and leaned into his hand. The warmth of his touch the most welcoming, comforting, and soothing in my world. As I closed my eyes, I let every molecule flee from my lungs. I reached for him, snaked my arms around his torso, and anchored him close. His presence consoled me and I drew myself tighter to his chest as his caress calmed me further with each stroke.

Officers Hawks said something, but I didn't hear her exact words. As I studied her lips, trying to decipher what she just asked, I saw two other officers grab Alan's arms and drag his body.

My stomach plummeted to my feet as nausea roiled in my gut, and my body convulsed. We stepped closer to the shower and lost sight of the bedroom. Once we halted, Jackson traced the line of my jaw with his fingers, so tender, and stopped under my chin. When he tipped my chin up, I registered the guilt written in paragraphs across his face. "I'm sorry I didn't get her sooner. I'm so sorry, babe."

My eyes heated, swelled with unshed tears, and the magnitude of what happened punched me in the gut. My eyes blinked and the tears spilled out, rolled down my cheeks and fell from my chin as my lips quivered uncontrollably.

"I should've listened to you. I shouldn't have been so stubborn. None of this would've happened if I'd only stayed here and waited, like you asked."

Shaking his head, his thumb stroked across my lower lip. "No, no, no. You do *not* get to shoulder the blame for this. This was *not* your fault. Do you hear me? This is *not. Your. Fault.*"

Utilizing every ounce of strength I could muster, I crashed into his embrace, and his lungs exhaled fully. He brought me closer to his chest and ran a hand down the length of my hair, the continuous strokes comforting me. I closed my eyes and allowed myself to get lost in the serenity he provided. His warmth. His kind-hearted nature. His love.

The rise and fall of his chest below me, the steady beat of his heart, soothed me more by the minute.

My eyes refocused on the room and Officer Hawks's voice just outside. "Ms. Bradley. Mr. Ember. We'd like to escort you to the hospital. Can we help you find some clothing? Be sure not to discard the towel. We'll need to confiscate it for evidence."

My entire apartment represented one large piece of

evidence. I never wanted to be near or touch my bed again. The bedding contaminated, I hoped the cops threw it in an inferno. Nothing about my apartment—revered as a safe haven once upon a time—resembled the life I desired for the future. Nothing was sacred anymore.

"Jackson, can you please grab me something to wear? I don't care what it is." I wanted out of this place as quickly as possible.

"Sure, babe."

Officer Hawks followed Jackson and told him to gather extra clothing, since I wouldn't be able to access my apartment for days. The notion perfectly acceptable with me. The only time I wanted to return here was to gather everything I owned and either pack it or burn it.

Jackson returned to me, handed me a pair of blue jeans, a loose cotton tee, and the necessary undergarments. "Officer Hawks had me pack some other clothes for you, since you can't stay here for a while. If you grab whatever you need from the bathroom, I'll pack it."

After getting dressed, I grabbed the basic necessities from the bathroom—shampoo, conditioner, face wash, hairbrush, toothbrush and toothpaste. If I missed anything vital, I'd go to the store. My sole focus right now was exiting this hell hole.

I handed everything to Jackson. He slipped it into a bag he'd grabbed and put it in the suitcase lined with days worth of clothing. I reached for my purse, made sure everything I needed was in there, picked my keys up from the floor in the living room, and headed out the door.

On my small patio, I saw my watch on the ground, the glass cracked and glinting in the fading sunlight. I started for it, wanting to take it with me.

"Babe, you need to leave it. For now." My eyes burned as tears threatened for the hundredth time today. "I'm sure they'll return it to you once they've taken care of everything here."

I nodded and ambled forward as Jackson's fingers snaked between mine and kept me glued to his side.

A few steps past the patio, a sound caught my attention, and I turned to locate the source. Two officers stood at one side of the patio, their hands rustling the tall shrub. Seconds later, one of them walked toward the other side of the patio as bright yellow tape screamed CRIME SCENE DO NOT ENTER now spanned the entryway.

I turned back to Jackson and hung my head. "As much as this whole situation sucks, I'm just glad it's over. I can deal with everything else as it comes."

His hand gripped mine tighter. "Me, too."

We traveled the sidewalk, almost to his Jeep, when screaming broke out. My eyes scanned the lot, and my stomach revolted when I stopped at its source. *Alan.* In the backseat of a police cruiser. Kicking and screaming, his face pressed to the glass. A wicked gleam in his eyes.

When I got to the passenger door of the Jeep, Jackson barricaded me from seeing my attacker. And then I heard the words no victim wanted to hear.

"I won't be in there forever. You can't hide from me.

I'll find you. I'll scour the earth for you. And when I do...
I'll finish what I started. You can bet on it!"

As much as I wanted to escape from all of this, I froze.
Rooted in place with fear. Yes, it all happened. And it
would haunt me for many years to come, no doubt about
it. But right now, it all seemed surreal. Like a living nightmare I couldn't erase.

"Come on, babe. Let's get you to the hospital. Officer
Hawks is waiting."

I stepped into the Jeep, fastened my seat belt, and
prayed to a higher power. *Please, I'll do anything. Just keep
that guy from ever finding me again.*

Being thoroughly examined by someone you don't
know—photos taken, swabs run over your skin, ointments
and medications given—after a traumatic situation... It's a
whole new version of hell.

When the female nurse stepped into the room, she
asked my permission for Jackson to stay. I granted it in a
heartbeat. She proceeded to explain the entire process of
the exam and everything that happened. I signed a docu-

ment once I agreed, the headline atop the page read *Rape Kit Analysis*.

Although there was no penal penetration by Alan, I wanted to do everything throughout the process. Not certain how all of this worked, but if the analysis was used to keep him in jail, I was one-hundred percent good with it.

Forty-five minutes later, the procedure finished and Officer Hawks entered the room. She sat on a chair, opposite me and Jackson, and said we would need to give formal statements. She retrieved a digital recorder from her pocket, checked the time, and pressed record.

"This is the testimony of Sarah Bradley. Today's date is April eighteenth. The time is currently nine-twenty-one in the evening. Sarah, when you are ready, you may give us your testimony."

Tears welled in my eyes, and at any moment they would spill. I was so tired of crying over this whole situation. Inhaling a deep breath, I held it a moment and vowed to myself this would be the last time I cried over this. I wouldn't allow this one inhumane person to ruin my life. And I would move on and live my life to the fullest.

When I exhaled, I let it all out. Every single moment. I sobbed while I relived the nightmare as Jackson held me and kept me grounded. When I finished, I wiped away the blubbering tears and listened while Jackson told his side of the story.

As difficult as it must have been for him to hear my side, I never thought it would be just as difficult to listen to him recount his testimony. His voice shook, guilt weighed on him immensely, tears rolled down to his jaw and lodged in the scruff. He was in absolute fear for my life. Devastated by the possibilities of what he might walk in on when he finally got to me.

Never again would I ignore anything this man told or asked of me. He loved me so profusely and I disregarded his requests, wanting to go somewhere and think. My selfishness resulted in me being violated in one of the worst possible ways. If he hadn't arrived when he did, I shuddered at the possibilities of what else could have happened.

My body noticeably shivered and Jackson glanced down at me. "You cold, babe?"

"No." But I curled into him, and his arm snaked around me and drew me closer.

After our statements were given, we left the hospital and went to Jackson's place. He set my suitcase by the dresser in the bedroom and took my hand. "Come with me." His voice soft and kind and full of adoration as he walked me into the bathroom.

We stopped in the middle of the room and his palms framed my face. He wanted to kiss me, but resisted, a war brewing in his eyes. I pushed up on my toes and pressed my lips to his. A gentle exchange between two lovers. Every touch from him healed me a little more. When he pulled away, he glanced down at my body and came back to my eyes. "Can I undress you? We need to shower."

I nodded and granted this wonderful man permission

to help me and provide me comfort when I needed it most. He took his time as he removed each piece and eased over the abused areas. He turned away from me and cranked the water on in the shower. A second later, he stripped his clothes, tested the water temperature, and walked us under the hot spray.

I had no recollection of a time when I enjoyed a shower as much as right now. The water mimicked something more potent, not just cleansing my skin, but also washing away everything that lingered from the last several hours. It purified parts of me I didn't realize were tainted. As each droplet hit my skin, a new form of tranquility washed over me. I felt safe. Protected. Loved.

Cupping Jackson's face in my palms, I lowered his lips to mine, kissed him without hurry, and showed him how much gratitude I held in my heart for him. As I broke the kiss, I peeked up and gasped as his sapphires burned into me with compassion and strength and vulnerability, his emotions on full display. Three of the most significant words lingered on the tip of my tongue. Three words I'd never expressed so deeply in my life.

"I love you."

TWENTY-THREE

SIXTEEN MONTHS LATER

"A COUPLE more days till the big day!"

In more ways than one, I missed the high-pitched excitement of Christy's voice when we were face-to-face. The squeaky voice I heard through my phone currently wasn't quite the same.

"Are you excited? What are you guys doing?" Christy spewed out in her usual inquisitive nature.

"I don't know yet. Jackson said it's a surprise. I wish you guys could be here. I miss you terribly," I confessed.

Music played in the background of the call alongside a crowd of chatter. "We miss you too, girl. I can't wait to fly out and see you. Christy and I are trying to coordinate vacation time and see if Marco's cool with it." Liz chimed in, her ear probably glued next to Christy's.

A man in the background started yelling something about someone keeping their hands off his woman.

"Where are you guys?"

"Bar life, bitch. It's cray-cray. There're some hotties up in here, but mostly crazy drunks. Nothing we can't handle."

"Sounds like it. I hope you guys can talk Marco into it. You'd love it here. There's so much to do, so much to see. In the time we've been here, I still feel like I haven't seen anything."

Moving out of Georgia had been both easy and difficult. Painless because it got me away from everything that occurred. Flashbacks infiltrated my mind whether I was awake or asleep, day-in and day-out. No matter how hard I tried, I couldn't escape them.

One night, about a month after Alan's arrest, Jackson made an amazing dinner and crept into the topic of us moving for my consideration. He didn't want to assume that I would want to move with him, but asked if us moving away would make me feel safer. When I didn't hesitate to say yes, we started scouting for places to live.

The most heartbreaking part of moving... I left my two favorite people in the world. Thousands of miles away, at that. When we looked into the various options, we took into consideration jobs for both of us as well as scenery and things to do. I loved working at Hammond Life, but I just couldn't stay there any longer, even after Bob and Marco offered to transfer me to a sister office near where we planned to move.

"Christy and I will see if we can talk any sense into him next week, but it might not be for weeks. A lot of coercion goes into letting two of us take a vacation at the same time." Liz's voice snapped me back to our conversation.

"I know, I know. Just keep me in the loop with what happens. I miss you guys like crazy. I really wish you could be here for my birthday."

Life hadn't been the same not seeing them every day, but Jackson and I knew moving was the best thing for us. We couldn't stay in that city any longer, not with the possibility of Alan being released from jail and scouring the city for me or him or both of us. We couldn't take that risk.

"Us too, bitch. We might just have to do a belated shindig. Besides, more parties are better. Am I right?"

As long as I got to see them, I didn't care what we did. "Sounds fantastic. I'm going to let you two get back to your bar life. Jackson's just finishing dinner. Love you guys."

"We love you, too." They were the Bobbsey twins when they answered in unison. It made me wonder if they practiced doing that, for laughs.

The noise of the bar vanished. My ear met with silence. The longing to see my friends grew to new heights. Things weren't the same without them.

My hand dropped to my side as I clutched my phone, trying to hold on to my friends a little longer. I stared out the window as the sun dipped in the early evening sky. Sunsets in California stole my breath. The same can be said about sunrises off the coast of Georgia. Something about the sun being close to the water, that monumental glowing ball of fire and energy setting the sky ablaze—rich blues, corals, pinks, oranges, and yellows burning the atmosphere for miles on end. No one could simulate beauty like that. And I couldn't get enough of it.

When we first settled, we spent half of our evenings on the beach at sunset. We packed food and joined the countless others who drove out for the exact same reason. In the process, we met a few other couples, people we saw repeatedly and found the courage to spark a conversation with, and made the start of our new life a little less daunting.

Before reaching Santa Barbara, we elected to never mention the topic of Alan or the stalking unless we'd heard something from the police worth concern. As of now, life was beautiful and fresh and new.

The scent of Asian food wafted my way, and I spun to see what exactly Jackson concocted for dinner. Walking into the kitchen—one more spacious than either of the kitchens we had in Georgia—I stepped up behind him, grazed my hands across his shoulders then down his back, and planted a kiss between his shoulder blades. He glanced over his shoulder, and his glorious sapphires smiled down on me.

"Whatever you're making, it smells unbelievable."

"Found a new recipe for vegan pad Thai online. I thought we'd give it a try, so..."

"If it tastes as good as it smells, it'll be amazing." Standing on my toes, I planted a kiss on his cheek. "Anything I can help with before Judy and Kendra get here?"

His eyes roamed the counter, his thoughts written in the lines of his forehead as he asked himself what else needed to be done. "Maybe open the wine? Let it breathe a little."

"On it." I set off to open the wine, carrying it to the table set for four.

Judy and Kendra were one of the few couples we met at our favorite beach sunset destination. On our fourth visit to watch the sunset, we'd set up our chairs, parked a basket full of cheese, crackers, fresh fruit, and wine between us, and absorbed the show nature displayed.

As we'd settled into our surroundings, the two of them walked onto the beach and laid out a blanket near us. The sun rested a breath above the horizon, and I retrieved my phone to snap a couple photos. One of them spoke up and asked if we'd like to have our photo taken with the sunset behind us. I jumped on the opportunity and returned the favor.

We spent a couple hours that night, talking and getting to know the two of them. Judy was a California native, but lived further north until a few years ago, moving south after she and Kendra met. Kendra had been visiting friends and, while she waited to meet up with them at a coffee shop, Judy walked in the door and the rest is history.

Since that night on the beach, we'd had couples date nights with Judy and Kendra several times. At first, we met up at various restaurants and got to know each other.

After becoming better acquainted and comfortable, our home became their home, and vice versa.

Although they could never fill the shoes of our Georgia friends, having them in our lives made us feel more at home than we had in a while. Judy had a brain that would give Liz a run for her money and Kendra had a smile that occasionally reminded me of Christy's laugh. Sometimes I wondered if it was fate that brought them to us, giving us something to remind us of those we missed.

"Wine is officially breathing." I checked my watch, noting we had a few minutes before our guests arrived. "What else can I do, angel?"

I glanced over to see the curve of Jackson's lips push up his cheeks as his tanned skin flushed. I loved watching his reaction to the nickname. Anyone overhearing would think it endearing. It was, but also so much more.

After the fiasco in Georgia quieted. After Alan went to jail. After the world felt like it was no longer spinning out of control. I had time. Time to absorb everything that happened. How Jackson saved me from who knows what, my body shuddering at the mere possibilities.

We sat in bed, he perused the internet on his tablet and I read. I slid my marker in the page, closed the book and laid it in my lap, staring across the room. He wrapped his hand around mine and asked if I was okay. I'd told him I was fine, but just realized something.

You're my guardian angel, I'd told him. He'd laughed before turning serious. So many times, guilt weighed us down over how that day had unfolded, but I'd told him, *you can't change fate. If it's meant to be, it's going to happen. It all happens for a reason.* I still believed that. The good, bad, and ugly.

We may not love all the circumstances that sent us to the opposite side of the country, but we were meant to come here. To experience this place. To make new friendships. We were meant to do these things together. I don't think any of that would've happened if something so life altering hadn't taken place and shook our world.

My guardian angel. Angel. He would forever be the love of my life. And I his. I would scour the planet to find him, plummet to the earth if I lost him, and lose my way without him. He was me and I was him. We would always be, forever, us.

The doorbell chimed, snapping me back to the present. "They're here."

Jackson tugged his *Kiss the Cook* apron over his head and followed me to the door. His hand rested on the door handle as his eyes met mine, the corners crinkled before his lips upturned.

"I love you, babe." A kiss grazed my temple.

"I love you, too. Angel." My cheeks plumped as I gave him a brilliant smile. "Now, let's not make our friends feel like we're ignoring them." My chin jutted forward and signaled him to open the door.

"Yes, ma'am." His sweet smile slipped into something a bit sexier and my insides puddled.

"So, what's new and exciting at the magazine, Sarah?" Kendra's inquisition, and eagerness for information on the daily activities of my life, felt like I was back in Georgia with Christy. A light, elated sensation warmed the center of my chest.

"Things are good. We're currently designing the October issue, which has been a blast with all the Halloween themed decor and recipes. Everybody is really getting into it. I think it's going to be my favorite since I've been there."

"I can't wait to see it." Bringing her spoon to her lips, the scoop loaded with apple-pear cobbler and coconut whipped cream, pure appreciation hummed in her throat when the treat hit her tongue. "Good, god. I don't know where you found this one, Sarah." She pointed her spoon toward Jackson. "Damn, he is definitely a keeper."

The three of us burst at the seams, and our laughter was sure to be heard outside the four walls of our home. It was the greatest gift—friends you couldn't live without.

Judy set a hand on her wife's shoulder. "Are you trying to tell me something, K?" Working her face into faux seriousness.

"What?" The singular word muffled by the latest shove of dessert between her lips, Kendra turned to meet Judy's eyes. "No, sweets. I was simply noting that Sarah was extremely fortunate to find someone who knows how to cook. That's kinda rare nowadays."

"That's true, I suppose. Lucky for me, I'm partially skilled in the ways of the kitchen, otherwise I might be watching for my replacement." She was joking around, but Judy made a damn good poker face and Kendra wasn't sure if she laid on the sarcasm or honesty.

"Sweets..." Kendra's hands encased her wife's, eyes locked on hers, her face earnest. "You know no one could, or will, ever replace you. Right? No matter what." Her voice dropped lower with each word. "They wouldn't be you. You're all that matters."

Warmth wrapped around my palm as it rested on my thigh, followed by a soft squeeze. I glanced away from the private moment Judy and Kendra shared and peered to the man beside me. His sapphires torched my body instantly.

It always astounded me how Jackson made me feel with just one brush against my skin or a single glance. It started beneath my breastbone, the heat magnifying with each contraction of my heart. Molten lava erupted from the epicenter, trickled its way to my limbs, warmed my fingers and toes, and continually flowed and circulated until it found the finish line. Within seconds, my core temperature was off the charts. I clamped my thighs together and tightened. The yearning for relief skyrocketed as my desire for Jackson clawed at my insides. A relief only he provided.

The walls appeared closer together, the furniture too big for the space, the number of people in the room too many. How did I politely ask my friends to leave? How did I end our evening with them so *our* evening could begin? *Think, think, think.* My mind considered hundreds of possible courtesies, but didn't find one that fit. I would simply have to wait and hope time didn't creep.

Wood scraped on tile, garnering my attention to the other side of the table, as Judy rose from her chair and Kendra mimicked her movements.

"I think we're going to head out. K had a long day, and she starts early again tomorrow. Another big shoot."

Thank heavens, Judy found her way to excuse the two of them for the evening. I'm sure Kendra was filming tomorrow, and that it was for hours on end, but I highly doubted that either of them was tired. Right now, though, I didn't care. The room overflowed with sexual tension and we all needed to end our shared time together.

"Sorry we kept you out so late. Let us walk you out." I scooted my chair back and stepped beside them. Before opening the door, I wrapped my arms around the pair of them. "Thanks for coming tonight. Give us a call and we'll do it again. Soon." Jackson gave each of them a brief hug.

"Soon. Thanks for having us. Everything was wonderful." Judy's voice quieted as she stepped onto the porch and joined the cicadas singing a melody in the darkness.

Jackson and I stood outside the open door, watched

our friends back out of the driveway, and waved goodbye. As soon as their car was out of sight, I reached for his hand, walked backward into the house, and tugged him with me.

After passing the threshold, his foot kicked up and shut the door. His fingers locked the bolt, but his eyes never left mine. "We'll clean everything up later." The simple statement set my body ablaze.

He hauled me forward and my chest crashed into him, his hands grabbing my cheeks and his lips crushing mine. Clothes were peeled away at a fevered pace, bits and pieces of fabric littered a trail from the living room to our bedroom.

My feet dangled above the floor as he broke the kiss and tossed me onto the plush cotton comforter on our bed. Instantly, his body blanketed mine. It had been almost two years and the heat and passion and longing for each other hadn't faded one ounce. If I were to describe it, I'd say it amplified with each day that passed.

Jackson worshipped me with his mouth as my hands pawed and scraped his backside. The room an echo chamber of our whimpers, heady breaths, cries for more. I loved the feel of him across every inch of my skin, but I needed more. My body screamed for his. "I need to feel you. Inside. Now."

His sapphires captured me as a growl ripped from his chest and his heat rubbed against me. His lips grazed mine a second before he broke away to observe as he slid deep inside me. My eyes rolled back and my back bowed off the mattress as his hips met mine. We sat unmoving for a beat, his breath hot on my neck as one hand encompassed my hip while the other laced through my hair, his forearm on the bed.

His hips retreated slowly, and then thrust forward once more in a methodical, soft rhythm. A breath later, he whispered in my ear. "I love you, Sarah." Another slow shift of his hips. "More than anything in this world." His hips pumped slowly as the pace grew more impassioned. "I couldn't imagine my life without you." The tempo built with each word he spoke. My orgasm closer to the precipice. His love igniting me. My nails bit his flesh, and his orgasm exploded with mine.

Pure, undiluted heaven. Wrapped in the arms of the person I loved. Our passion an accessory. Our souls united. I couldn't imagine life getting better.

TWENTY-FOUR

JACKSON

My phone alarm went off, and the metal case buzzed and danced over the wooden bedside table. I snatched it up and prayed it didn't wake Sarah. Silencing the alarm, I slowly peeled back the covers and slipped out of bed. Fingers crossed my absence wouldn't disturb her.

Slipping on a pair of lounge pants, I exited and closed the door behind me. Today's to-do list ran a lap around the block with every minute packed. Thankfully, I recruited help and it would be seamless.

Unlocking my phone, I typed out a new message—one I would delete after it's sent. My fingers tapped across the keyboard on the screen. I peeked up every other second to double check Sarah hadn't wandered out.

Jackson: Morning. Just wanted to check we're on task. She's still asleep. Let me know if you need anything. My phone will be on silent, but I'll answer as soon as I'm able.

I pressed send, waited until the 'delivered' message popped up under the blue bubble, then deleted the message and tucked the phone in my pants pocket. I headed into the kitchen for the first task of the day—make breakfast in bed for my woman. My phone buzzed incessantly against my leg, reply after reply from the friends I entrusted with today's deeds.

After Sarah woke, I'd figure out a way to check them. Until then, I couldn't risk her walking out and wondering who I texted. Raiding the cabinets, drawers, and fridge, I retrieved the necessary ingredients and went about whipping up her first gift.

Moving from Georgia to California was a huge step for us. When we moved here, we'd known each other all of five months. Although, deep in the fiber of my being, it felt as if we had known each other our entire lives. When you had an all-consuming, I-don't-want-to-spend-a-day-without-you connection, translating or comparing that connection to words was impossible. Sarah was a million fireflies buzzing and sparking in my soul. Friends—hers and mine —questioned us moving to the other side of the country, thousands of miles away, together, not knowing how our relationship would pan out.

We spent countless hours discussing the intricacies of our plan, sifted through every possible scenario or outcome, and had a resolution for each. Never once did the mention of us not being together come into the equation. We loved each other. For us, it was that simple. Neither of us pictured life without the other, so we didn't.

We sat down one weekend and looked at all the potential places to live. Both of us decided we wanted to be in a populous area. Somewhere near water, not specifically the ocean, but that's where we landed. And lastly, we wanted to be in an area that supported all walks of life—young, old, healthy, modern, classic, a little bit of this, a little bit of that.

The internet morphed into a tiresome annoyance, one I wanted to rip out of the computer and incinerate. Who knew it'd be so challenging to find what we were looking for? So we paused a few days, rested our brains and started fresh after time out of the house.

The mini break of city searching triggered opportunity to land in our lap. A client I hadn't seen in months booked an appointment on short notice. During our session, I asked how life was treating him since I'd last seen him. He shared tales of his work travels, how he'd flown all over the country, recruiting new clients and visiting new places.

At the mention of travels, I shared my intent to move out of state in the near future, but hadn't nailed down the where yet. He understood my need for privacy, but asked what was stopping us.

After a long list of details, he threw a couple of suggestions my way. "Have you looked at Colorado or Santa Barbara, California?" We had looked into Colorado extensively—the area both beautiful and populous. The only turn off. Snow. Lots and lots of snow. Sure, we'd seen snow in Georgia, but it was nothing compared to Colorado.

His other suggestion—Santa Barbara—was where we landed. After some research, we automatically fell in love with the area. The next day, we booked a flight, took a long weekend trip and discovered our new home. Within a month and a half, we secured jobs and a place to live. Everything happened so seamlessly, it was hard to believe it wasn't meant to be.

Sarah in my life was an incomprehensible dream. The sight of her hair fanned across the pillow each morning when I woke. Her warm skin that lit a thousand fires across my skin when we touched. How her eyes sparkled when she looked at me. The way her voice slightly stuttered when she said my name... Sarah was all I wanted. All I ever needed.

The blueberry pancake slid off the spatula and stacked atop the two on the plate. Fresh cut strawberries, melon, and pineapple piled high beside the maple covered cakes. Then I finished it off with strips of tempeh bacon. I positioned the plate on a serving tray alongside a small glass of orange juice, a napkin, cutlery, and fresh daisies to decorate the perimeter. Grabbing the handles of the tray, I set off to accomplish the first task of the day.

Shortly after we moved to California, we made one other big change in our lives. How we lived. We took nothing for granted and experienced everything life offered. Some might say we changed into two completely different people. We say, we simply became a better version of ourselves.

Setting the tray on the table beside the bed, I lit a

small candle and kneeled on the floor beside her. Sarah laid curled on her side; her pillow crushed in her embrace, head on the edge of mine as her golden locks splayed across the cotton. Soft, fair lashes rested above her cheek-bones and accentuated the light smattering of freckles below them. Her chest rose and fell in a whisper.

With a slight shift, the sheet slipped down to her navel. Her pale breasts on full display, and I studied her golden tan lines in the dim light. I hoped she'd wake up, roll over, notice breakfast, and the day would begin. But now... plans changed. Even with a to-do list longer than Santa's at Christmas, there was no resisting the primal beast clawing inside me.

I lowered my head, wrapped my lips around her areola, and lavished the tender flesh. Her body stirred awake and pressed further into my greedy mouth. I slid a hand beneath the sheet and trailed down her body. From her navel, trekking through the small patch of curls, I traced over her slit and coated myself in her moisture.

One of her hands slid into my hair, curled into a fist, and held on for dear life. Her other slid over mine, and coaxed my fingers to slip inside. I kissed a path across her chest and sucked the other nipple between my lips. She gasped and bowed her back, and pressed her breast farther into my mouth as I dipped a finger inside. I hooked my finger in a *come hither* motion and rubbed against her walls.

"Oh god, Jackson," she moaned, tugging my hair harder.

A light sheen pierced her bare flesh as I explored her with my mouth. I inserted another finger and circled her clit with my thumb as my free hand shoved my pants to the floor. A second later, I joined her on the bed and hovered inches above her. I shifted hands and picked up speed. Within a beat, red blotches bloomed between her breasts, up her throat, and over her cheeks as her body clamped down on my fingers. I leaned down and bit her shoulder as her orgasm ricocheted from her core.

Kissing my way to her mouth, I absorbed her heady breaths and became intoxicated. After coating my erection with her release, I positioned the head of my dick at her folds and stilled as her body trembled under me. Smoldering emeralds magnetized to my sapphires. Her jaw slackened, breath panting. I kissed the corner of her lips, her jawline, the sweet spot beneath her ear. "Happy birthday, babe," I whispered in her ear as I thrust forward. Moments later, we both came unraveled.

"What tricks you got up your sleeve today?" Sitting up on the bed, Sarah's eyes squinted in deep thought, studying me as if trying to read my thoughts. Not happening today.

Today, I was on lockdown. A sealed vault. Poker face securely in place.

"I checked the weather yesterday. It's supposed to be nice all day, so I thought we'd go to the beach for a bit. Pack a picnic, soak up the sun. Maybe see a movie after. Later, though, we've got a dinner reservation."

The cutest and most peculiar expression lit her face. Was she confused or trying to read deeper into the context? *Best of luck*, I thought. I had planned today for weeks. Every detail locked up tight like Fort Knox. No way in, baby.

"Sounds good. Need help with anything before we go?" Desperation laced her words.

"Nope. Just get ready. I've got everything else under control."

Flipping the sheet off her legs, she scooted off the bed and stood a foot away, her sculpted curves on full display. She traipsed a hand over her hip, across her navel and up to her breast, and pinched her nipple. An obvious attempt to distract me. "Are you *sure* you don't need *any* help? You have *everything* under control?"

She toyed with me. Tried to make me cave under pressure. The only thing I'd give into today... fucking her as much as possible. I pushed off the bed, rose to my full height, and molded my body to hers. I gripped her ass with both hands and hoisted her off the floor, warranting a squeal from her.

I carried her into the bathroom, set her down, and turned on the shower. "You know, we don't have to leave the house today, if that's what you want. I'll gladly spend the day fucking you over every surface in the house. It's *your* birthday."

I slid my fingers between her folds and inserted two. Sarah was insatiable. She gasped, "*Yes...*" A command on her lips.

"Yes, what?"

A moan bubbled deep in her chest. "Take me. In the shower. Now." Each word jagged.

"As you wish." I swept her off the floor, and her ankles hooked above my ass as I carried her into the raining water.

In every direction, the beach was blanketed with bodies. The sun shone bright and warm in the practically cloudless sky. After another hour of side-tracking, we'd finally dressed and left the house. The day mapped out for weeks, I was more than willing to spend Sarah's birthday naked in bed, if she wished it.

The only part that had to stick was dinner. Dinner

involved more than us, and it would be selfish of me to leave everyone out. She didn't know it yet, but she'd remember this birthday for years to come.

I laid back against the soft blanket, propped up on my elbows, the sun partially hidden by the dark blue beach umbrella shading my face. Sarah walked out of the surf, feet sloshing along the salty water shallows, hands twisting her wet hair into a bun at the crown of her head. The sun shimmered the water droplets on her body and accentuated her curves. A balloon inflated my chest as a lion growled in my groin.

"The water feels great. You should join me," she pleaded, a gorgeous smile highlighting her cheeks.

The cool Pacific didn't tempt me as much as Sarah, but it was hot as fuck out today.

She stood in front of me as her body shadowed my legs. "Yeah, sure." Extending my hand to her, she helped me up and dragged me toward the surf.

If you'd ever dipped your toes in the Pacific, one thing was certain. It was cold as fuck. Even on a hot summer day, it was frigid. Back in Georgia, every once in a while, we'd drive to the Atlantic beaches. It was incomparable. Sure, it was cold, but not like the Pacific. The occasional trips to the Gulf of Mexico warmer, most likely because it was a smaller body of water.

I waded my way slowly into the water, hissing as I adapted to the temperature.

"You know it's better if you just take the plunge," she giggled.

"What?" I questioned, confused. The frigid water had my thoughts scrambled. *Did she know about later?*

"Just dunk your whole body under the water at once. Get the initial shock of it over and done with." Then she demonstrated.

"It's like ripping a band-aid off. Just be quick about it, huh?" She nodded and waited for me to submerge.

Inhaling deep, I leapt forward and took us both under the water. When we breached the surface, she panted and playfully smacked my arm.

"I wasn't ready for that."

I wrapped her arms around my neck, her legs around my waist, and held her close. "I know. That's why I did it, silly." My lips crushed against hers and pushed all her playfulness aside.

I walked us farther into the water. The depth breaking the water at our shoulders, and the crowd thinning around us. Our lips danced and tongues stroked as the water cooled our heated flesh.

I drew back, the dark lenses of my sunglasses reflecting against hers. "Is this what you want for your birthday? Us, making love and fucking all day?" My question serious and not-so-serious at the same time. "Everywhere we go today, you want us to leave our mark?" The idea stirred deep in my bones. Marking and claiming the city had an unimaginable appeal.

Her arm dipped below the water, her hand sunk between my board shorts and skin, and my dick stiffened further. Her hand stopped when her fingers wrapped around my shaft. She pressed her cheek to mine, her lips a breath away from my ear.

"It seems as if you're good with the whole idea." Her tongue traced the shell of my ear before she sucked the lobe. "I want you to fuck me. Right here. Right now," she whispered. The demand an electrical impulse straight to my cock.

"Put your hands around my neck, babe." As her hand abandoned my dick, I inched my shorts beneath my ass and exposed myself to the elements. I traced her bikini bottoms, ground through the material over her clit before pushing it to the side.

I slid two fingers inside her. *Fuck, she was wet.* I slid my fingers out and positioned her over me. Something about the thought of anyone realizing what we were doing turned me on immensely. Voyeurism had never been a desire or fetish—I never wanted another person getting off watching us—but it was more the adrenaline rush of being caught with our pants down.

I pushed into her, and the water created an unfamiliar friction. Withdrawing a fraction, I thrust forward again and our bodies found an unnoticeable rhythm. She leaned her cheek against mine, the side least visible to the beach goers. Her hot breath panted in my ear as soft whimpers rippled over the waves. I quaked under her as she quietly demanded more.

I widened my stance, trying to gain more leverage, and thrust my hips as I drove her down my shaft. Sex in a body of water was a wholly new experience. Strange and foreign, but also unbelievable and exciting.

Her breathing accelerated as small, high-pitched cries wept from her lips. *Don't stop. Don't stop. Don't stop.* She repeated it as if she knew no other words. A moment later, her body tightened around me and held me in place as my release followed.

"Holy shit!" She pressed her forehead against mine. "That was…"

"Fucking amazing…" I finished her sentence. Exhilaration flooded my veins.

"Yeah." She pulled back and studied me through her sunglasses. "You know I'm never going to look at the beach the same again, right?"

I laughed, thinking how I'll never see the ocean in the same way either. The thought made me love her even more.

"Where are we going?" Sarah asked.

I reached across the center console of the Jeep and encased her hand in mine. I brought her soft, delicate fingers to my lips and kissed each proximal phalanx. My lips had devoured every square inch of her flesh today, but right now, this small intimate touch… beyond perfection.

My eyes veered back to the road as I turned right at a random intersection. I purposely drove us all over the city, burned time, and threw her off to where we were going. Apparently, it worked. In my periphery, Sarah stared out the window and then back at me, her brow furrowed.

She was lost. But me? Not one bit.

"It's a surprise," I replied.

Her reaction exactly what I expected. I felt her eyes roll as she sighed heavily and exhaled with every iota of drama she owned. A gleaming smile split my lips as I worked diligently to suppress my laughter.

"Can I at least get some sort of hint as to where we're going?" Her brilliant emeralds seared my flesh and attempted to seduce me.

Tempted to toy with her, maybe I'd give her a tidbit. A great deal of time and effort went into planning today, no way I'd ruin the surprise. Others would have my head on a platter.

I wanted this birthday to be one she remembered. Always.

We pulled up to a red light, and I glanced over at her and kissed her knuckles. "You'll love it. We should be there in ten minutes or less."

"That's a crappy hint. I don't even know where we are. How can I guess where we're going?"

I shrugged and faced forward as the traffic light

turned green. "Sorry, babe. I might get murdered for ruining the surprise."

A quick glimpse at her expression and I laughed loud. Her eyes squinted, brows bunched in, and lips pursed. Her irritation with me absolutely adorable. After she discovered why I kept the surprise on lockdown, she'd overlook any irritation.

I turned the Jeep into the parking lot of Bella and Daisy's Bistro and parked in a space near the entrance. I discovered the restaurant through a client. His endless bragging about how great the food was and how his wife loved the vibe piqued my interest. Days later, I drove by and scoped it out.

I cut the engine and tugged the handle on the door, stepping around the front of the Jeep to open her door. She stared at me, dumbstruck, and then back to the restaurant.

"What is this place?" Her eyes scanned every surface as I took her hand and helped her from the passenger seat.

"Bella and Daisy's Bistro. It came recommended, and I checked it out. I think you'll like it."

She faced me, eyes alight with excitement, her expression softening after a minute. Facing forward again, she squeezed my hand in hers. "It looks wonderful."

I glimpsed the restaurant with her, wanting to see everything how she saw it. From where we stood, the right half of the building was visible, the left masked by a large pergola decorated with vines, small flowers peeking between the leaves. Strewn along the ground, under the pergola, was a mass of colorful river rocks. Different sized wooden tables scattered throughout the gravel. Between all the tables was a fire pit. Adirondack chairs crowded the flickering flames.

To the right of the outdoor seating a small, winding walkway, each slate stepping stone a different shape. To the left of the walkway were tall ornamental grasses with small tufts on the tops. A small pond trickled down a towering stack of rocks on the right. Rows of compact, Edison-style bulbs hung above us as we walked toward the entrance.

Her expression mesmerized me. I loved her awe and excitement as we stepped closer to a set of large glass doors.

I opened the door and gestured her inside ahead of me. Fun, eclectic music crooned from hidden speakers. The scent of fresh herbs and citrus wafted in the air. Walking past a handful of long benches, we approached the hostess.

"Welcome to Bella and Daisy's. Two for dinner?" the brunette asked as her eyes darted between us.

"We have a reservation. Ember."

She ran a finger over the reservations as another fidgeted with her ponytail. She froze a second before her eyes peered up again and her hospitality smile slipped in place. "Right this way, please."

Outside, the restaurant appeared small, as if it could hold ten or fifteen tables max. When I first checked it out, I got a brief tour and found it perfect for tonight. But now

I had the opportunity to really check it out and was more than pleased with my choice.

The restaurant had several tables spread throughout the interior—some for two, others for more. The tables were distressed like the ones outside. Along the ceiling, more of the same Edison bulbs lit the space. With a modern and intimate appearance, I knew my girl loved every part of it.

We wove through a few more tables before turning and walking toward a pair of aged, oak doors, **PRIVATE** decoratively burned into each. The hostess paused in front of the doors, turned to face me, and gave me a knowing look. I smiled in thanks and she retreated.

I faced Sarah, her expression bewildered as she stared back at me. I closed the gap between us and kissed her delicate lips briefly. "Happy birthday, babe."

I opened the door, the room pitch black, and gestured Sarah to step into the room ahead of me. Shutting the door behind us, I flipped a switch on the wall and a group of voices screamed.

"Surprise!"

Her expression went from recognition to shocked to awed to elation... I'd pay every cent I earned for that to happen again.

TWENTY-FIVE

JACKSON OPENED the door and gestured for me to step inside the dark and secretive room. After he shut the door, it was like an endless tunnel without light. His hand patted along the wall in search of the light switch.

A second later, while I stood in the dark and my other senses heightened, a whiff of a familiar scent struck my nose. One ingrained in several memories. One not around often anymore. Before I asked what was happening, lights blinded me, and a sea of friendly faces grinned ear to ear.

"Surprise!"

I rubbed my eyes in disbelief. Everyone I held near and dear to my heart stood in front of me; their excitement and joy to see me flooded me with a rainbow of emotions. My face heated as the corners of my mouth perked up, smiling so hard my cheeks stung. Tears pricked my eyes as a boulder of adoration clogged my throat. I wanted to cry and squeal and jump up and down, but also squeeze the heck out each person here.

I spun to face Jackson, wrapped my arms around his neck, and whispered into his ear. "Thank you for bringing everyone here. This is the best present anyone ever gave me." I kissed the angle of his jaw then retreated and gazed into the eyes of all the beautiful, smiling faces.

Without a word, everyone filed into a zigzag line, ready to hug me and hug or shake hands with Jackson. Christy and Rick, Liz and Tiffany, Marco, Eric, Rob, Judy and Kendra, Peter and Mark (another couple we met during our sunsets on the beach), my parents—Sally and George—and a man I assumed was Jackson's father because of his striking resemblance.

My mom and dad stepped forward, wrapped me in their embrace, and squeezed me with ferocity. I hadn't seen them since we left Georgia. And although I talked with my mom often—phone calls and FaceTime at least two to three times a week—I missed them terribly. Thousands of miles apart versus twenty minutes was an odd feeling. The three of us separated, and I hooked Jackson's arm with mine. "Mom. Dad. This is Jackson. Jackson, these are my parents. Sally and George Bradley."

Mom stepped to my right; the top of her head barely reached Jackson's chin as she looked up at him with a beaming smile. With her arms outstretched and welcoming, she yanked him into her for a hug. "It's so good to finally meet you in person, Jackson."

"You, too, Mrs. Bradley." His hold on her one of the most tender things I witnessed in our time together.

Mom stepped out of the hug and moved aside as dad took her place with his hand held out, firmly shaking hands with Jackson before he drew him in for a man hug and a strong pat on the back. "Jackson. Great to meet you, son. I've heard nothing but amazing things about you." His dark, amber eyes glanced my way before focusing on the forest greens set in my mother's features. "Thank you for inviting us out tonight. It means the world to the both of us."

"Certainly, sir. I wouldn't want it any other way."

Jackson's formality and expression befuddled me. An abnormal exchange for my father and Jackson. A secret between two men. A quiet sentiment from a father to the man who held his daughter's heart. I had zero time to mull it over as my body was hauled into a tall man's chest and the wind knocked out of me.

I wrapped my arms around his frame. Strong and older, yet familiar. Giving him a tight hug, I took a deep breath and relaxed, his earthy scent comforting. As he broke the hug, his palms rested along my biceps with nearly straight elbows. "Hey, sweetheart. I'm Bill, Jackson's old man. It's wonderful to meet you. Although it feels like I've known you years, seeing how Jackson talks about you like a schoolgirl."

He smiled, and I instantly knew Jackson's genetics mirrored his father. I studied Bill a moment—the sharp angle of his jaw, the salt-and-pepper sprinkled in his short, black hair, his broad chest. As I examined him, it dawned on me this would be Jackson in the future. The notion plucked at my heartstrings. The only noticeable difference —his eyes. Where Jackson had the most intense sapphires, Bill's resembled more of a steel, metallic swirl. Quite striking.

"It's great to finally meet you, too. I've heard some stories, all good ones, from Jackson. Maybe you can fill me in on stories I haven't heard." I peeked over at Jackson as my brows danced up and down.

"Sure thing, sweetheart. I always love embarrassing my boy. Too bad I didn't bring any old photos. Then we could have some real fun." His laughter shook against me, a deep, throaty bellow. I loved him immediately.

After a mass of hugs are exchanged, everyone took their seat—a table front and center for us faced the group. We headed for our table and Jackson drew out a chair for me while he remained standing.

He picked up a glass of wine from the table, raised it, and cleared his throat; his other hand on my shoulder.

"I wanted to take a moment and thank everyone for being here tonight. I know some of you had to travel farther than others, but it means the world to us you could be here. To our Georgia friends and family, we've missed you deeply. Thank you. We love you." He lifted his glass higher and bellowed out *cheers* before he brought it to his lips.

"Cheers!" Our friends and family echoed.

Jackson sat down beside me, placed his glass on the

table, and wrapped his arm around my shoulders. His breath hot on my ear, he whispered, "Happy birthday, babe. Were you surprised?"

"Totally surprised. *You did all this?* This is… *amazing.* Thank you." This birthday would definitely be stored in my memory bank.

"Only for you." He pressed a sweet, tender kiss on my forehead. "Now let's enjoy some great company and delicious food."

Over the next couple of hours, we mingled with our friends and ate a plethora of appetizers before our dinner arrived. I learned more about Jackson's father—he was a retired carpenter, although he never really stopped working. He loved working with his hands. More or less, he worked as a hobby now and made art for people.

One of the most amazing bits of news, Christy and Liz planned on transferring to the California Hammond Life office. Although it was a two-hour drive from where Jackson and I lived, it was closer—and cheaper—than a long flight across the country. If everything went according to plan, they'd be in California before the year ended. Both of them paused their transfer while Rick and Tiffany sorted out jobs and they all found a place to live.

Life got better with each passing day. My heart was on cloud nine. Ecstatic to have more family closer. Of all the things heavy on my heart when we moved, not being near my parents or friends resonated the worst. At least I would get a chunk back.

Jackson fidgeted next to me—his leg bounced, his attention shifted from Eric to me out of the corner of his eye, then back to Eric. Under the tablecloth, I placed my hand on his thigh and sent calming energy his way. His eyes darted to mine, searching, and a million thoughts flitted across the lines of his face. He rested his palm over mine—his palm sweaty and cool to the touch. His leg stopped bouncing as he gazed into my eyes, a forced, tight smile replaced the nervousness he worked to hide.

I mouthed. "You okay?" Unsure if he had eaten something bad and felt sick. He nodded, but didn't answer.

I watched him another minute. Small beads of sweat glistened the ridged lines of his forehead. His Adam's apple bobbed a beat before he closed his eyes. The wooden legs of his chair screeched against the tile floor, and everyone stopped talking and focused on Jackson.

Peering up at him, I worried over his pallor and dampened skin. "Are you sure you're okay?"

He bent down and placed a kiss on my cheek. "I'm fine, babe."

Taking him at his word, I turned back to my mother, ready to resume our conversation about how different the beaches are in California versus Georgia. I assumed Jackson got up to use the restroom, that was until I heard him clear his throat. My attention returned to him, curious what he was up to.

Dwarfed under his height beside me, I strained to peek up and assess him. Sweat painted his face as his eyes danced over everyone in the room as he stood silent. Everyone except mine. Nervous energy cascaded off him in waves. I didn't know what was happening, but I suddenly had a knot in the pit of my stomach.

When he spoke, it was a rattled sound. A stutter on his tongue. "Hey, everyone. Can I have your attention for a moment or two?"

Everyone stopped their chit-chat and directed their attention to Jackson. I gazed at where his fingers rested by his side, the ends tapping his thigh repeatedly.

"Thank you, again, for being here tonight. I know it means the world to Sarah." He locked eyes with me for a second. "It means everything to me, too. It took a lot of man hours, and woman hours," he looked over at Christy and Liz, smiled and tipped his head in their direction, "to get tonight put together. Countless hours and weeks of planning. I couldn't have done it without help. So, thank you. You are the best friends we could ask for."

Christy and Liz lifted their wine glasses and returned the sentiment to Jackson.

"Sarah's birthday isn't the only reason I wanted everyone here tonight." He must have read the confusion on my face, because his smile radiated at my obvious lack of Intel. "I brought you all here tonight for another reason as well. I wanted all of you here, the people who hold the highest level of importance to both of us—individually or together—on this memorable evening." Jackson faced me, slid his chair farther back, and dropped to one knee, his hands trembling at his sides. My mouth fell open, hands slapping to cover it as I gasped and my eyes welled with tears.

"Sarah, since the day I met you, a little over a year and a half ago, you have turned my life into this astonishing place. You made me see things a little brighter, your aura like a glowing ray of sunlight. Before you, my skies were gray and life was monotonous. Now, everything is brilliant and bold and screaming with life. You make me feel whole. You make life worth living."

Pausing a moment, his hand dug into his right pocket. A second later, light glimmered off the ring he fished out. Attempting to steady his hold on the band, he held the ring up and presented it.

He glanced over at his father, his eyes wetting before he continued. "This ring belonged to my mother, Mary-Anne. I wish you could have met her. She would have loved you immensely." Tears rolled down his cheek, my thumbs swiping them away before they reached his jaw. "But nowhere near as much as I love you. Sarah, today I invited our family and closest friends here for two reasons. The first... to celebrate your birthday. A day that is definitely worth rejoicing over because without it you wouldn't be in my world. The second... I could have held the door open for anyone that day. I was in such a rush to meet up with my client, I didn't have time to pause at the gym doors or say anything to anyone. I thought, in that moment, I'd missed the opportunity of a lifetime. I thought I'd missed my one chance to talk to the most stunning woman I ever laid eyes on. But I didn't know luck was on my side. I didn't know we were meant to see each other again. I wallowed for days, told my friends about the woman I saw at the gym. I tried to make more appointments with the clients that lived in your complex, hoping to cross paths with you again. But nothing happened. Not until days later. I'd been bumming around for days, and Eric was having way too much fun giving me shit for acting like such a girl."

He takes a minute, looking over at Eric and they both laughed a moment before he continued.

"He told me he was going to a party and asked me to come along, that maybe I'd feel better afterwards. Just after we walked in the door to Liz's party, I saw you. Standing in the kitchen. You noticed Eric, but hadn't seen me. Someone had dropped something, and you went into cleanup mode, ignoring everything else. I watched you, waiting for the right moment to approach you and start a conversation. When I did... it was all downhill from there. I was hooked. I've been hooked every moment since. Sarah, I couldn't ever imagine my life without you in it. I never want to. When we're not together, I feel as if a part of me is absent. You fill in all the gaps. You make me whole. You make me a better man. Life without you... it would be cold and dark and empty. You are my light. You are my reason for... *everything*. You make the sun shine and the moon glow. On this day—your day—I ask you the most important question I will ever ask. Sarah Lynn Bradley, will you marry me? Will you be mine forever?"

The spacious room faded away, replaced with a gray fog that clouded everything from sight. Everything except him. It was only me and Jackson. His bold sapphires glassy with unshed tears. Wetness fell down my cheeks as my eyes dropped from his and locked onto the ring clasped between his first finger and thumb.

A silver band, not too thin nor too thick. In the band's center rested a rich, dark sapphire baguette, the precious stone a little longer than wide. Three thin baguette diamonds nestled along both sides of the stone, accentuating the piece and giving it a classic look. The sight of it stole my breath, had my eyes swelling with unshed tears, and froze my voice. Not only did the ring remind me of the specific pair of blues I could never get enough of, but it also held more meaning to him than anything I could ever understand.

My eyes slid up from the ring and locked back onto his. I opened my mouth, tried to form words past the lump in my throat. Never had I been at such a loss for words. My eyes dropped briefly, another batch of tears fell at the quick closing and reopening of my eyes, caught on my lashes and blurred my view.

I waded through the thick layer of emotion that filled the space between us and swallowed. The world around me lightened as if someone lifted a weight off me I didn't know existed. The corners of my mouth perked up, my cheeks rosy from the love and adoration I had for this man. The connection we shared unlike any I had with anyone else. I never imagined my world without him in it. Never wanted to. Ever. He breathed life into me. Was the reason I woke with a smile every morning. The reason I existed. My world was his world and his was mine.

"*Yes*. Yes, Jackson, I will marry you."

TWENTY-SIX

OCTOBER—THE FOLLOWING YEAR

I SPIRALED the last fallen length of hair around the curling iron and followed it with a heavy spritz of hairspray. Relaxed spirals loosely framed my face while the remainder of my hair sat secured in an artfully messy bun at my nape. Christy stood behind me and added final touches—a handful of daisies and sprigs of baby's breath. Once finished with my hair, she twisted me in the chair and studied my face.

"Makeup looks fine. Closer to natural is better," I said.

I never wore a lot of makeup. Honestly, the less on my skin, the happier I was.

"Yeah, yeah. Shut up, bitch. This is my time to shine." Christy giggled and it crowded the small dressing room as she playfully shoved my shoulder.

"Be nice now." Liz poked her head out around the tri-fold dressing wall, her eyes pinging between me and

Christy like a game of table tennis. "This dress feels all wrong."

"What do you mean? You tried it on and said it was perfect." A tsunami of panic surged from my belly and gnawed its way through my limbs.

Shit! Shit! Shit!

"That's not what I meant." She stepped out from behind the barrier, the soft, teal chiffon complemented her hazelnut skin. A stunning visual I couldn't resist smiling at. "What I meant is... I'm just not a dressy-dress kinda girl." She pivoted side-to-side and the sheer top layer flowed more freely than the thicker fabric below it.

"I think you look stunning. Wait till Tiffany sees you." I glanced up at Christy, her eyes pinched at the corners, and her smile bright. "You're up. Time to change."

"No messing up your hair or makeup while I'm changing," Christy said with a pointed finger and cocked hip.

I stuck my tongue out and saluted her. "Yes, ma'am."

"No need for sarcasm, bitch. The time for you to change is coming soon."

In less than an hour, the ceremony would begin. Instantly, my palms slickened as I stood on the edge of a cliff. I had zero reservations about marrying Jackson. I wanted to be his wife more than I wanted to breathe. The dark cloud of anxiety hovered around my fear of falling on my way down the aisle.

In record time, Christy stepped out from behind the panels and twirled in her dress. In the bust, the material hugged her curves like a glove. From the waist down, it billowed out slightly. Both Christy's and Liz's dresses ghosted the ground when they walked and their shoes peeked out.

"Rescue me. I think I'm going to cry." I fanned my eyes while Christy rushed to my side with a tissue to blot the corners of each eye.

"No tears. Not until pictures are taken and everyone has seen you. Just because the makeup says it's water-proof, doesn't mean shit."

"Okay, I promise. No tears."

Christy and Liz stood back a few feet and studied me. This moment one of the best I shared with them both. Beyond lucky to have them here and sharing another monumental occasion.

Liz squeezed my shoulder. "It's time."

I stared at her and nodded. "Will you guys help me?"

"Wouldn't have it any other way." Christy rested her hand on my other shoulder, the three of us connected. Sisters.

I slid off the creamy, cotton robe, and stood in a nude thong and nude bra adhesives. Liz walked to the garment rack and unzipped the heavy, white dress bag. The three of us had seen my dress a few times, but when the split zipper exposed the material below, we each gasped at my wedding dress.

Some parts of Jackson and I are traditional; other parts, not so much. My dress fell under the less traditional side. It was a soft, creamy rosé hue. The bottom layer of the dress a thick, matte satin fabric, cutting across my bust and sloping down at the sides and plunging to a point at my low back, my bare back exposed. The dress flared out gradually down my legs—not snug; not puffy—and danced across the floor. A thin, delicate layer of matching lace covered the dress as well as the exposed area of my back up to the tops of my shoulder blades, above my breasts to my collarbones, and down my arms. The pattern intricate, the lace hand stitched by an Italian family.

This dress more formal than anything I'd worn prior, yet still wielded my bohemian style. The moment I laid eyes on it on the hanger, I stopped scanning the racks. The moment I tried it on, every particle in my body screamed this was *the* dress.

Gently sliding the dress from the garment bag, Liz carried the dress over to me—Christy noticeably bounced beside me—the length draped over an arm. They both held one side of the dress, Liz's thin fingers trembled slightly as she unlatched the lacy, round buttons down the spine. Once she reached the last button, her hazel eyes gazed at my emeralds as a sweet smile spread across her face and ignited her eyes. The silent exchange between us inflated my heart with joy—she was as happy for me as I was for her.

Most brides got jittery on their wedding day. Although you've seen your wedding dress umpteen times, luxuriated in the fabric against your skin during the several fittings, and smiled like a fool every time you saw it—some women lost all sense of peace the instant the dress left the garment bag.

But I wasn't most women. I definitely wasn't most brides.

My eyes glazed over as I stared at the stunning layers of fabric. All I saw was forever. Forever with Jackson. And forever in love. A bubble of serenity encircled me at wearing this dress and walking toward my forever. If one truth was absolute in my life, it was that marrying Jackson Ember was set in the stars. Love of my life. Guardian angel. The key to my heart.

Stepping into the gown, my arms dipped into the soft, lace sleeves and I wiggled the dress up my body. As I held the lace to my chest, Liz and Christy fastened each button along my spine. As each one connected, a glimpse of my future flashed like an old picture movie. Breathtaking and beautiful and fulfilling. A sharp tug snapped me out of my daydream as Christy and Liz made sure the gown sat in place on my curves. When Liz reached the top button, Christy grabbed my heels—basic nudes with the toe open and a strap around the heel.

I slid my feet into each shoe and held up the dress for Christy to hook them. Once in place, I added one last piece to my ensemble. Grabbing a black box from the vanity, I inhaled deep and lifted the lid. A classic piece nestled in soft satin. My fingers skimmed the precious stone at the heart of a silver chain. A magnificent sapphire rested high atop an intricate silver design. Jackson purchased the necklace. It paired with the ring that once belonged to his mother and now rested on my left ring finger.

With the necklace latched around my neck, the pendant rested at the hollow above my sternum. Liz and Christy slowly spun us to face the three mirrors in the room. No longer concerned about falling over the lace of my dress, I peeked up and digested the three angled reflections staring back at me.

Completely awestruck with my best friends at my side. Tears stung behind my eyes and threatened to spill. I tipped my face to the ceiling and kept them at bay. Again. Overwhelmed by the enormity of my love for Jackson, my best friends held my hands and laughed with me as I refused to shed a tear. Life was complete. Whole.

"Is it time yet? Not sure how much more I can take?" My body trembled with laughter.

Two sets of arms embraced me as *awes* cooed nearby. When we parted, Christy checked the time and announced we should get in position—the ceremony a couple minutes away.

In the blink of an eye, the door opened. Liz and Christy walked out and my father stepped in. My heart a gooey, toasty marshmallow as he stood in awe before me. After a bated breath, Dad swathed me in love and adoration before kissing my cheek softly. "You are stunning, baby girl. Your mother and I are so happy for you."

I gazed into his weepy, amber eyes and noticed soft lines crinkling the corners. "Thank you, Daddy," I whispered as emotion choked me.

His strong, calloused fingers secured mine and held me tight. "We should make our way toward the aisle. There is a strapping young gentleman waiting for you at the end." A smile that matched my own, one I inherited from the man embracing me, beamed back at me. Pride and love and joy reverberated from his aura and merged with mine. Love only a father possessed for his little girl.

We exited the intimate dressing room and wandered down a pathway to an open set of doors. Outside the building, our shoes clicked along the cobblestone walkway as the muted wedding music played in the foreground. After a hundred rapid heartbeats, we approached an archway blanketed in small red roses, stopped and waited.

Our arms hooked at the elbow, Dad rested his free hand over my exposed elbow and gave me an affirmative squeeze. The music shifted as he locked eyes with me, and his broad smile like a million fireflies brightening the sky. The happiest I'd ever seen him.

"Here we go, baby girl."

I lifted my bouquet—an ornate arrangement of sunflowers, daisies, purple calla lilies, and wildflowers. Had I been in charge of the bouquet, it'd be a hot mess. The florist was our saving grace. I readied myself, took a deep, relaxing breath, and signaled I was ready.

The next thirty-seven steps—yes, I counted each and every one of them—were somewhat of a blur. I remembered people in my periphery, but had no clue who was who and where exactly they were in the ocean of chairs.

The only person I cared to see the entire time was

Jackson. His sharp charcoal suit. The teal button-down under his jacket—same as Christy and Liz—unbuttoned at the collar. A boutonniere on the right breast of his jacket matched my bouquet. His black hair spiked, the line of his jaw layered with a thin line of trimmed hair. His hands clamped together in front of him at the groin.

But once I locked eyes with him, everything vanished. No family, no friends, no elaborate decor. It was only me and him. And the glow of his sapphires... their luminescence as I closed the space between us able to vanquish all darkness.

The moment I stood inches from him, the music and chatter faded to white noise. Jackson's hands unlocked, reached forward, and took hold of mine, steadying me. All my buzzing mind thought was—after saying yes in the correct places and speaking our vows—this gorgeous, extraordinary, loving man belonged to me forever. Love exploded in my chest, the shrapnel fiery in my bloodstream as it fueled my soul.

As if psychic, his sapphires glazed over and he mouthed *I love you*. A quiet tear broke the dam and rolled down my cheek just before I mouthed back *I love you forever*.

EPILOGUE

ONE YEAR LATER

I GRABBED another collapsible stadium chair from the back of the Jeep and set it on the beach cart beside me. Towels. Blankets. A bag loaded with several tubes of sunscreen.

"Need a hand?"

I spun around and spotted Tiffany shielding her sunglasses-covered eyes. "Sure. Grab the cooler?"

Sliding the oversized, blue cooler from the Jeep, she set it on the ground and tugged the handle up. Closing the Jeep tailgate, we ambled through the parking lot until the coarse sand warmed our feet.

I paused and scanned the beach for my husband. He—along with Liz, Judy, and Kendra—erected the beach canopy we recently purchased. Seeing as we spent so much time here, especially with friends, it was a great investment.

I trekked toward everyone as Tiffany hauled the cooler

beside me. "So, how have things been with you two since the move?" A silly question, but I felt compelled to ask and check on my best friend, as well as her other half. Liz and Tiffany had been living in California for the last year-and-a-half. But I only ever heard Liz's side of life. I wanted to hear Tiffany's, too. It was a big transition for them both.

"It's been really great. At first, I worried I wouldn't find a job. But after a bit of research, I discovered there was tons of opportunity. Probably wouldn't have been as fortunate back home. Us moving here... it was meant to be. And we couldn't be happier."

Her words meant the world to me. Liz assured me everything was fantastic between them—romantically, as well as their careers. Knowing Tiffany echoed the same sentiment put my heart at ease. Beyond happy to see my best friend get her slice of the pie. Liz deserved nothing except the best and it warmed my heart she found her happiness with Tiffany.

As we approached the group, they staked the last corner of the canopy into the sand. Everyone grabbed chairs and blankets and set up our plot of the beach. Jackson stepped forward, wrapped his arms around my waist, dropped his lips to mine and left me wanting when he backed away.

"Is there anything else left in the car, babe?"

"No. Tiffany and I got everything."

Jackson peered over my shoulder. Sand crunched

loud, and I turned to Christy and Rick approaching the group.

"Rick, need a hand getting the table?" Jackson spun me so we both faced them.

"Yeah, man. If you don't mind."

The two of them trudged off to Rick's truck, heaved a large banquet table out of the bed, and returned and set it up under the makeshift gazebo canopy.

Moments later, drinks circulated, conversation halted, and Jackson cleared his throat, reining in the group. "Thanks for coming out and sharing our anniversary with us." Jackson leaned in and placed a tender kiss on my temple. "It means everything, to both of us, that we have so many great people in our life. And on that note..."

He paused and left everyone hanging. Tantalizing sapphires sparkled when he pushed his sunglasses into his hair and rested them atop his head. Our next announcement left for me to share.

No pressure. Not really.

After a long pull from my water bottle, I inhaled deep as the cool liquid quenched my nerves a fraction. With my sunglasses in place, the dark lenses a safety net against the knot in my stomach, I peered back at Jackson a second. His smile burned brighter than the sun, and the knot untwisted and my anxiety vanished.

I glanced back to my anxious friends as my lips kicked up at the corner. "We're pregnant!" I announced cheerfully.

For a moment, I swore the earth silenced. But before

my mind shifted to overdrive, cheers erupted from everyone. Hugs were exchanged. After everything died down,
Liz stated she had news as well.

Beside her, Tiffany glowed brighter by the second. Liz
lifted Tiffany's left hand, a diamond rested atop a rose gold
band parked on the finger next to her pinky. "We're
engaged!"

"Holy shit!" Christy slapped her hand to her mouth
before she jumped up and down. "I can't fucking believe
it! Soon, we'll all be married." Tears rolled down Christy's
cheeks, stress over her and Rick's wedding next month
temporarily evaporating.

"Must be something in the water here." I laughed at
Christy's exuberance and everyone followed suit, our
laughter echoed for miles.

Within minutes, bodies zigzagged here and there,
setting up the table with plates and cutlery and mountains
of food. I hung out at one corner, shade masking me from
the chest up, and ogled the most wonderful people in my
life as they shuffled around one another like they knew
each other all their lives.

I glanced down at my stomach, a bump protruded an
inch, and rested my hand just below my navel. Excited to
become a mother, to meet the person who would be a
sliver of me and a sliver of Jackson. Eager to teach him or
her all the wonderful things I loved about this place.

As overjoyed as I was, a grain of sadness came along
with pregnancy and having a baby. My parents lived thou-

sands of miles away and the opportunity for them to see their grandchild would be much less than preferred.

I would more than love to travel back home to Georgia with the baby, but the remote possibility of seeing Alan or him finding out I was there if he got released… it wasn't a risk worth taking.

I hate to say one person still ruled a part of my life, it's not that. Not really. Somewhere, in the depths of my mind, I forgave Alan for what he did. Perhaps it was all he knew. I wasn't the one who needed to worry about such things anymore.

Jackson walked up behind me, his strong arms curved around my mid-section as his hands covered mine on my belly. "You okay, babe?" A whisper of a kiss pressed below my ear.

"Yeah, just thinking about how excited I am to meet our little bundle." I turned my head toward his and our lips met.

"Me, too. Do you want to know the sex ahead of time? So we can plan his or her whole future." His smile beamed, and his dimple peeked out.

"I don't know. I don't think so. Think I'd rather be more focused on what I need to do to be the best for him or her. Unisex stuff isn't so horrible when they're little."

"Whatever you want, babe. Have you thought of any names?"

Both of us stared out at the water, the white-crested waves crashed along the surf. Had I thought of names yet? I hadn't sat down and surfed the web.

"Maybe Alex. For short. That way, if it's a girl, Alexandria. Or if it's a boy, Alexander. What d'ya think?"

His hands rubbed back and forth over my belly, eyes focused as he pondered. "I like it. It's perfect, babe. Baby Alex."

"Baby Alex," I repeated. "Now that we have that sorted out... middle names are your job." I ducked out of his clutches and jogged toward our friends with a wicked grin plastered on my face.

Jackson sat in the chair next to mine and took hold of my hand. In this moment, everyone in my life happy... This was the best love on earth.

Leaning over to his ear, I whispered. "This life, our life, is perfect. And it's all because of you. I love you, angel."

"I love you, too, babe." And then he kissed me as if six of our closest friends were nowhere in sight.

Thank you so much for reading Distorted Devotion!

I hope you loved Sarah and Jackson's gripping romance. Ready for more in the Devotion world? Start Undying Devotion, Christy and Rick's steamy, secret life romance.

THANK YOU

Thank you so much for reading **Distorted Devotion**, book one in the **Devotion Series**. If you would take a moment to leave a review on the retailer site where you made your purchase, Goodreads and/or BookBub, it would mean the world to me.

Reviews help other readers find and enjoy the book as well.

Much love,
    Persephone

MORE BY PERSEPHONE

Undying Devotion

A long-term couple with a secret life. Their friends envy the bond they share, but remain oblivious to their lifestyle and how deep the bond lies. A turn of events has her wanting to spill every secret.

Darkest Devotion

At an underground rave, the last thing either plans is a hook up. When he takes her home the next day, an unexpected confrontation threatens to keep them apart.

Beloved Devotion

She asks the love of her life to marry her. When her girlfriend hesitates, then says yes, she is determined to learn why. As the pieces start to fall in place, she discovers she doesn't know her fiancée at all.

The Insomniac Duet

He was her high school bully. She was the outcast that secretly crushed on him. More than ten years later, he's her boss, completely oblivious to their shared past, and wants no one but her. More importantly, he doesn't understand her animosity toward him.

The Click Duet

High school sweethearts torn apart. When fate gives them a second chance, one doesn't trust they won't be hurt again. Through the Lens (Click Duet #1) and Time Exposure (Click Duet #2) is an angsty, second chance, friends to lovers romance with all the feels.

The Inked Duet

A man with a broken heart and a woman scared to put herself out there. Love is never easy. Sometimes love rips you apart. Fine Line (Inked Duet #1) and Love Buzz (Inked Duet #2) is a second chance at love, single parent romance with a pinch of angst and dash of suspense.

Depths Awakened

A small town romance which captivates you from the start. Two broken souls have sworn off love. Vowed to never lose anyone else. But their undeniable attraction brings them together and refuses to let go.

DISTORTED DEVOTION PLAYLIST

Here are some of the songs from the **Distorted Devotion** playlist. You can listen to the entire playlist on Spotify!

In the House In a Heartbeat | Metro Exodus
Need Some1 | The Prodigy
Joanne (Where Do You Think You're Going?) – Piano version | Lady Gaga
Into You | Ariana Grande
Electric | Alina Baraz, Khalid
High For This | The Weeknd
Wicked Game | Emika
Only Love | Ben Howard
Mercy (Acoustic) | Shawn Mendes
Mine | Bazzi
All We Do | Oh Wonder
Every Breath You Take (Re: Imagined) | Denmark + Winter

DISTORTED DEVOTION PLAYLIST

Release The Psycho | Rowan McLaughlin
Die For You | The Weeknd

CONNECT WITH PERSEPHONE

Connect with Persephone
www.persephoneautumn.com

Subscribe to Persephone's newsletter
www.persephoneautumn.com/newsletter

Join Persephone's reader's group
Persephone's Playground

Follow Persephone online

instagram.com/persephoneautumn

facebook.com/persephoneautumnwrites

tiktok.com/@persephoneautumn

goodreads.com/persephoneautumn

bookbub.com/authors/persephone-autumn

amazon.com/author/persephoneautumn

pinterest.com/persephoneautumn

twitter.com/PersephoneAutum

ACKNOWLEDGMENTS

First and foremost, thank you to everyone who picks up this book (and my previous)! Your support astounds me and I bow down to you. Readers are invaluable humans and I love you!

Wife! You are the most supportive human I know. You put up with my crazy hours and timelines and read all my words. Really, you're the best! And I can never thank you enough.

To the readers, authors, and bloggers reading my words! Starting an author career isn't a walk in the park. Thank you for being there for me and supporting me. Without any of you, things would be so much different.

Ellie and Rosa at My Brother's Editor! Thank you for editing and proofing this book. Thank you for questioning things I wrote and making me look at it from a different perspective. When I'm in the zone, sometimes I don't see how ridiculous something is. Many thanks.

To everyone in the Inkers Group for answering questions I've had throughout this journey. No author ever has all the answers and I'm so grateful for this group of amazing people who always help one another.

To my family who supports and roots for me! Sometimes it freaks me out when I hand a copy of my book to a family member. Although I'm proud of my accomplishment, it's strange to have someone so close to you reading your work.

ABOUT THE AUTHOR

Persephone Autumn lives in Florida with her wife, crazy dog, and two lover-boy cats. A proud mom with a cuckoo grandpup. An ethnic food enthusiast who has fun discovering ways to veganize her favorite non-vegan foods. If given the opportunity, she would intentionally get lost in nature.

For years, Persephone did some form of writing; mostly journaling or poetry. After pairing her poetry with images and posting them online, she began the journey of writing her first novel.

She mainly writes romance, but on occasion dips her toes in other works. Look for her poetry publications, and a psychological horror under P. Autumn.

9 781951 477035